PHANTOMS
AND OTHER STORIES

PHANTOMS
AND OTHER STORIES

BY

IVÁN TURGÉNIEFF

TRANSLATED FROM THE RUSSIAN BY
ISABEL F. HAPGOOD

Short Story Index Reprint Series

BOOKS FOR LIBRARIES PRESS
FREEPORT, NEW YORK

First Published 1904
Reprinted 1971

1194/5

INTERNATIONAL STANDARD BOOK NUMBER:
0-8369-4029-6

LIBRARY OF CONGRESS CATALOG CARD NUMBER:
79-169566

PRINTED IN THE UNITED STATES OF AMERICA
BY
NEW WORLD BOOK MANUFACTURING CO., INC.
HALLANDALE, FLORIDA 33009

CONTENTS

PHANTOMS

(1863)

PHANTOMS

A FANTASY

One instant . . . and the magic tale is o'er—
And with the possible the soul is filled once more.

A. FET.[1]

I

I COULD not get to sleep for a long time, and kept tossing incessantly from side to side. " May the devil take those table-tipping follies! " —I thought:—" they only upset the nerves."— Drowsiness began to overpower me. . .

Suddenly it seemed to me as though a chord had twanged faintly and lugubriously in the room.

I raised my head. The moon was hanging low in the sky, and staring me straight in the eye. White as chalk its light lay on the floor. . . . The strange sound was clearly repeated.

I leaned on my elbow. A slight alarm nipped at my heart.—One minute passed, then another. . . . . A cock crowed somewhere in the distance; still further away another answered.

I dropped my head on my pillow. " Just see

[1] The pseudonym of Afanásy Afanásievitch Shénshin (1820–1892).—TRANSLATOR.

3

to what one can bring one's self," I began my reflections again:—" my ears will begin to ring."

A little later I fell asleep—or it seemed to me
that I did. I had a remarkable dream. It seemed
to me as though I were lying in my bedroom, in
my bed, but I was not asleep, and could not close
my eyes. . . . I turned over. . . . The streak of
moonlight on the floor softly began to rise up,
to straighten itself, to become slightly rounded at
the top. . . . Before me, transparent as mist,
a white woman stood motionless.

" Who art thou? "—I asked with an effort.

The voice which replied was like the rustling
of leaves.—" It is I . . . . I . . . . I . . . . I have come
for thee."

" For me? But who art thou? "

" Come by night to the corner of the forest,
where the old oak stands. I shall be there."

I tried to get a good look at the features of
the mysterious woman—and suddenly I gave an
involuntary start: I felt a chill breath on me.
And now I was no longer lying in my bed, but
sitting on it—and there, where the spectre had
seemed to stand, the moonlight lay in a long
streak on the floor.

II

THE day passed after a fashion. I remember
that I tried to read, to work . . . . it came to no-

thing. Night arrived. My heart beat violently within me, as though I were expecting something. I went to bed and turned my face to the wall.

"Why didst thou not come?"—an audible whisper rang out in the room.

I glanced round swiftly.

It was she again . . . . the mysterious phantom. Motionless eyes in a motionless face, and a gaze full of grief.

"Come!"—the whisper made itself heard again.

"I will come,"—I replied, with involuntary terror. The phantom quietly swayed forward, and became all mixed up, undulating lightly like smoke;—and the moonlight again lay white upon the polished floor.

III

I PASSED the day in a state of agitation. At supper I drank almost a whole bottle of wine, and started to go out on the porch; but returned, and flung myself on my bed. My blood was surging heavily through my veins.

Again a sound made itself heard. . . . I shuddered, but did not look round. Suddenly I felt some one clasp me in a close embrace from behind, and whisper in my ear: "Come, come, come!" . . . . Trembling with fright I groaned:

"I will come!"—and straightened myself up.

5

PHANTOMS

The woman stood bending over me, close beside the head of my bed. She smiled faintly and vanished. But I had succeeded in scrutinising her face. It seemed to me that I had seen her before; —but where? when? I rose late and roamed about the fields all day long, approached the old oak-tree on the border of the forest, and made an attentive inspection of the surroundings.

Toward evening I seated myself at an open window in my study. The old housekeeper set a cup of tea before me—but I did not taste it. . . . . I kept wondering and asking myself: "Am not I losing my mind?" The sun had only just set—and not only did the sky grow red, but the whole air suddenly became suffused with an almost unnatural crimson; the leaves and grass, as though covered with fresh varnish, did not stir; in their stony immobility, in the sharp brilliancy of their outlines, in that commingling of a strong glow and death-like tranquillity, there was something strange, enigmatical. A rather large grey bird flew up without any sound, and alighted on the very edge of the window. . . . I looked at it—and it looked at me askance with its round, dark eye. "I wonder if she did not send thee in order to remind me?"—I thought.

The bird immediately fluttered its soft wings, and flew away, as before, without any noise. I sat for a long time still at the window, but I no longer gave myself up to wonder: I seemed to have got into a charmed circle, and an irresistible though quiet power was drawing me on, as the onrush of the torrent draws the boat while still far away from the falls. At last I gave a start. The crimson had long since disappeared from the air, the hues had darkened, and the enchanted silence had ceased. A breeze was beginning to flutter about, the moon stood out with ever-increasing distinctness in the sky which was turning darkly blue,—and soon the leaves on the trees began to gleam silver and black in its cold rays. My old woman entered my study with a lighted candle, but the draught from the window blew on it and extinguished the flame. I could endure it no longer; I sprang to my feet, banged my cap down on my head, and set out for the corner of the forest, for the aged oak.

IV

MANY years before, this oak had been struck by lightning; its crest had been shattered and had withered away, but it still retained life enough for several centuries. As I began to draw near to it, a dark cloud floated across the moon: it was very dark under its wide-spreading boughs. At first I did not notice anything peculiar; but I glanced to one side—and my heart sank within me; a white figure was standing motionless beside

7

a tall bush, between the oak-tree and the forest. My hair rose slightly on my head; but I summoned my courage, and advanced toward the forest.

Yes, it was she, my nocturnal visitor. As I approached her, the moon shone forth again. She seemed all woven of semi-transparent, milky vapour,—through her face I could see a branch softly waving in the wind,—only her hair and eyes shone dimly-black, and on one of the fingers of her clasped hands gleamed a narrow gold ring. I halted in front of her, and tried to speak; but my voice died in my breast, although I no longer felt any real terror. Her eyes were turned upon me; their gaze expressed neither grief nor joy, but a certain lifeless attention. I waited to see whether she would utter a word; but she stood motionless and dumb, and kept gazing at me with her deadly-intent look. Again I began to feel uneasy.

" I have come!"—I exclaimed at last with an effort. My voice had a dull, queer ring.

" I love thee,"—a whisper became audible.

" Thou lovest me!"—I repeated in amazement.

" Give thyself to me,"—rustled the voice again in reply to me.

" Give myself to thee! But thou art a phantom—thou hast no body."—A strange sensation overpowered me.—" What art thou,—smoke, air, vapour? Give myself to thee! Answer me first—

who art thou? Hast thou lived upon earth?
Whence hast thou revealed thyself?"

"Give thyself to me. I will do thee no harm.
Say only two words: 'Take me.'"

I looked at her. "What is that she is saying?"
I thought. "What is the meaning of all this?
And how will she take me? Shall I try the ex-
periment?"

"Well, very good,"—I uttered aloud, and
with unexpected force, as though some one had
given me a push from behind. "Take me!"

Before I had finished uttering these words, the
mysterious figure, with a sort of inward laugh,
which made her face quiver for an instant, swayed
forward, her arms separated and were outstretched. . . . I tried to spring aside; but I was
already in her power. She clasped me in her embrace, my body rose about fourteen inches from
the earth—and we both soared off, smoothly and
not too swiftly, over the wet, motionless grass.

V

AT first my head reeled, and I involuntarily closed
my eyes. . . . A minute later, I opened them
again. We were floating on as before. But the
forest was no longer visible; beneath us lay outspread a level plain dotted with dark spots. With
terror I convinced myself that we had risen to a
fearful height.

"I am lost—I am in the power of Satan," flashed through me like lightning. Up to that moment, the thought of obsession by an unclean power, of the possibility of damnation, had not entered my head. We continued to dash headlong onward, and seemed to be soaring ever higher and higher.

"Whither art thou carrying me?"—I moaned at last.

"Wherever thou wishest,"—replied my fellow-traveller. She was sticking close to me all over; her face almost rested on my face. Nevertheless, I barely felt her touch.

"Let me down to the earth; I feel giddy at this height."

"Good; only shut your eyes and do not take breath."

I obeyed—and immediately felt myself falling, like a stone which has been hurled. . . . the wind whistled through my hair. When I came to myself, we were again floating close above the ground, so that we caught in the tips of the tall plants.

"Set me on my feet,"—I began.—"What pleasure is there in flying? I am not a bird."

"I thought it would be agreeable to you. We have no other occupation."

"You have not? But who are you?"

There was no answer.

"Thou dost not dare to tell me that?"

A plaintive sound, like that which had awakened me on the first night, trembled on my ear. In the meantime, we continued to move almost imperceptibly through the night air.

" Let me go! "—I said. My companion bent backward, and I found myself on my feet. She came to a halt in front of me and again clasped her hands. I recovered my equanimity and looked her in the face: as before, it expressed submissive grief.

" Where are we? "—I queried. I did not recognise my surroundings.

" Far from thy home, but thou mayest be there in one moment."

" In what manner? Am I to trust myself to thee again? "

" I have not done and will not do thee any harm. We shall float together until dawn, that is all. I can carry thee whithersoever thou wishest —to all the ends of the earth. Give thyself to me; say again: ' Take me! ' "

" Well, then . . . . take me! "

Again she fell upon my neck, again my feet left the earth—and away we flew.

VI

" Whither? "—she asked me.

" Straight ahead, ever straight ahead."

" But the forest lies in that direction."

"Let us rise above the forest—only, very gently."

We soared aloft, like wood-snipe flying upon a birch-tree, and again floated on in a straight line. Instead of grass, the crests of the trees flitted past under our feet. It was wonderful to see the forest from above, its bristling spine all illuminated by the moon. It seemed some sort of a vast slumbering wild beast, and accompanied us with a broad, incessant rustling, resembling an unintelligible growl. Here and there we came across small glades; a dentated strip of shadow stood out finely in black on one side of them. . . . . Now and then a hare cried pitifully below; up above, an owl whistled, also in plaintive wise; there was an odour of mushrooms, of buds, of lovage abroad in the air; the moonlight fairly poured in a flood in all directions—coldly and severely; the myriad stars glittered directly above our heads.

And now the forest was left behind; athwart the plain stretched a strip of mist; a river flowed there. We floated along one of its shores, above the bushes, rendered heavy and immovable by humidity. The waves on the river now glistened with a blue gleam, now rolled on darkly and as though they were vicious. In places a thin vapour moved strangely above it, and the cups of the water-lilies shone out with the virginal and sump-tuous whiteness of all their unfolded petals, as though they knew that they were inaccessible. I took it into my head to pluck one of them—and lo! I immediately found myself directly over the smooth surface of the river. . . . The dampness struck me unpleasantly in the face as soon as I had broken the strong stem of a large blossom. We began to flit from shore to shore, like the sand-pipers, which we kept waking, and which we pursued. More than once it happened that we flew down upon a little family of wild ducks, disposed in a circle· on a clear spot among the reeds—but they did not stir; perhaps one of them would hastily take its head out from under its wing, look and look, and then anxiously thrust its bill back again into its downy feathers; or another would quack faintly, its whole body quivering the while. We frightened one heron; it rose out of a willow bush, with dangling legs, and flapped its wings with awkward vigour; it really did seem to me then to resemble a German. Not a fish splashed anywhere—they, too, were asleep. I began to get used to the sensation of flying, and even found a certain pleasure in it; any one who has chanced to fly in his sleep will understand me. I took to watching with great attention the strange being, thanks to whom such improbable events were happening to me.

VII

SHE was a woman with a small, non-Russian face. Greyish-white, semi-transparent, with barely-defined shadows, it reminded one of the figures on an alabaster vase illuminated from within—and again it seemed to be familiar to me.

" May I talk with thee? "—I said.

" Speak."

" I see that thou hast a ring on thy finger; so thou hast dwelt on earth—thou hast been married? "

I paused. . . . There was no reply.

" What is thy name—or what was thy name, at least? "

" Call me Ellis."

" Ellis! That is an English name? Art thou an English woman? Thou hast known me before? "

" No."

" Why didst thou reveal thyself to me in particular? "

" I love thee."

" And art thou content? "

" Yes; we are floating, we are circling, you and I, through the pure air."

" Ellis! "—I said suddenly,—" perchance thou art a guilty, a damned soul? "

14

My companion's head dropped.—" I do not understand thee,"—she whispered.

" I adjure thee, in God's name . . . ." I was beginning.

" What art thou saying? "—she said with surprise.—" I do not understand."—It seemed to me that the arm which lay about my waist like a girdle, was moving gently. . . .

" Fear not,"—said Ellis,—" fear not, my dear one! "—Her face turned and moved closer to my face. . . . I felt on my lips a strange sensation, like the touch of a soft, delicate sting. . . . Leeches which are not vicious take hold in that way.

VIII

I GLANCED downward. We had again managed to rise to a very considerable height. We were flying over a county capital with which I was unfamiliar, situated on the slope of a broad hill. The churches reared themselves amid a dark mass of wooden roofs and fruit orchards; a long bridge lowered black at a curve in the river; everything was silent, overwhelmed with sleep. The very domes and crosses seemed to glitter with a dumb gleam; dumbly the tall poles of the wells reared themselves aloft beside the round clumps of willows; the whitish highway dumbly plunged, like a narrow dart, into one end of the town—and dumbly emerged from the other side upon the gloomy expanse of the monotonous fields.

" What town is that? "—I queried.

" ***off, in the *** Government."

" ***off, in the *** Government? "

" Yes."

" Well, I am very far from home! "

" For us distance is nothing."

" Really? "   Sudden boldness flashed up within me.—" Then carry me to South America! "

" I cannot go to America. It is day there now."

" While you and I are night birds? Well, somewhere or other, only as far off as possible."

" Close thine eyes and do not draw breath,"—replied Ellis,—and we dashed headlong onward with the swiftness of the whirlwind. The wind rushed into my ears with a crashing noise.

We halted, but the noise did not cease. On the contrary, it had become converted into a sort of menacing roar, a thunderous din. . . .

" Now thou mayest open thine eyes,"—said Ellis.

IX

I OBEYED. . . . My God, where was I?

Overhead were heavy, smoky clouds; they were crowding together, and flying like a herd of vicious monsters . . . . and yonder, below, was another monster: the raging, just that,—raging sea. . . . The white foam was glistening convulsively, and seething in it in mounds,—and rearing aloft in shaggy billows, it was pounding with harsh thunder on the pitch-black cliffs. The howling of the storm, the icy breath of the heaving deep, the heavy dashing of the surf, in which, at times, one seemed to hear something resembling howls, the distant firing of cannon, the ringing of bells, the torturing shriek, and the grinding of the pebbles on the shore, the sudden scream of an invisible gull, on the troubled horizon the reeling remains of a ship—everywhere death, death and horror. . . . My head began to reel, and swooning, I again closed my eyes. . . .

" What is this? Where are we? "

" On the southern shore of the Isle of Wight, in front of the Blackgang Cliff, where ships are so frequently dashed to pieces,"—said Ellis, this time with peculiar distinctness and, as it seemed to me, not without malicious joy. . . .

" Take me away, away from here. . . . home! Home! "

I shrank together utterly, I clutched my face in my hands. . . . I felt that we were floating still more swiftly than before; the wind no longer howled nor whistled—it shrieked through my hair, in my garments. . . . I gasped for breath. . . .

" Now stand on thy feet,"—rang out the voice of Ellis.

I tried to control myself, my consciousness. . . .

17

PHANTOMS

I felt the ground under foot, but heard nothing,
as though everything round about had died . . . .
only the blood beat irregularly in my temples, and
my head still reeled with a faint, internal sound.
I straightened myself up and opened my eyes.

X

WE were on the dam of my pond. Directly in
front of me, athwart the pointed leaves of the
willows, its broad expanse was visible with fila-
ments of feathery mist clinging to it here and
there. On the right a field of rye glinted dully;
on the left the trees of the garden reared themselves aloft, long, motionless, and damp in appearance. . . . Morning had not yet breathed
upon them. Across the sky two or three clouds
were stretched, obliquely, like wreaths of smoke;
they seemed yellowish, and the first faint reflection of the dawn fell on them, God knows
whence: the eye could not yet detect on the whit-
ening horizon the spot from which it must be bor-
rowed. The stars had disappeared; nothing was
stirring yet, although everything was already
awake in the enchanted stillness of early morning.

"The morning! Yonder is the morning!"—
exclaimed Ellis in my very ear. . . . "Farewell!
until to-morrow!"

I turned. . . . Lightly quitting the ground,

18

she floated past,—and suddenly raised both arms above her head. The head, and the arms, and the shoulders instantly flushed with warm, corporeal light; in the dark eyes quivered living sparks; a smile of mysterious delicacy flitted across the reddening lips. . . . A charming woman suddenly made her appearance before me. . . . But she instantly threw herself backward, as though falling into a swoon, and melted away like vapour.

I stood motionless.

When I came to my senses and looked about me, it seemed to me that the corporeal, pale-rosy flush which had coursed over the figure of my phantom had not yet vanished and, dispersed through the air, was flooding me on all sides. . . . It was the dawn flushing red. I suddenly became conscious of extreme fatigue and wended my way homeward. As I passed the poultry-yard I heard the first matutinal quacking of the goslings (no bird wakes earlier than they) ; along the roof, at the tip of each projecting stake, perched a daw; and all of them were diligently and silently pluming themselves, distinctly outlined against the milky sky. From time to time, they all rose into the air simultaneously and, after flying about a little while, alighted again in a row, without croaking. . . . From the forest near at hand was wafted, twice, the hoarsely-fresh cry of the black-cock, which had just flown up from the dewy grass all overgrown with berries. . . . With a light shiver all over my body, I gained my bed and speedily sank into a sound sleep.

XI

On the following night, when I began to draw near to the ancient oak, Ellis floated to meet me, as to a friend. I was not afraid of her as on the preceding day; I was almost delighted to see her. I did not even attempt to understand what had happened with me: all I cared about was to fly as far as possible, through curious places.

Again Ellis's arm was wound about me—and again we darted off.

"Let us go to Italy,"—I whispered in her ear.

"Whithersoever thou wilt, my dear one,"— she replied solemnly and softly—and softly and solemnly she turned her face toward me. It seemed to me to be less transparent than on the day before; more feminine and more dignified; it reminded me of that beautiful creature who had flashed before my vision in the dawn before our parting.

"To-night is a great night,"—went on Ellis. —"It rarely comes,—only when seven times thirteen . . . ."

At this point I lost several words.

"Now that can be seen which is invisible at other times."

"Ellis!"—I pleaded,—"who art thou? Tell me!"

She silently raised her long, white hand.

In the dark heaven, at the point to which her finger pointed, in the midst of tiny stars, a comet gleamed in a reddish streak.

"How am I to understand thee?"—I began. —"Dost thou mean that thou soarest like that comet, between the planets and the sun,—that thou soarest among men . . . . and how?"

But Ellis's hand was suddenly clapped over my eyes. . . . Something akin to the grey mist from a damp valley enveloped me. . . .

"To Italy! to Italy!"—I heard her whisper.— "This night is a great night!"

XII

THE mist disappeared from before my eyes, and I beheld beneath me an interminable plain. But I was able to understand, from the very touch of the warm, soft air on my cheeks, that I was not in Russia; and neither did that plain resemble our Russian plains. It was a vast, dim expanse, apparently devoid of grass and empty; here and there, throughout its entire length, gleamed small stagnant pools, like tiny fragments of a mirror; far away the inaudible, motionless sea was visible. Great stars glittered in the intervals between the large, beautiful clouds; a thousand-voiced, unceasing, yet not clamorous trill, arose in all directions; and wonderful was that penetrating and dreamy rumble, that voice of the nocturnal desert. . . .

"The Pontine Marshes,"—said Ellis.—"Dost thou hear the frogs? Dost thou discern the odour of sulphur?"

"The Pontine Marshes . . . ." I repeated, and a sensation of majestic sadness took possession of me.—"But why hast thou brought me hither, to this mournful, deserted region? Let us rather fly to Rome."

"Rome is close at hand,"—replied Ellis. . . . "Prepare thyself!"

We descended and dashed along the ancient Roman road. A buffalo slowly raised from the ooze his shaggy, monstrous head with short whorls of bristles between the crooked horns which curved backward. He rolled the whites of his eyes sideways, and snorted heavily with his wet nostrils, as though he scented us.

"Rome, Rome is near," . . . . whispered Ellis.—"Look, look ahead."

I raised my eyes.

What was that which rose darkly against the night sky? The lofty arches of a huge bridge? What river did it span? Why was it rent in places? No, it was not a bridge, it was an ancient aqueduct. Round about lay the sacred land of Campania, and yonder, far away, were the Alban

Hills; and their crests and the great back of the ancient aqueduct gleamed faintly in the rays of the moon which had just risen. . . .

We suddenly soared upward and hung suspended in the air before an isolated ruin. No one could have told what it had formerly been: a tomb, a palace, a tower. . . . Black ivy enveloped the whole of it with its deadly power—and below, a half-ruined arch yawned like jaws. A heavy, cellar-like odour was wafted in my face from that heap of small, closely-packed stones, from which the granite facing of the wall had long since fallen off.

"Here,"—said Ellis, raising her hand;— "here!—Utter loudly, thrice in succession, the name of a great Roman."

"But what will happen?"

"Thou shalt see."

I reflected.—"Divus Cajus Julius Cæsar!"— I suddenly exclaimed:—"Divus Cajus Julius Cæsar!" I repeated slowly:—"Cæsar!"

XIII

BEFORE the last echoes of my voice had had time to die away I heard. . . .

It is difficult to say precisely what. At first I heard a confused burst of trumpet notes and of hand-clapping, barely perceptible to the ear, but endlessly repeated. It seemed as though somewhere, immensely far away, in some bottomless abyss, an innumerable throng were suddenly beginning to stir, and rise, rise, undulating and exchanging barely audible shouts, as though athwart a dream, athwart an oppressive dream many ages in duration. Then the air began to blow and darken above the ruin. . . . Shadows began to flit past me, myriads of shadows, millions of outlines, now rounded like helmets, now long like spears; the rays of the moon were shivered into many bluish sparks on these spears and helmets—and the whole of that army, that throng, moved nearer and nearer, grew greater, surged mightily. . . . An indescribable effort, a tense effort sufficient to lift the whole world, could be felt in it; but not a single figure stood out distinctly. . . . And suddenly it seemed to me as though a tremor ran through it all, as though certain huge billows had surged back and parted. . . . . " Cæsar! Cæsar venit! "—rustled voices like the leaves of the forest upon which a whirlwind has suddenly descended . . . . a dull shock surged along, and a pallid, stern head in a laurel wreath, with drooping lids,—the head of the emperor,—began slowly to move forward from the ruin. . . .

There are no words of mortal tongue to express the dread which gripped my heart. It seemed to me that if that head were to open its eyes, to unseal its lips, I should fall dead on the spot.—" Ellis! "—I moaned:—" I do not wish it, I cannot, I do not want Rome, coarse, menacing Rome. . . . Away, away from here! "—" Pusillanimous! "—she whispered, and we dashed headlong away. Once more I heard behind me the iron shout of the legions, like thunder now . . . . then all grew dark.

XIV

" Look about thee,"—said Ellis to me,—" and calm thyself."

I obeyed; and I remember that my first impression was so sweet that I could only heave a sigh. Something smoky-blue, silvery-soft encompassed me on every side. At first I could distinguish nothing: that azure splendour blinded me. But lo! little by little the outlines of beautiful mountains and forests began to start forth before me; a lake lay outspread before me, with stars quivering in its depths, and the caressing murmur of the surge. The fragrance of orange-blossoms enveloped me in a billow, and along with it, also in a billow, as it were, the strong, pure tones of a youthful feminine voice reached my ears. That fragrance, those sounds, fairly drew me downward, and I began to descend . . . . to descend to a luxurious marble palace, which gleamed white and in friendlywise amid a cypress grove, The sounds were welling forth from its wide-open windows; the waves of the lake, dotted with a dust of flowers, plashed against its walls—and directly opposite, all clothed in the dark-green of orange-trees and laurels, all bathed in radiant mist, all studded with statues, slender columns, and porticoes of temples, a circular island rose from the bosom of the lake. . . .

"Isola Bella!"—said Ellis. . . . "Lago Maggiore. . . ."

I articulated only: "Ah!" and continued to descend. The feminine voice rang out ever more loudly, ever more clearly in the palace; I was irresistibly drawn to it. . . . I wanted to gaze into the face of the songstress who was warbling such strains on such a night. We halted in front of a window.

In the middle of a room decorated in Pompeian style, and more resembling an ancient temple than the newest sort of a hall, surrounded by Greek statues, Etruscan vases, rare plants, precious stuffs, and lighted from above by the soft rays of two lamps enclosed in crystal globes, sat a young woman at the piano. With her head thrown slightly backward, and her eyes half-closed she was singing an Italian aria; she was singing and smiling, and, at the same time, her features were expressive of seriousness, even of severity . . . . a sign of complete enjoyment. She smiled . . . . and the Faun of Praxiteles, indolent, as young as she, effeminate, sensual

26

also, seemed to be smiling at her from one corner, from behind the branches of an oleander, athwart the thin smoke which rose from a bronze perfuming-pan upon an antique tripod. The beauty was alone. Enchanted by the sounds, the beauty, the glitter and perfume of the night, shaken to the very depths of my soul by the spectacle of that young, calm, brilliant happiness, I totally forgot my companion, forgot in what strange wise I had become a witness of that life which was so distant, so remote, so strange to me—and I wanted to step through the window, I wanted to enter into conversation. . . .

My whole body quivered from a forcible blow —as though I had touched a Leyden jar. I glanced round. . . . Ellis's face was gloomy and menacing, despite all its transparency; wrath glowed dully in her eyes, which had suddenly been opened to their full extent. . . .

" Away! "—she whispered furiously; and again there was the whirlwind and gloom and dizziness. . . . Only this time it was not the shout of the legions, but the voice of the songstress, broken short off on a high note, which lingered in my ears. . . .

We halted. A high note, that same high note, continued to ring out and did not cease to resound, although I felt an entirely different air, a different odour. . . . Invigorating freshness breathed upon me, as from a great river, and

27

there was the scent of hay, of smoke, of hemp. The long-drawn note was followed by a second, then by a third, but with such an indubitable shading, such a familiar turn characteristic of my native land, that I immediately said to myself: " That is a Russian man singing a Russian song," —and at that moment everything round about me grew clear.

XV

WE found ourselves above a flat shore. On the left, stretched out, losing themselves in infinity, lay mowed meadows, dotted with huge haystacks; on the right, to an equally unlimited extent, spread out the level expanse of a vast river abounding in water. Not far from the shores huge, dark barges were rocking quietly at anchor, slightly moving the tips of their masts like index-fingers. From one of these barges were wafted to me the sounds of a flowing voice, and on it burned lights, quivering and rocking in the water with their long, red reflections. Here and there both on the river and in the fields twinkled other lights—the eye was unable to discern whether near at hand or far away; now they blinked, again they stood forth in large, radiant spots; numberless katydids shrilled ceaselessly— quite equal to the frogs on the Pontine Marshes; and beneath the cloudless, but low-hanging, dark sky invisible birds uttered their calls from time to time.

"Are we in Russia?"—I asked Ellis.

"This is the Volga,"—she replied.

We soared along the bank.—"Why hast thou torn me thence, from that beautiful land?"—I began.—"Wert thou envious, pray? Did not jealousy awake in thee?"

Ellis's lips quivered faintly, and a menace again flashed in her eyes. . . . But her whole face immediately grew rigid once more.

"I want to go home,"—I said.

"Wait, wait,"—replied Ellis.—"To-night is a great night. It will not soon return. Thou mayest be the spectator. . . . Wait."

And suddenly we flew across the Volga, in a slanting direction, close above the water, low and abruptly, like swallows before a storm. The broad waves gurgled heavily below us, the keen river wind beat us with its cold, strong wing . . . . the lofty right shore soon began to rise before us in the semi-darkness. Steep hills with great clefts made their appearance. We approached them.

"Shout, 'Tow-path men to the prow!'" Ellis whispered to me.

I remembered the dread which I had experienced at the appearance of the Roman spectres, I felt fatigue and a certain strange anguish, as though my heart were melting within me—and

PHANTOMS

I did not wish to utter the fateful words. I knew beforehand that in reply to them something monstrous would appear, like Freischütz, in the Volga Valley.—But my lips parted against my will, and I shouted in a weak, strained voice: " Tow-path men to the prow!"[1]

XVI

AT first all remained dumb, as before the Roman ruin.—But suddenly close to my very ear, a coarse bark-hauler's[2] laugh rang out, and something fell with a bang into the water and began to choke. . . . I glanced round: no one was anywhere to be seen, but an echo rebounded from the shore, and instantly and from all quarters a deafening uproar arose. What was there not in that chaos of sounds! Shouts and whines; violent swearing and laughter, laughter most of all; strokes of oars and of axes; the crash as of breaking in doors and chests; the creaking of rigging and wheels, and the galloping of horses; the sound of alarm-bells and the clanking of chains; the rumble and roar of conflagrations, drunken songs and interchange of hurried speech; inconsolable, despairing weeping, and imperious ex-

[1] According to tradition, this was the war-cry of the Volga brigands when they captured vessels. —TRANSLATOR.

[2] Before the introduction of steamers on the Volga, all vessels were hauled up-stream from Ástrakhan to Nízhni-Nóvgorod—or even further—by men walking along the tow-paths on the shore. —TRANSLATOR.

30

clamations; the death-rattle, and audacious whistling; the yelling and trampling of the dance. . . . "Beat! Hang! Drown! Cut his throat! That's fine! That's fine! So! Show no pity!"—were distinctly audible; even the broken breathing of panting men was audible;—and nevertheless, everywhere round about, as far as the eye could see, nothing came into sight, nothing underwent any change. The river flowed past mysteriously, almost morosely; the very shore seemed more deserted and wild than before—that was all.

I turned to Ellis, but she laid her finger on her lips. . . .

"Stepán Timoféitch! Stepán Timoféitch is coming!"—arose a rustling round about;—"our dear little father is coming, our atamán, our nourisher!"—As before, I saw no one, but it suddenly seemed to me as though a huge body were moving straight at me. . . . "Frólka! Where art thou, dog?"—thundered a terrible voice.—"Set fire on all sides—and put them under the axe, my little White-hands!"[1]

The heat of a flame close at hand breathed upon me, and the bitter reek of smoke,—and at the same moment something warm, like blood, spattered upon my face and hands. . . . Wild laughter roared round about. . . .

[1] The bandit chief, generally known in history as Sténka Rázin and Frol or Frólka, his younger brother and inseparable companion, captured and laid waste great stretches of the Volga. Their memory still lives in epic ballads and among the peasants.—TRANSLATOR.

I lost consciousness, and when I recovered my senses, Ellis and I were slipping along the familiar verge of my forest, straight toward the old oak-tree. . . .

" Seest thou yonder path? "—Ellis said to me, —" yonder where the moon is shining dimly and two small birch-trees are bending over? . . . Dost thou wish to go thither? "

But I felt so shattered and exhausted, that in reply I could say only:—" Home. . . . home! " . . . .

" Thou art at home,"—answered Ellis.

In fact, I was standing in front of the door of my house—alone. Ellis had vanished. The watch-dog was about to approach, glared suspiciously at me—and fled howling.

With difficulty I dragged myself to my bed, and fell asleep, without undressing.

XVII

On the following morning I had a headache, and could hardly move my feet; but I paid no attention to my bodily indisposition. I was gnawed by penitence, stifled with vexation.

I was extremely displeased with myself. " Pusillanimous! "—I kept repeating incessantly:— " Yes—Ellis is right. What did I fear? How could I fail to profit by the opportunity? . . . . I might have beheld Cæsar himself—and I swooned with terror, I squealed, I turned away, like a child from the rod. Well, Rázin—that is quite a different matter. In my quality of noble-man and land-owner . . . . However, what was the actual cause of my fright in that case also? Pusillanimous, pusillanimous!" . . . .

"But is it not in a dream that I am seeing all this?"—I asked myself at last. I called my housekeeper.

"Márfa, at what time did I go to bed last night?—dost thou remember?"

"Why, who knows, my benefactor. . . . Late, I think. In the gloaming thou didst leave the house; and thou were clattering thy heels in thy bedroom after midnight. Just before dawn—yes. And this is the third day it has been like that. Evidently, something has happened to worry thee."

"Ehe-he!"—I thought.—"There can be no doubt as to the flying."—"Well, and how do I look to-day?"—I added aloud.

"How dost thou look? Let me look at thee. Thy cheeks are somewhat sunken. And thou art pale, my nourisher; there now, there is n't a drop of blood in thy face."

I winced slightly. . . . I dismissed Márfa.

"If thou goest on like this thou wilt surely die or lose thy mind,"—I reasoned, as I sat meditat-ing by the window. "I must abandon all this. It is dangerous. And, here now, how strangely my heart is beating! And when I am flying, it constantly seems to me as though some one were sucking it, or as though something were seeping out of it—like the spring sap from a birch, if you thrust an axe into it. And yet I feel sorry. And there is Ellis. . . . She is playing with me as a cat plays with a mouse . . . . but it is unlikely that she wishes any evil to me. I 'll surrender myself to her for the last time—I 'll gaze my fill —and then. . . . But what if she is drinking my blood? This is terrible. Moreover, such swift motion cannot fail to be injurious; they say that on the railways in England it is forbidden to go more than one hundred and twenty versts an hour. . . ."

Thus did I meditate—but at ten o'clock in the evening I was already standing before the aged oak.

XVIII

THE night was cold, dim, and grey; there was a scent of rain in the air. To my surprise, I found no one under the oak; I made the circuit of it several times, walked as far as the verge of the forest, and returned, staring assiduously into the darkness. . . . Everything was deserted. I waited a while, then uttered Ellis's name several times in succession, with ever-increasing loudness . . . . but she did not show herself. I was seized with sadness, almost with anguish; my former apprehensions vanished; I could not reconcile myself to the thought that my companion would never return to me.

"Ellis! Ellis! Do come! Wilt thou not come?"—I shouted for the last time.

A crow which had been awakened by my voice suddenly began to fidget about in the crest of a neighbouring tree, and becoming entangled in the branches, set to flapping its wings. . . . But Ellis did not appear.

With drooping head I wended my way homeward. Ahead of me the willows on the dam stood out in a black mass, and the light in the window of my room twinkled among the apple-trees of the garden,—twinkled and vanished, like the eye of a man watching me,—when suddenly the faint swish of swiftly-cloven air became audible behind me, and something with one swoop embraced and seized hold of me from below upward: that is the way a buzzard seizes, "smashes" a quail. . . . It was Ellis who had flown upon me. I felt her cheek on my cheek, the girdle of her arms around my body—and like a keen chill the whisper of her mouth pierced my ear: "Here am I!" I was simultaneously alarmed and delighted. . . . We floated off not far above the ground.

"Thou didst not mean to come to-day?"—I said.

"But thou didst languish for me! Thou lovest me? Oh, thou art mine!"

Ellis's last words disconcerted me. . . . I did not know what to say.

"I was detained,"—she went on;—"they set a guard over me."

"Who could detain thee?"

"Whither dost thou wish to go?"—queried Ellis, not replying to my question, as usual.

"Carry me to Italy, to that lake—dost thou remember?"

Ellis drew back a little and shook her head in negation. Then for the first time did I perceive that she had ceased to be transparent. And her face seemed to have grown rosy; a crimson flush spread over its cloudy whiteness. I looked into her eyes . . . . and dread came upon me: in those eyes something was moving—with the slow, unceasing and vicious motion of a serpent which has coiled itself and, congealed in that position, is beginning to grow warm in the sunshine.

"Ellis!"—I exclaimed:—"Who art thou? Tell me, who art thou?"

Ellis merely shrugged her shoulders.

I was vexed. . . . I wanted to punish her;—and suddenly it occurred to me to order her to carry me to Paris. "That 's where thou wilt have occasion for jealousy,"—I thought.—"Ellis!"—I said aloud;—"thou art not afraid of large cities, Paris, for example, art thou?"

"No."

" No? Not even of those places where it is bright, as on the boulevards? "

" That is not the light of day."

" Very good; then carry me immediately to the Boulevard des Italiens."

Ellis threw over my head the end of her long, flowing sleeve. I was immediately enveloped in a sort of white mist, with a soporific scent of poppies. Everything disappeared instantaneously; all light, all sound—and almost consciousness itself. The sensation of life alone remained —and it was not unpleasant. Suddenly the mist vanished; Ellis had removed her sleeve from my head, and I beheld before me a huge mass of buildings crowded together, brilliancy, movement, din. . . . I beheld Paris.

XIX

I HAD been in Paris before, and therefore immediately recognised the spot to which Ellis had shaped her course. It was the garden of the Tuileries, with its aged chestnut-trees, iron fences, fortress-moat, and beast-like Zouaves on guard. Passing the palace, passing the Church of St. Roch, on whose steps the first Napoleon shed French blood for the first time, we halted high above the Boulevard des Italiens, where the third Napoleon did the same thing, and with equal success. Crowds of people—young and old

dandies, workmen, women in sumptuous attire—
were thronging the sidewalks; the gilded restau-
rants and cafés were blazing with lights, carriages of all sorts and aspects were driving up
and down the boulevard; everything was fairly
seething and glittering, in every direction, where-
ever the eye fell. . . . But, strange to say, I did
not feel like quitting my pure, dark, airy height;
I did not wish to approach that human ant-hill.
It seemed as though a hot, oppressive, copper-
coloured exhalation rose up thence, not precisely
fragrant, nor yet precisely stinking; a very great
deal of life had been collected there in one heap.
I wavered. . . . But now the voice of a street-
courtesan, sharp as the screech of iron rails, suddenly was wafted to my ear; like a naked blade
it thrust itself out upward, that voice; it stung
me like the fangs of a viper. I immediately pictured to myself the stony, greedy, flat Parisian
face, with high cheek-bones, the eyes of a usurer,
rouge, powder, curled hair, and a bouquet of
bright-hued artificial flowers on the high-peaked
hat, the scraped nails in the shape of claws, the
monstrous crinoline. . . . I pictured to myself
also a steppe-dweller like myself pursuing the
venal doll with detestable tripping gait. . . . I
pictured to myself how, confused to the point of
rudeness, and lisping with his efforts, he en-
deavours to imitate in his manners the waiters at
Véfour's, squeals, keeps on the alert, wheedles—

and a feeling of loathing took possession of me.
. . . . " No,"—I thought,—" Ellis will have no
occasion to feel jealous here. . . ."

In the meantime, I noticed that we were beginning gradually to descend. . . . Paris rose to
meet us with all its din and reek. . . .

" Halt! "—I turned to Ellis.—" Dost thou not
find it stifling here, oppressive? "

" It was thou thyself who asked me to bring
thee hither."

" I was wrong, I recall my word. Carry me
away, Ellis, I entreat thee. Just as I thought:
yonder goes Prince Kulmamétoff, hobbling along
the boulevard; and his friend Baráksin is waving
his hand at him and crying: ' Iván Stepánitch,
allons souper, as quickly as possible, and engage
Rigolbosch itself! ' Carry me away from these
Mabilles and Maisons Dorés, away from fops,
both male and female, from the Jockey Club and
Figaro, from the closely-clipped soldiers' heads
and the polished barracks, from the *sergents de
ville* with their goatees and the glasses of turbid
absinthe, from the players of domino in the cafés
and the gamblers on 'Change, from the bits of red
ribbon in the buttonhole of the coat and the
buttonhole of the overcoat, from Monsieur de
Foi, the inventor of ' the speciality of wed-
dings,' and from the free consultations of Dr.
Charles Albert, from liberal lectures and governmental pamphlets, from Parisian comedies and

Parisian operas and Parisian ignorance. . . .
Away! Away! Away!"

"Look down,"—Ellis answered me:—"thou
art no longer over Paris."

I lowered my eyes. . . . It was a fact. A dark
plain, here and there intersected by whitish lines
of roads, was running swiftly past beneath us,
and only behind, on the horizon, like the glow
of a huge conflagration, the reflection of the innumerable lights of the world's capital throbbed
upward.

XX

AGAIN a veil fell across my eyes. . . . Again I
lost consciousness. It dispersed at last.

What was that yonder, below? What park
was that with avenues of clipped lindens, isolated
spruce-trees in the form of parasols, with porticoes and temples in the Pompadour taste, and
statues of nymphs and satyrs of the Bernini
school, and rococo Tritons in the centre of curving ponds, rimmed by low balustrades of black-
ened marble? Is it not Versailles? No, it is not
Versailles. A small palace, also in rococo style,
peers forth from clumps of curly oak-trees. The
moon shines dimly, enveloped in a haze, and an
extremely delicate smoke seems to be spread over
the earth. The eye cannot distinguish what it is:
moonlight or fog. Yonder on one of the ponds

a swan is sleeping; its long back gleams white, like the snow of the steppes gripped by the frost, and yonder the glow-worms are burning like diamonds in the bluish shadow at the foot of the statues.

" We are close to Mannheim,"—said Ellis.— " That is the Schwetzingen Park."

" So we are in Germany,"—I thought, and began to listen. Everything was dumb; only somewhere a slender stream of falling water was plashing and babbling, isolated and invisible. It seemed to be repeating the same words over and over again: " Yes, yes, yes," always " yes." And suddenly it seemed to me as though in the very middle of one of the avenues, between the walls of shorn greenery, affectedly offering his arm to a lady in powdered coiffure and a gay-coloured farthingale, there stepped forth on his red heels a cavalier in a golden coat and lace cuffs, with a light, steel sword on his hip. . . . They were strange, pale figures. . . . I wanted to get a look at them. . . . But everything had vanished, and only the water babbled on as before.

" Those are dreams roaming abroad,"—whispered Ellis.—" Yesterday a great deal might have been seen—a great deal. To-day even dreams shun the eye of mortal man. On! On!"

We soared upward and flew further. So smooth and even was our flight that we did not seem to be moving, but everything, on the contrary, appeared to be coming toward us. Mountains made their appearance, dark, undulating, covered with forests; they augmented and floated toward us. . . . Now they are already flowing past beneath us, with all their sinuosities, ravines, narrow meadows, with the fiery points in the slumbering villages along the swift rivers at the bottom of the valleys; and ahead of us again other mountains loom up and float past. . . . We are in the heart of the Schwarzwald.

Mountains, nothing but mountains . . . . and forest, the splendid, old, mighty forest. The night sky is clear; I can recognise every variety of tree; especially magnificent are the firs with their straight, white trunks. Here and there on the borders of the forests chamois are to be seen; stately and alert they stand on their slender legs and listen, with their heads finely turned, and their large, trumpet-shaped ears pricked up. The ruin of a tower sadly and blindly displays on a peak of naked crag its half-demolished battlements; above the ancient, forgotten stones a golden star glows peacefully. From a small, almost black lake, the moaning croak of tiny frogs rises up like a wail. I seem to hear other sounds, long, languid, like the sounds of a golden harp. . . . . Here it is, the land of legend! That same delicate shimmer of moonlight which had impressed me at Schwetzingen is here disseminated everywhere, and the further the mountains stand apart the thicker does that smoke become. I distinguish five, six, ten, different tones of the different layers of shadow on the slopes of the mountains, and over the silent diversity pensively reigns the moon. The air ripples on softly and lightly. I feel at ease and in a mood of lofty composure and melancholy as it were. . . . .

" Ellis, thou must love this land! "

" I love nothing."

" How is that? And how about me? "

" Yes . . . . thee! "—she replies indifferently.

It strikes me that her arm clasps my waist more closely than before.

" On! On! "—says Ellis, with a sort of cold enthusiasm.

" On! "—I repeat.

XXI

A MIGHTY fluctuating, ringing cry suddenly resounded overhead and was immediately repeated a little way in advance.

" Those are belated cranes flying to your land, to the north,"—said Ellis:—" wouldst thou like to join them? "

" Yes, yes! raise me to them."

We soared upward and in the twinkling of an eye found ourselves alongside of the flock which had flown past.

The huge, handsome birds (there were thirty

43

of them in all) were flying in a wedge form abruptly and rarely flapping their inflated wings. With head and legs intently ahead and breast thrust sternly forward, they were forging onward, and that so swiftly that the air whistled around them. It was wonderful to see such hot, strong life, such unflinching will, at such a height, at such a distance from all living things. Without ceasing triumphantly to plough their way through space the cranes exchanged calls, from time to time, with their comrades in the vanguard, with their leader; and there was something proud, dignified, something invincibly confident in those loud cries, in the conversation under the clouds. " We shall fly to our goal, never fear, however difficult it may be," they seemed to be saying, encouraging one another.

And at this point it occurred to me that there are very few people in Russia—why do I say in Russia?—in the whole world—like those birds.

" We are now flying to Russia,"—said Ellis. This was not the first time I had noticed that she almost always knew what I was thinking about.— " Dost thou wish to return? "

" Let us return . . . . or, no! I have been in Paris; take me to Petersburg."

" Now? "

" This instant. . . . Only cover my head with thy veil or I shall become dizzy."

44

Ellis raised her arm . . . . but before the mist enveloped me I felt on my lips the touch of that soft, dull sting. . . .

XXII

" At-te-e-e-e-ention ! "—a prolonged cry resounded in my ears. " At-te-e-e-e-ention ! " came the response, as though in despair, from the distance. " At-te-e-e-e-ention ! " died away somewhere at the end of the world. I started. A lofty golden spire met my eye: I recognised the Peter-Paul Fortress.

A pale, northern night! Yes, but was it night? Was it not a pale, ailing day? I have never liked the Pétersburg nights; but this time I was even terrified: Ellis's form disappeared entirely, melted like the mist of morning in the July sun, and I clearly descried her whole body as it hung heavily and alone on a level with the Alexander column. So this was Petersburg! Yes, it really was. Those broad, empty, grey streets; those greyish-white, yellowish-grey, greyish-lilac, stuccoed and peeling houses with their sunken windows, brilliant sign-boards, iron pavilions over their porches, and nasty little vegetable-shops; those façades; those inscriptions, sentry-boxes, watering-troughs; the golden cap of St. Isaac's Cathedral; the useless, motley Exchange; the granite walls of the fortress and the broken wooden pavement; those barks laden with hay and firewood; that odour of dust, cabbage, bast-matting and stables; those petrified yard-porters in sheepskin coats at the gates, those cab-drivers curled up in death-like sleep on their rickety carriages,—yes, it was she, our Northern Palmyra. Everything was visible round about; everything was clear, painfully clear and distinct; everything was sleeping mournfully, strangely heaped up and outlined in the dimly-transparent air. The glow of sunset—a consumptive glow—has not yet departed, and will not depart until morning from the white, starless sky. It lies on the silky surface of the Nevá, and the river barely murmurs and barely undulates as it hastens onward its cold, blue waters. . . .

" Let us fly away,"—pleaded Ellis.

And, without awaiting my answer, she bore me across the Nevá, across the Palace Square, to the Litéinaya. Footsteps and voices were audible below: along the street a cluster of young men were walking with drink-sodden faces and discussing dancing-classes. " Sub-lieutenant Stolpakóff the seventh! " suddenly cried out in his sleep a soldier, who was standing on guard at the pyramid of rusty cannon-balls,[1] and a little further on, at the open window of a tall house I caught sight of a young girl in a crumpled silk gown without sleeves, with a pearl net on her hair and a ciga-

---

[1] At the Artillery Barracks.—TRANSLATOR.

rette in her mouth. She was devoutly perusing a book: it was the work of one of the most recent Juvenals.

" Let us fly on! "—I said to Ellis.

A minute more, and the little forests of decaying spruce-trees and mossy swamps which surround Petersburg were flitting past us. We directed our course straight for the south; sky and earth gradually grew darker and darker. The diseased night, the diseased day, the diseased city —all were left behind.

XXIII

WE flew more slowly than usual, and I was able to watch how the broad expanse of my native land unrolled before me like a series of interminable panoramas. Forests, bushes, fields, ravines, rivers—now and then villages and churches—and then again fields, and forests, and bushes, and ravines. . . . I grew melancholy,—and melancholy in an indifferent sort of way, somehow. And I was not melancholy and bored because we were flying over Russia in particular. No! The land itself, that flat surface which spread out beneath me; the whole earthly globe with its inhabitants, transitory, impotent, crushed by want, by sorrow, by diseases, fettered to a clod of contemptible earth; that rough, brittle crust, that excrescence on the fiery grain of sand of our planet, on which has broken out a mould dignified by us with the appellation of the organic, vegetable kingdom; those men-flies, a thousand times more insignificant than flies; their huts stuck together out of mud, the tiny traces of their petty, monotonous pother, their amusing struggles with the unchangeable and the inevitable,—how loathsome all this suddenly became to me! My heart slowly grew nauseated, and I did not wish to gaze any longer at those insignificant pictures, at that stale exhibition... Yes, I felt bored—worse than bored. I did not even feel compassion for my fellow-men: all emotions within me were drowned in one which I hardly venture to name: in a feeling of aversion; and that aversion was strongest of all and most of all toward myself.

" Stop,"—whispered Ellis:—" Stop, or I will not carry thee. Thou art becoming heavy."

" Go home."—I replied in the same sort of a tone with which I was accustomed to utter those words to my coachman on emerging, at four o'clock in the morning, from the houses of my Moscow friends with whom I had been discussing the future of Russia and the significance of the commune ever since dinner.—" Go home,"—I repeated, and closed my eyes.

XXIV

But I speedily opened them again. Ellis was pressing against me in a strange sort of way; she was almost pushing me. I looked at her, and the blood curdled in my veins. Any one who has chanced to behold on the face of another a sudden expression of profound terror the cause of which he does not suspect, will understand me. Terror, harassing terror, contorted, distorted the pale, almost obliterated features of Ellis. I have never beheld anything like it even on a living human face. A lifeless, shadowy phantom, a shadow . . . . . and that swooning terror . . . .

"Ellis, what ails thee?"—I said at last.

"'T is she . . . . 't is she. . . . ." she replied with an effort;—"'t is she!"

"She? Who is she?"

"Do not name her, do not name her,"—hurriedly stammered Ellis.—"We must flee, or there will be an end to all—and forever. . . . Look: yonder!"

I turned my head in the direction which she indicated to me with trembling hand,—and saw something . . . . something really frightful.

This something was all the more frightful because it had no definite form. Something heavy, gloomy, yellowish-black in hue, mottled like the belly of a lizard,—not a storm-cloud, and not

smoke,—was moving over the earth with a slow,
serpentine motion. A measured, wide-reaching
undulation downward and upward,—an undulation which reminded one of the ominous sweep
of the wings of a bird of prey, when it is in
search of its booty; at times an inexpressibly re-
volting swooping down to the earth,—that is the
way a spider swoops down to the captured fly.
. . . . Who art thou, what art thou, threatening
mass? Under its influence—I saw it, I felt it—
everything was annihilated, everything grew
dumb. . . . A rotten, pestilential odour emanated
from it—and a chill that caused the heart to grow
sick, and made things grow dark before the eyes,
and the hair to stand on end. It was a power
which was advancing;—the power which cannot
be resisted, to which all are subject, which, without sight, without form, without thought, sees
everything, knows everything, and like a bird of
prey chooses out its victims, like a serpent crushes
them and licks them with its chilly sting. . . .

" Ellis! Ellis! "—I shrieked like a madman.—
" That is Death! Death itself! "

The wailing sound which I had already heard,
burst from Ellis's mouth—this time it bore more
resemblance to a despairing, human scream—and
we dashed away. But our flight was strange and
frightfully uneven; Ellis kept turning somer-
saults in the air; she fell downward, she threw
herself from side to side, like a partridge which

is mortally wounded, or which is desirous of lur-
ing the hound away from her brood. And yet,
long, wavy offshoots, separating themselves from
the inexpressibly-dreadful mass, rolled after us,
like outstretched arms, like claws. . . . The huge
form of a muffled figure on a pale horse rose up
for one moment, and soared up to the very sky.
. . . . Still more agitatedly, still more despair-
ingly did Ellis throw herself about. " She has
seen me! All is over! I am lost!" . . . . her
broken whisper became audible. " Oh, unhappy
one that I am! I might have enjoyed, I might
have acquired life . . . . but now . . . . Annihilation, annihilation!"

This was too unbearable. . . . I lost consciousness.

XXV

WHEN I came to myself I was lying prone upon
the grass, and felt a dull pain all through my
body, as though from a severe injury. Dawn
was breaking in the sky: I was able to distinguish
objects clearly. Not far away, along the edge
of a birch-coppice, ran a road fringed with willows; the surroundings seemed familiar to me.
I began to recall what had happened to me,—
and I shuddered all over, as soon as the last, monstrous vision recurred to my mind. . . .

51

" But of what was Ellis afraid? " I thought.
" Can it be possible that she also is subject to *its*
power? Can it be that she is not immortal? Can
it be that she is doomed to annihilation, to destruction? How is that possible? "

A soft moan resounded close at hand. I turned
my head. Two paces distant from me lay, outstretched and motionless, a young woman in a
white gown, with dishevelled hair and bared shoulders. One arm was thrown up over her head, the
other fell upon her breast. Her eyes were closed,
and a light crimson foam had burst forth upon
the closely-compressed lips. Could that be Ellis?
But Ellis was a phantom, while I beheld before
me a living woman. I approached her, bent
over. . . .

" Ellis? Is it thou? "—I exclaimed. Suddenly, with a slow quiver, the broad eyelids were
lifted; dark, piercing eyes bored into me—and at
that same moment the lips also clung to me,
warm, moist, with a scent of blood . . . . the soft
arms wound themselves tightly round my neck,
the full, burning bosom was pressed convulsively
to mine.—" Farewell! Farewell forever! "—a
dying voice articulated distinctly,—and everything vanished.

I rose to my feet staggering like one intox-
icated, and passing my hands several times across
my face, I gazed attentively about me. I was
close to the *** highway, a couple of versts from

my manor-house. The sun had already risen when I reached home.

ALL the following nights I waited—and not without terror, I admit—for the appearance of my phantom; but it did not visit me again. I even went one day, in the twilight, to the old oak-tree; but nothing unusual occurred there either. I did not grieve overmuch, however, at the cessation of the strange friendship. I pondered much and long over this incomprehensible, almost inexplicable affair—and I became convinced that not only is science unable to elucidate it, but that even in the fairy-tales, the legends, there is nothing of the sort to be encountered. What was Ellis, as a matter of fact? A vision, a wandering soul, an evil spirit, a sylph, a vampire? Sometimes it seemed to me once more that Ellis was a woman whom I had formerly known, and I made strenuous efforts to recall where I had seen her. . . . . There now, there,—it sometimes seemed to me,—I shall recall it directly, in another moment. . . . In vain! again everything deliquesced like a dream. Yes, I pondered a great deal, and as was to be expected, I arrived at no conclusion. I could not make up my mind to ask the advice or opinion of other people, for I was afraid of gaining the reputation of a madman. At last I have cast aside all my surmises: to tell the truth, I am in no mood for them. On the one hand, the

53

Emancipation has taken place, with its division of arable land, and so forth, and so on; on the other hand, my health has failed; my chest has begun to pain me, I am subject to insomnia, and have a cough. My whole body is withering away. My face is yellow as that of a corpse. The doctor declares that I have very little blood, and calls my malady by a Greek name—" anæmia "—and has ordered me to Gastein. But the Arbiter of the Peace [1] fears that he " will not be able to deal with " the peasants without me. . . .

So you see how matters stand!

But what signify those keen, piercingly-clear sounds,—the sounds of a harmonica,—which I hear as soon as people begin to talk to me about any one's death? They grow ever louder and more piercing. . . . And why do I shudder in such torturing anguish at the mere thought of annihilation?

[1] An official who was appointed after the Emancipation to arbitrate differences of opinion as to the division of the land between the landed proprietors and the serfs.—TRANSLATOR.

YÁKOFF PÁSYNKOFF

(1855)

YÁKOFF PÁSYNKOFF

I

IT happened in Petersburg, in winter, on the first day of the carnival-week. I had been invited to dine by one of my boarding-school comrades, who had borne the reputation in his youth of being a pretty girl, and had later on turned out a man who was not in the least bashful. He is dead now, like the majority of my comrades. In addition to myself, Konstantín Alexándrovitch Asánoff, and a literary celebrity of the day had promised to come to dinner. The literary celebrity kept us waiting for him, and at last sent word that he would not come, but in his stead a small, fair-haired gentleman presented himself,—one of those everlasting unbidden guests in which Petersburg abounds.

The dinner lasted a long time; the host did not spare his wine, and our heads gradually got heated. Everything that each one of us had concealed in his soul—and who has not something concealed in his soul?—came out. The host's face suddenly lost its modest and reserved expression; his eyes began to glitter insolently, and an insipid grin distorted his lips; the fair-haired gentleman began to laugh in a pitiful sort of way, with a stupid whine; but Asánoff surprised me most of all. That man had always been distinguished for a sense of decorum; but on this occasion he suddenly began to pass his hand across his brow, to put on airs, and to brag of his powerful connections, incessantly making mention of some uncle of his, a very influential man. . . . I decidedly failed to recognise him; he was openly jeering at us . . . . he almost expressed his contempt for our society. Asánoff's insolence enraged me.

" See here,"—I said to him:—" if we are so insignificant in your eyes, march off to your influential uncle. But perhaps he does not admit you to his presence? "

Asánoff made me no reply, and continued to draw his hand across his brow.

" And what sort of folks are these! "—he said again.—" Why, they never go in any decent society, they are n't acquainted with a single well-bred woman, while I,"—he exclaimed, drawing from his side-pocket a wallet, and banging the table with it,—" have here a whole bunch of letters from a young girl whose like you will not find in all the world! "

The host and the fair-haired gentleman paid no heed to Asánoff's last words; they were clutching each other by the button,—and both of them were narrating some story; but I pricked up my ears.

" Well, you are bragging in good sooth, Mr. Nephew of an important personage! "—I said, moving closer to Asánoff:—" you have n't any letters, whatsoever."

" You think so? "—he retorted, glancing loftily down upon me.—" What 's this, then? "—He opened the wallet, and showed me about half a score of letters addressed to him. . . . " The handwriting is familiar! "—I thought. . . .

I feel the flush of shame start out on my cheeks . . . . my self-love suffers acutely. . . . What possesses me to confess so ignoble a deed? . . . . But there is no help for it. I knew when I began my tale that I should be forced to blush to the very ears. So, then, summoning up all my forces, I am bound to confess that . . . .

Here is the point: I took advantage of Asánoff's tipsy condition, and when he carelessly flung the letters on the table-cloth, which was drenched with champagne (my own head was buzzing pretty hard, too), I swiftly ran my eye over one of the letters. . . .

My heart sank within me. . . . Alas! I myself was in love with the young girl who had been writing to Asánoff, and now I could no longer cherish any doubt that she loved him. The whole letter, which was written in French, breathed forth tenderness, devotion. . . .

" *Mon cher ami Constantin!* "—that was the

way it began .... and it wound up with the words:
" be cautious, as of yore, and I will be yours or
no one's."

Stunned, as though by a clap of thunder, I sat
motionless for a few moments, but recovered myself at last, sprang to my feet, and rushed from
the room. . . .

A quarter of an hour later I was in my own
lodgings.

THE Zlotnítzky family was one of the first with
which I had become acquainted after my removal
from Moscow to Petersburg. It consisted of father, mother, two daughters, and a son. The
father, already a grey-haired but still fresh man,
formerly in the army, occupied a rather important post, spent the morning at his service, slept
after dinner, and in the evening played cards at
the club. . . . He was rarely at home, he con-
versed little and reluctantly, gazed askance from
under his brows in a manner which was not precisely surly nor yet precisely indifferent, and
never read anything except books of travel and
geographies, and when he was ill he coloured pictures, having locked himself in his study, or
teased the old grey parrot Pópka. His wife, an
ailing and consumptive woman, with sunken black
eyes and a sharp nose, never quitted her couch for
days together, and was always embroidering cush-
ions on canvas; so far as I was able to observe,

she was afraid of her husband, exactly as though she were culpable toward him in some way. The eldest daughter, Varvára, a plump, rosy, chestnut-haired girl, eighteen years of age, was perpetually sitting at the window and scrutinising the passers-by. The son was being educated in a government institution, made his appearance at home only on Sunday, and was not fond of wasting words for nothing either; even the younger daughter, Sófya, the young girl with whom I fell in love, was of a taciturn disposition. Silence always reigned in the Zlotnítzkys' house; only Pópka's piercing screams broke it; but visitors speedily became accustomed to it, and again felt the burden and oppression of that eternal silence weighing upon them. However, visitors rarely looked in at the Zlotnítzkys': it was tiresome there. The very furniture, the red wall-paper, with yellowish patterns, in the drawing-room; the multitude of chairs, with plaited seats, in the dining-room; the faded worsted pillows, with representations of young girls and dogs, on the divans; the horned lamps and gloomy portraits, on the walls—all inspired an involuntary melancholy, all emitted a cold, sour sort of atmosphere. On reaching Petersburg, I had regarded it as my duty to call upon the Zlotnítzkys: they were distantly related to my mother. With difficulty did I sit out the hour, and for a long time I did not return; but gradually I took to going

more and more frequently. I was attracted by
Sófya, whom I had not liked at first, and with
whom I ultimately fell in love.

She was a girl of short stature, almost gaunt,
with a pale face, thick, black hair, and large,
brown eyes, which were always half-closed. Her
features, which were regular and sharp-set, especially her tightly-compressed lips, expressed
firmness and force of will. At home she was
called a girl with character. . . . " She resembles
her eldest sister, Katerína,"—said Madame Zlotnítzky one day, when she was sitting alone with
me (she never ventured to refer to that Katerína
in her husband's presence).—" You do not know
her; she is in the Caucasus, married. At the age
of thirteen,—just imagine it!—she fell in love
with the man who is now her husband, and then
announced to us that she would marry no one
else. Do what we would,—nothing was of any
avail! She waited until she was twenty-three, enraged her father,—and married her idol all the
same. It would be the easiest thing in the world
for a catastrophe to happen with Sónetchka also!
May the Lord preserve her from such stubbornness! But I 'm apprehensive for her; she is only
sixteen, but already it is impossible to control
her. . . ."

Mr. Zlotnítzky entered; his wife immediately
fell silent.

Strictly speaking, Sófya did not attract me by

her force of will—no; but, with all her dryness, and lack of animation and imagination, she possessed the charm of straightforwardness, honourable sincerity, and spiritual purity. I respected her as much as I loved her. . . . It seemed to me that she was well-inclined toward me; it was painful to me to be undeceived as to her attachment, to become convinced of her love for another.

The unexpected discovery which I had made astounded me all the more, because Mr. Asánoff visited the Zlotnítzkys' house infrequently, much more rarely than I did, and showed no particular preference for Sófya. He was a handsome, dark-complexioned man, with expressive, although rather heavy features, prominent, brilliant eyes, a large, white brow, and plump, red little lips beneath a delicate moustache. He bore himself very modestly, but rigorously, talked and pronounced judgment with self-confidence, and held his peace with dignity. It was obvious that he thought a great deal of himself. Asánoff laughed rarely, and that through his teeth, and he never danced. He was very badly built. He had once served in the *** regiment, and had borne the reputation of an active officer.

" Strange! "—I reflected, as I lay on my divan: —" why have I not noticed anything of this? " The words of Sófya's letter suddenly recurred to my mind.—" Ah! "—I thought:—" that 's it! What a crafty little girl! And I had thought

her frank and sincere. . . . Well, just wait, and
I 'll show you! . . . ."

But at this point, so far as I can recall the
circumstances, I fell to weeping bitterly, and
could not get to sleep until morning.

On the following day, at two o'clock, I set out for
the Zlotnítzkys'. The old man was not at home,
and his wife was not sitting in her accustomed
place; her head had begun to ache after she had
eaten pancakes,[1] and she had gone to lie down in
her bedroom. Varvára was standing with her
shoulder leaning against the window, and staring
into the street; Sófya was pacing to and fro in the
room, with her arms folded across her breast;
Pópka[2] was shrieking.

"Ah! good morning!"—said Varvára, lan-
guidly, as soon as I entered the room, and immediately added, in an undertone: "yonder goes a
man with a tray on his head. . . ." (She had a
habit of making remarks about the passers-by,
occasionally, and as though to herself.)

"Good morning,"—I replied.—"Good morning, Sófya Nikoláevna. And where is Tatyána
Vasílievna?"

---

[1] Pancakes, served with melted butter and caviare (never with sweet
syrup), are the principal feature of the Russian "butter-week" or
carnival-tide, and are seldom or never eaten at any other time. —
TRANSLATOR.

[2] Equivalent to Polly, in the case of parrots.—TRANSLATOR.

"She has gone to lie down,"—replied Sófya, continuing to pace the room.

"We had pancakes,"—remarked Varvára, without turning round.—"Why did n't you come? . . . Where is that clerk going?"

"I had no time."—("Po-li-iice!" yelled the parrot, harshly.)—"How your Pópka does screech to-day!"

"He always screeches like that,"—said Sófya. We all maintained silence for a while.

"He has turned in at the gate,"—said Varvára, suddenly climbing on the window-sill and opening the hinged pane.

"What art thou about?"—inquired Sófya.

"A beggar,"—replied Varvára, bent down, picked up a copper five-kopék piece, on which the ashes of a fumigating pastile still rose in a mound, flung the coin into the street, slammed to the pane, and jumped heavily to the floor. . . .

"I passed the time very pleasantly last night," —I began, as I seated myself in an arm-chair:— "I dined with a friend; Konstantín Alexándritch was there. . . ." (I looked at Sófya; she did not even contract her brows.)—"And, I must confess,"—I went on,—"that we got rather convivial; the four of us drank eight bottles."

"You don't say so!"—calmly ejaculated Sófya, shaking her head.

"Yes,"—I went on, slightly nettled by her indifference;—" and do you know what, Sófya Nikoláevna,—'t is not without reason that the proverb says that when the wine is in the truth comes out."

" How so? "

" Konstantín Alexándritch made us laugh greatly. Just picture to yourself: he suddenly took to passing his hand across his forehead like this, and saying: ' What a fine, dashing fellow I am! I have an uncle who is a distinguished man. . . .' "

" Ha, ha! "—rang out Varvára's short, abrupt laugh. . . . " Pópka, pópka, pópka! " rattled the parrot in response.

Sófya halted in front of me, and looked into my face.

" And what did you say? "—she asked:— " don't you remember? "

I blushed involuntarily.

" I don't remember! I must have been in a fine state also. As a matter of fact,"—I added, with significant pauses:—" it is a dangerous thing to drink wine; the first you know, you babble secrets, and say that which no one ought to know. You will repent afterward, but then it is too late."

" And did you babble secrets? "—inquired Sófya.

" I 'm not talking about myself."

Sófya turned away, and again began to walk up and down the room. I gazed at her, and raged inwardly. "Just look at you,"—I said to myself, —" you 're a baby, a mere child, yet what control you have over yourself! You 're like a stone, simply. But just wait a bit. . . ."

" Sófya Nikoláevna . . . ." I said aloud.

Sófya stood still.

" What do you want? "

" Will not you play something on the piano? By the way, I have something to tell you,"—I added, lowering my voice.

Sófya, without uttering a word, went into the hall; I followed her. She stopped beside the piano.

" What shall I play for you? "—she asked.

" What you please . . . a nocturne by Chopin."

Sófya began the nocturne. She played rather badly, but with feeling. Her sister played only polkas and waltzes, and that rarely. She would lounge up to the piano, with her lazy gait, seat herself, drop the burnous from her shoulders to her elbows (I never saw her without a burnous), start up a polka thunderously, fail to finish it, begin another, then suddenly heave a sigh, rise and return to the window. A strange being was that Varvára.

I sat down beside Sófya.

" Sófya Nikoláevna,"—I began, gazing intently at her askance:—" I must impart to you a bit of news which is very disagreeable to me."

" News? What is it? "

" This. . . . Up to this time I have been mistaken in you, utterly mistaken."

" How so? "—she returned, continuing to play, and fixing her eyes on her fingers.

" I have thought that you were frank; I have thought that you did not know how to be crafty, to be sly. . . . ."

Sófya put her face close to her music. . . .

" I don't understand you."

" But the principal thing is,"—I went on:— " that I could not possibly imagine, that you, at your age, were already capable of playing a part in so masterly a manner. . . ."

Sófya's hands trembled slightly on the keys.

" What are you saying? "—she said, still without looking at me:—" I am playing a part? "

" Yes, you." (She laughed. . . . Fierce wrath took possession of me.) . . . . " You feign to be indifferent to a certain man and . . . and you write letters to him,"—I added in a whisper.

Sófya's cheeks blanched, but she did not turn toward me; she played the nocturne to the end, rose, and shut the lid of the piano.

" Where are you going? "—I asked, not without confusion.—" You will not answer me? "

" What answer have I to make to you? I don't know what you are talking about. . . . And I don't know how to dissemble."

She began to put the music together. . . .

The blood flew to my head.

" Yes, you do know what I am talking about,"
—I said, rising also:—" and if you like, I will
immediately remind you of several expressions
in one of those letters:—' be cautious as of
yore.' . . . "

Sófya gave a slight start.

" I had not in the least expected this from you,"
—she said at last.

" And I had not in the least expected,"—I
interposed,—" that you, Sófya Nikoláevna,
deigned to bestow your attention upon a man
who . . . ."

Sófya turned swiftly toward me; I involuntarily retreated a pace; her eyes, always half-
closed, were so widely opened that they appeared huge, and sparkled angrily under her
brows.

" Ah! In that case,"—said she,—" you must
know that I love that man, and that your opinion
of him and of my love for him is a matter of
perfect indifference to me. And where did you
get the idea? . . . . What right have you to say
that? And if I have made up my mind to anything . . . ."

She stopped short, and swiftly left the room.

I remained. I suddenly felt so awkward and
conscience-stricken, that I covered my face with
my hands. I comprehended all the impropriety,
all the baseness of my conduct, and panting with
shame and penitence, I stood like one branded

with disgrace. "My God!"—I thought:—
"what have I done?"

"Antón Nikítitch,"—the maid's voice became
audible in the anteroom,—"please get a glass of
water as quickly as possible for Sófya Nikoláevna."

"Why, what's the matter?"—asked the butler.

"I think she's weeping. . . ."

I gave a start, and went into the drawing-room
to get my hat.

"What were you talking about with Sónetchka?"—Varvára asked me indifferently, and
after a brief pause, she added in an undertone:
—"there goes that notary's clerk again."

I began to take my leave.

"Where are you going? Wait, mamma will
come out of her room directly."

"No; I can't now,"—said I:—"it would be
better for me to return some other time."

At that moment, to my terror,—precisely that,
—to my terror, Sófya entered the drawing-room
with firm steps. Her face was paler than usual,
and her eyelids were slightly red. She did not
even glance at me.

"Look, Sófya,"—said Varvára:—"some clerk
or other keeps walking about our house."

"Some spy or other," . . . . remarked Sófya,
coldly and scornfully.

This was too much! I departed, and, really,
I do not remember how I got home.

YÁKOFF PÁSYNKOFF

I was very heavy at heart, more heavy and bitter than I can describe. Two such cruel blows in the space of four-and-twenty hours! I had learned that Sófya loved another, and had forever forfeited her respect. I felt myself so annihilated and put to shame, that I could not even be indignant with myself. As I lay on the divan, with my face turned to the wall, I was surrendering myself with a sort of burning enjoyment to the first outbursts of despairing anguish, when I suddenly heard footsteps in the room. I raised my head and beheld one of my most intimate friends—Yákoff Pásynkoff.

I was ready to fly into a passion with any man who entered my room that day, but never could I be angry with Pásynkoff; on the contrary, in spite of the grief which was devouring me, I inwardly rejoiced at his coming, and nodded to him. According to his wont, he strode up and down the room a couple of times, grunting and stretching his long limbs, stood silently for a little while, in front of me, and silently seated himself in one corner.

I had known Pásynkoff a very long time, almost from childhood. He had been reared in the same private boarding-school, kept by a German named Winterkeller, in which I had spent three years. Yákoff's father, a poor, retired major, a very honourable man, but somewhat unhinged mentally, had brought him, an urchin of

71

seven years, to this German, paid a year's tuition in advance, had gone away from Moscow, and vanished, without leaving a trace. From time to time dark, strange rumours concerning him arrived. Only after the lapse of seven years was it learned with certainty that he had been drowned in a freshet, as he was crossing the Irtýsh. What had taken him to Siberia, the Lord only knows. Yákoff had no other relatives. So he remained on Winterkeller's hands. It is true that Yákoff had one distant relative,—an aunt, who was so poor, that at first she was afraid to go to see her nephew, lest they should cast him on her shoulders. Her alarm proved to be unfounded; the kind-hearted German kept Yákoff with him, permitted him to learn with the other pupils, fed him (but they passed him over at dessert on week-days), and made over clothing for him from the camelot morning-gowns (chiefly snuff-coloured) of his mother, a very aged, but still alert and active Liflyand [1] woman. The result of all these circumstances, and the result of Yákoff's inferior position in the boarding-school was, that his comrades treated him slightingly, looked down on him, and called him sometimes " woman's wrapper," sometimes " the mob-cap's nephew " (his aunt constantly wore a very queer cap, with a tuft of yellow ribbons in the shape of an artichoke, sticking out at the top), sometimes " the

[1] Livonia. — TRANSLATOR.

son of Yermák[1] (because his father had been drowned in the Irtýsh). But, in spite of these nicknames, in spite of his absurd garments, in spite of his extreme poverty, they all loved him greatly, and it was impossible not to love him; a kinder, more noble soul never existed on earth, I think. He also studied extremely well.

When I saw him for the first time, he was sixteen years of age, while I had just passed my thirteenth birthday. I was an extremely conceited and spoiled urchin, had been reared in a fairly wealthy home, and therefore when I entered the boarding-school I made haste to get intimate with a certain little Prince, the object of Winterkeller's special solicitude, and with two or three other small aristocrats, while I put on pompous airs with all the rest. I did not even deign to notice Pásynkoff. That long, awkward young fellow, in his hideous round-jacket and short trousers, from beneath which peeped thick, knitted thread stockings, seemed to me something in the nature of a page-boy from the house-serfs' class, or the son of a petty burgher. Pásynkoff was very polite and gentle to everybody, although he fawned on no one; if they repulsed him, he did not humble himself, and did not sulk, but held himself aloof, as though grieving and waiting. Thus did he behave with me also. About two months

---

[1] The conqueror of Siberia, in the reign of Iván the Terrible. He was drowned (1584) while trying to swim the Irtysh. — TRANSLATOR.

elapsed. One clear summer day, as I was passing from the courtyard into the garden, after a noisy game of ball, I saw Pásynkoff sitting on a bench, under a tall lilac-bush. He was reading a book. I cast a glance, in passing, at the cover, and read on the back the title: " Schiller's Werke." I stopped short.

" Do you know German? "—I asked Pásynkoff. . . .

To this day I feel mortified, when I recall how much scorn there was in the sound of my voice. . . . . Pásynkoff gently raised his small but expressive eyes to mine, and answered:

" Yes, I do; do you? "

" I should think so! "—I retorted, already affronted; and was on the point of proceeding on my way, but something kept me back.

" And what in particular are you reading from Schiller? "—I inquired with as much haughtiness as before.

" I am now reading ' Resignation '; it is a very beautiful poem. I 'll read it to you if you like— shall I? Sit down here beside me, on the bench."

I hesitated a little, but sat down. Pásynkoff began to read. He knew German much better than I did; he was obliged to explain to me the sense of several lines; but I was no longer ashamed either of my ignorance, or of his superiority to myself. From that day forth, from that reading together in the garden, in the shade of the lilac-bush, I loved Pásynkoff with all my soul; I got intimate with him, I submitted wholly to him.

I vividly recall his personal appearance at that epoch. However, he changed very little afterward. He was tall, thin, long-bodied, and decidedly clumsy. His narrow shoulders and sunken chest gave him a sickly aspect, although he had no reason to complain of his health. His large head, arched on top, was inclined slightly on one side, his soft, chestnut hair hung in thin locks around his thin neck. His face was not handsome, and might even appear ridiculous, thanks to his long, thick and reddened nose, which seemed to hang over his broad, straight lips; but his open brow was very fine, and when he smiled, his small, grey eyes beamed with such gentle and affectionate good-nature, that everyone felt warm and blithe at heart, from merely looking at him. I recall his voice, also, soft and even, with a peculiarly agreeable hoarseness. He talked little, as a general thing, and with obvious difficulty; but when he grew animated his speech flowed freely and,—strange to say!—his voice grew even softer, his glance seemed to retreat within and become extinguished, and his whole face flushed faintly. In his mouth the words: "good," "truth," "life," "science," "love," never had a false ring, no matter how enthusiastically he uttered them. He entered into the realm of the ideal without a strain, without an effort; his chaste soul was ready at all times to present itself before " the shrine of beauty "; it waited only for the greeting, the touch of another soul. . . . Pásynkoff was a romanticist, one of the last romanticists whom I have chanced to meet. The romanticists, as every one knows, have died out now; at all events, there are none among the young people of the present day. So much the worse for the young people of the present day!

I spent about three years with Pásynkoff, soul to soul, as the saying is. I was the confidant of his first love. With what grateful attention and sympathy did I listen to his avowal! The object of his passion was Winterkeller's niece, a fair-haired pretty little German, with a plump, almost childish little face, and trustful, tender blue eyes. She was very kind-hearted and sentimental, loved Mattieson, Uhland, and Schiller, and recited their verses very agreeably, in her timid, melodious voice. Pásynkoff's love was of the most platonic sort; he saw his beloved only on Sunday (she came to play at forfeits with the Winterkeller children) and talked very little with her; on the other hand, one day, when she said to him, " *Mein lieber, lieber Herr Jacob!*" he could not get to sleep all night from excess of happiness. It never entered his head then, that she said " *mein lieber* " to all his comrades. I remember, too, his grief and dejection, when the news suddenly spread abroad, that Fräulein Frederika (that was her name), was going to marry Herr Kniftus, the owner of a rich meat-shop, and marry solely out of obedience to her parents' wishes, but not for love. That was a difficult time for Pásynkoff, and he suffered especially on the day when the newly-wedded pair made their first call. The former Fräulein, now already Frau Frederika, introduced him again by the name of " *lieber Herr Jacob,*" to her husband, everything about whom was glistening: his eyes, and his black hair curled into a crest, and his forehead, and his teeth, and the buttons on his dress-suit, and the chain on his waistcoat, and the very boots on his decidedly large feet, whose toes were pointed outward. Pásynkoff shook hands with Herr Kniftus, and wished him (and wished it sincerely—I am convinced of that) full and long-continued happiness. This took place in my presence. I remember with what surprise and sympathy I gazed at Yákoff then. He seemed to me a hero! . . . And afterward, what sad conversations took place between us!—" Seek consolation in art,"—I said to him.—" Yes,"—he answered me,—" and in poetry."—" And in friendship,"—I added.— " And in friendship,"—he repeated. Oh, happy days! . . .

It was painful to me to part from Pásynkoff! Just before my departure, he finally got his papers, and entered the university, after long wor-

rying and trouble, and a correspondence which
was often amusing He continued to exist at
Winterkeller's expense, but in place of the camelot round-jackets and trousers, he received the
customary clothing in return for lessons in various subjects, which he gave to the younger pupils.
Pásynkoff never changed his mode of conduct
to me to the very end of my stay in the boarding-
school, although the difference in our ages had
already begun to tell, and I, I remember, had
begun to be jealous of several of his new com-
rade-students. His influence on me was of the
most beneficial nature. Unfortunately, it was
not of long duration. I will cite one instance
only. In my childhood, I had a habit of lying.
. . . . In Yákoff's presence my tongue never
turned to falsehood. But especially delightful to
me was it to stroll with him, or to pace by his
side to and fro in the room, and listen to him
recite verses in his quiet, concentrated voice, without glancing at me. Really, it seemed to me then,
that he and I were gradually leaving the earth
behind us and soaring away into some radiant,
mysteriously-beautiful region. . . . I remember
one night. He and I were sitting under the same
lilac-bush: we had grown fond of the spot. All
our comrades were already asleep; but we had
risen softly, dressed ourselves by the sense of feeling, in the dark, and stealthily gone out "to
dream awhile." It was quite warm out of doors,

but a chilly little breeze blew in gusts now and then, and made us nestle up closer to each other. We talked, we talked a great deal, and with fervour, so that we even interrupted each other, although we were not wrangling. In the sky shone myriads of stars. Yákoff raised his eyes, and, pressing my hand closely, softly exclaimed:

> " Above us
> Lies Heaven with its eternal stars. . . .
> And above the stars is their Creator. . . ."

A devout tremor coursed through me; I turned cold all over, and sank down on his shoulder. . . . My heart was filled to overflowing. . . .

Where are those raptures now? Alas! in the place where youth is also.

I encountered Yákoff in Petersburg eight years later on. I had just obtained a position in the government service, and some one had got him a petty post in some department or other. Our meeting was of the most joyous character. Never shall I forget that moment when, as I was sitting at home one day, I suddenly heard his voice in the anteroom. . . . How I started, with what a violent beating of the heart did I spring to my feet and throw myself on his neck, without giving him time to take off his fur coat and unwind his scarf! How eagerly did I gaze at him athwart bright, involuntary tears of delight! He had aged somewhat in the course of the last seven years; wrinkles, fine as the trace of a needle, had furrowed his brow here and there, his cheeks had grown slightly sunken, but his beard had hardly increased at all in thickness, and his smile remained the same as of yore, and his laugh, his charming, inward laugh, which resembled a drawing-in of the breath, was the same as ever. . . .

Great heavens! what was there that we did not talk over that day! . . . . How many favourite poems we recited to each other! I began to urge him to come and live with me, but he would not consent; but, on the other hand, he promised to come to see me every day, and he kept his promise.

And Pásynkoff had not changed in soul, either. He presented himself before me the same romanticist as I had formerly known him. In spite of the way in which life's chill, the bitter chill of experience, had gripped him, the tender flower, which had blossomed early in the heart of my friend had retained all its pristine beauty. No sadness, no pensiveness even, were perceptible in him: as of old, he was gentle, but ever blithe in soul.

He lived in Petersburg as in a desert, taking no heed for the future, and consorting with hardly any one. I made him acquainted with the Zlotnítzkys. He called on them with tolerable frequency. Without being conceited, he was not shy: but with them, as everywhere else, he talked little, although he liked them. The heavy old

man, Tatyána Vasílievna's husband, even treated
him affectionately, and both the taciturn girls
speedily got used to him.

He would come bringing with him, in the back
pocket of his overcoat, some newly-published
work, and take a long time to make up his mind
to read it, but keep twisting his neck to one side,
like a bird, and peering to see whether it were
possible; and, at last, he would ensconce himself
in a corner (he was fond, in general, of sitting in
corners), pull out the book, and set to reading
aloud, now and then interrupting himself with
brief comments or exclamations. I noticed that
Varvára was more given to sitting down beside
him and listening than her sister was, although,
of course, she did not understand him clearly:
literature did not interest her. She would sit opposite Pásynkoff, with her chin propped on her
hands, and gaze,—not into his eyes, but into his
whole face,—and not give utterance to a single
word, but merely heave a sudden, noisy sigh.—In
the evening, we played at forfeits, especially on
Sundays and feast-days. We were then joined
by two young ladies, sisters, distant relatives of
the Zlotnítzkys,—small, plump girls, and frightful gigglers; also by several cadets and yunkers,
very quiet, good-natured lads. Pásynkoff always
seated himself beside Tatyána Vasílievna, and
helped her devise what the person who drew the
forfeit should do.

YÁKOFF PÁSYNKOFF

Sófya was not fond of the caresses and kisses with which forfeits are usually redeemed, while Varvára was vexed when she was compelled to hunt up anything or guess a riddle. The young ladies giggled incessantly,—heaven knows what about,—and I was sometimes seized with vexation when I looked at them, while Pásynkoff merely smiled and shook his head. Old Zlotnítzky took no part in our games, and even glowered at us in none too gracious wise from behind the door of his study. Once only, quite unexpectedly, did he come out to us, and suggest that the person whose forfeit was drawn should waltz with him; of course, we assented. Tatyána Vasílievna's forfeit was drawn; she flushed all over, grew confused and shy as a fifteen-year-old girl,—but her husband immediately bade Sófya to seat herself at the piano, stepped up to his wife, and took a couple of turns with her, in old-fashioned style, in three-time. I remember how his sallow, dark face, with unsmiling eyes, now appeared, now disappeared, as he revolved slowly, and without altering his stern expression. In waltzing he took long steps, and skipped, while his wife took quick little steps and pressed her face to his breast, as though in terror. He led her to her seat, made his bow to her, went off to his own room, and locked himself in. Sófya was on the point of rising. But Varvára begged her to continue the waltz, stepped up to Pásynkoff, and, extending her hand, said with an awkward grin: "Will you?" Pásynkoff was astounded, but sprang to his feet nevertheless,—he was always distinguished for his refined courtesy,—took Varvára round the waist, but slipped at the very first step, and hastily freeing himself from his lady, rolled straight under the pedestal on which stood the parrot's cage. . . . The cage fell, the parrot was frightened, and began to shriek: " Po-li-iice!" A universal roar of laughter rang out. . . . Zlotnítzky made his appearance on the threshold of his study, gave a surly stare, and clapped to the door. From that time forth, all that was necessary was to allude to this incident in Varvára's presence, and she would forthwith begin to laugh, with an expression on her face, as she glanced at Pásynkoff, which seemed to say that nothing more clever than what he had done on that occasion could possibly be devised.

Pásynkoff was extremely fond of music. He frequently asked Sófya to play something for him, seated himself a little apart, and listened, from time to time chiming in with his thin voice on the tender notes. He was especially ˉfond of Schubert's " The Constellations." He declared that when " The Constellations " was played in his presence, it always seemed to him as though, along with the sounds, some long, sky-blue rays poured down from on high, straight into his breast. To this day, at the sight of the cloudless sky at night, with its softly-twinkling stars, I always recall that melody of Schubert and Pásynkoff. . . . A certain stroll in the suburbs also recurs to my mind. The whole company of us had driven out in two double-seated, hired carriages, to Párgolovo.[1] I remember that we got the carriages in Vladímir street; they were very old, light-blue in colour, mounted on round springs, with broad boxes for the coachmen, and tufts of hay inside; the dark-bay, broken-winded horses drew us along at a ponderous trot, each limping on a different foot. For a long time we roamed through the pine groves surrounding Párgolovo, drank milk from earthen jugs, and ate strawberries and sugar. The weather was splendid. Varvára was not fond of walking much: she soon wearied; but on this occasion she did not lag behind us. She took off her hat, her hair fell out of curl, her heavy features grew animated, and her cheeks flushed crimson. On encountering two peasant maidens in the forest, she suddenly seated herself on the ground, called them to her, and did not caress them, but made them sit down beside her. Sófya stared at them from afar with a cold smile, and did not approach them. She was walking with Asánoff, while Zlotnítzky remarked that Varvára was a

[1] A Finnish village, situated a little more than ten miles north of St. Petersburg. There are many summer villas, and numbers of the former dwellings of the Finns have been converted into summer residences by literary and artistic people. — TRANSLATOR.

regular setting hen. Varvára rose and walked on. In the course of the stroll she approached Pásynkoff several times and said to him: " Yákoff Ivánitch, I have something to say to you," —but what she wanted to say to him remained a secret.

However, it is high time for me to return to my story.

I was delighted at Pásynkoff's arrival; but I recalled what I had done on the preceding day; I felt inexpressibly conscience-stricken, and hastily turned my face to the wall again. After waiting awhile, Yákoff asked me if I were well.

" Yes,"—I replied through my teeth:—" only, my head aches."

Yákoff made no reply, and picked up a book. More than an hour passed; I was already on the point of making a clean breast of the whole thing to Yákoff . . . when, suddenly, the bell in the anteroom began to ring.

The door on the staircase opened. . . I listened. . . . . Asánoff was asking my man whether I was at home.

Pásynkoff rose; he did not like Asánoff, and whispering to me that he would go and lie down on my bed, he betook himself to my sleeping-room.

A minute later, Asánoff entered.

From his flushed face, from his curt and dr⌐

bow alone, I divined that he had not come to me
for any ordinary call. "What 's in the wind?"
I thought.

"My dear sir,"—he began, swiftly seating
himself in an arm-chair,—" I have presented myself to you for the purpose of having you solve
for me a certain doubt."

"What is it, precisely?"

"This: I wish to know whether you are an
honourable man?"

I flared up.

"What does this mean?"—I asked.

"This is what it means," . . . . he returned,
pronouncing each word with clear-cut distinctness: "Yesterday evening I showed you a wallet
containing the letters of a certain person to me.
. . . . To-day you have repeated to that person
with reproach,—observe, with reproach,—several
expressions from those letters, without having the
slightest right to do so. I wish to know how you
will explain this?"

"And I wish to know, what right *you* have to
catechise me?"—I replied, trembling all over
with rage and inward shame.—"Why did you
brag of your uncle, of your correspondence?
What had I to do with that? All your letters are
intact, are n't they?"

"The letters are intact; but I was in such a condition last night that you might easily have . . . ."

"In short, my dear sir,"—I interposed, intentionally speaking as loudly as I could,—" I request you to leave me in peace, do you hear? I don't want to know anything about it, and I shall explain nothing to you. Go to that person for explanations!" (I felt my head beginning to reel.)

Asánoff darted at me a glance to which he, obviously, endeavoured to impart an expression of sneering penetration, plucked at his moustache, and rose without haste.

"I know now what I am bound to think,"—said he:—" your face is the best proof against you. But I must observe to you that well-bred persons do not behave in this manner. . . . To read a letter by stealth, and then to go to a well-born young girl and worry her is . . . ."

"Go to the devil!"—I shouted, stamping my foot:—" and send your second to me; I have no intention of discussing the matter with you."

"I beg that you will not instruct me,"—retorted Asánoff, coldly:—" and I was intending to send my second to you."

He went away. I fell back on the divan, and covered my eyes with my hands. Some one touched me on the shoulder; I removed my hands—in front of me stood Pásynkoff.

"What is this? Is it true?" . . . he asked me.—" Hast thou read another person's letter?"

I had not the strength to answer him, but nodded my head affirmatively.

Pásynkoff walked to the window, and, standing with his back to me, said slowly: " Thou hast read a letter from a young girl to Asánoff. Who is the girl? "

" Sófya Zlotnítzky,"—I replied, as a condemned man answers his judge.

For a long time Pásynkoff did not utter a word.

" Passion alone can excuse thee, to a certain extent,"—he began, at last.—" Art thou in love with Miss Zlotnítzky? "

" Yes."

Again Pásynkoff held his peace for a while.

" I thought so. And to-day thou didst go to her and begin to upbraid her. . . ."

" Yes, yes, yes . . . ." I said in desperation.— " Now thou mayest despise me. . . ."

Pásynkoff paced up and down the room a couple of times.

" And does she love him? "—he asked.

" She does. . . ."

Pásynkoff dropped his eyes, and stared for a long time immovably at the floor.

" Well, this must be put right,"—he began, raising his head:—" things cannot be left like this."

And he picked up his hat.

" Whither art thou going? "

" To Asánoff."

I sprang from the divan.

" But I will not permit thee. Good heavens! how canst thou do so?! What will he think? "

Pásynkoff cast a glance at me.

" And is it better, in thy opinion, to let his folly proceed, to ruin thyself, and disgrace the girl? "

" But what wilt thou say to Asánoff? "

" I shall try to bring him to his senses; I shall say that thou dost beg his pardon. . . ."

" But I won't beg his pardon! "

" Thou wilt not? Art not thou guilty? "

I looked at Pásynkoff: the calm and stern though sad expression of his face impressed me; it was a new one to me. I made no reply, and sat down on the divan.

Pásynkoff left the room.

With what torturing anguish did I wait his return! With what cruel sluggishness did the time pass! At last he returned—late.

" Well, how are things? "

" God be thanked! "—he replied.—" Everything is made up."

" Hast thou been to Asánoff? "

" I have."

" Well, how about him? He made wry faces, I suppose,"—I said with an effort.

" No, I will not say that. I expected more. . . . . He . . . . is not the vulgar man I had thought him."

" Well, and hast thou not been to see any one except him? "—I asked, after waiting a little.

" I have been to see the Zlotnítzkys."

" Ah! " . . . . (My heart began to beat violently. I did not dare to look Pásynkoff in the eye.) — " Well, and how about her? "

" Sófya Nikoláevna is a sensible girl, a kind-hearted girl. . . . Yes, she is a good girl. At first it was awkward for her, but afterward she recovered her composure. However, our entire conversation did not last more than five minutes."

" And didst thou . . . . tell her . . . . everything . . . . about me? "

" I told her what was necessary."

" Henceforth, I shall not be able to go to see them! " — I said dejectedly. . . .

" Why not? Yes, yes; thou mayest occasionally. On the contrary, thou must call on them, without fail, lest they should imagine something. . . ."

" Akh, Yákoff, thou wilt despise me now! " — I exclaimed, hardly restraining my tears.

" I? Despise thee? " . . . (His affectionate eyes warmed up with love.) — "Despise thee . . . . stupid man! Was it easy for thee, pray? Didst not thou suffer? "

He extended his hand to me; I rushed to him and fell, sobbing, on his neck.

AFTER the lapse of several days, in the course of which I was able to observe that Pásynkoff was very much out of sorts, I finally made up my mind to call on the Zlotnítzkys. It would be difficult to convey in words what I felt when I entered their drawing-room. I remember that I could barely distinguish faces, and that my voice broke in my throat. And Sófya was no more at ease than I was: she evidently forced herself to converse with me, but her eyes avoided mine just as my eyes avoided hers, and in her every movement, in her whole being, there peered forth constraint, mingled with . . . why conceal the truth? . . . with a secret repulsion. I endeavoured as speedily as possible, to free both her and myself from such painful sensations. This meeting was, happily, the last . . . . before her marriage. A sudden change in my fate took me to the other end of Russia, and I bade farewell for a long time to Petersburg, to the Zlotnítzky family, and, what was more painful to me than all else, to kind Yákoff Pásynkoff.

II

SEVEN years elapsed. I do not consider it necessary to relate precisely what happened to me in the course of all that time. I wore myself out with travelling all over Russia; I went into the wilds and the remote parts—and, thank God! the wilds and the remote parts are not so dreadful as some people think, and in the most hidden nooks of the forest, dreaming in primeval dense-ness, under fallen trees and thickets, grow fragrant flowers.

One day in spring, as I was passing, on business connected with the service, through the small county town of one of the remote Governments of eastern Russia, through the dim little window of my tarantás I caught sight of a man on the square, in front of a shop,—a man whose face seemed extremely familiar to me. I took a second look at this man and, to my no small delight, recognised in him Elisyéi, Pásynkoff's servant.

I immediately ordered my postilion to halt, sprang out of the tarantás, and approached Elisyéi.

"Good morning, brother!"—I said, with difficulty concealing my agitation:—"art thou here with thy master?"

"Yes,"—he replied slowly, then suddenly cried out:—"Akh, dear little father, is it you? And I did n't recognise you!"

"Art thou here with Yákoff Ivánitch?"

"I am, dear little father, I am. . . . And with whom else should I be?"

"Lead me to him as speedily as possible."

"Certainly, certainly! This way, please, this way. . . . We are stopping here in the inn."

And Elisyéi conducted me across the square, incessantly repeating: "Well, and how delighted Yákoff Ivánitch will be!"

This Elisyéi, of Kalmýk extraction, a man of extremely hideous and even fierce aspect, but the kindest of souls, and far from stupid, was passionately attached to Pásynkoff, and had been in his service for ten years.

" How is Yákoff Ivánitch's health? "—I asked him.

Elisyéi turned toward me his small, dark-yellow face.

" Akh, dear little father, 't is bad . . . bad, dear little father! You will not recognise him. . . . I don't believe he has long to live in this world. That 's the reason we settled down here, for we were on our way to Odessa for the cure." [1]

" Whence come you? "

" From Siberia, dear little father."

" From Siberia? "

" Just so, sir. Yákoff Ivánitch has been in the service there. And it was there he received his wound, sir."

" Has he been in the military service? "

" Not at all, sir. He was in the civil service, sir."

" What marvels are these? ! " I thought. In the meantime, we had drawn near the inn, and Elisyéi ran on ahead to announce me. During the first years of our separation, Pásynkoff and I had written to each other pretty frequently, but

---

[1] The famous salt-water and mud baths in the vicinity of Odessa.—TRANSLATOR.

I had received his last letter four years previous to this, and from that time onward had known nothing about him.

"Please come in, sir; please come in, sir!"—Elisyéi shouted to me from the staircase:—"Yákoff Ivánitch is very anxious to see you, sir."

I ran hastily up the rickety stairs, entered a dark little room—and my heart sank within me. . . . On a narrow bed, under his uniform cloak, pale as death, lay Pásynkoff, stretching out to me his bare, emaciated hand. I rushed to him and clasped him in a convulsive embrace.

"Yásha!"—I cried at last:—"What ails thee?"

"Nothing,"—he replied in a weak voice.—"I am not very well. How in the world do you come to be here?"

I sat down on a chair beside Pásynkoff's bed and, without releasing his hands from mine, I began to gaze into his face. I recognised the features which were so dear to me: the expression of his eyes and his smile had not changed, but how sickness had altered him!

He noticed the impression which he produced on me.

"I have not shaved for three days,"—he said:—"well, and my hair is not brushed either, but otherwise I . . . . I 'm all right."

"Tell me, please, Yásha,"—I began:—"what

is this Elisyéi has been telling me. . . . Thou art wounded?"

"Ah! yes; that's a whole history in itself,"—he replied.—"I'll tell thee about that later on. I really was wounded, and just fancy by what? An arrow."

"An arrow?"

"Yes, an arrow; only not the mythological one, not the dart of love, but a real arrow made from some extremely supple wood, with an artful sharp tip on the end. . . . Such an arrow produces a very unpleasant sensation, especially when it lands in the lungs."

"But how did it happen? Good gracious. . . ."

"This way. As thou knowest, there has always been a great deal that was ridiculous about my fate. Dost thou remember my comical correspondence in connection with demanding my papers? Well, and so I was wounded in an absurd way also. And, as a matter of fact, what well-bred man, in our enlightened century, permits himself to deal wounds with an arrow? And not accidentally—observe, not during some games or other, but in conflict."

"Yes; but still thou dost not tell me. . . ."

"Here now, wait a bit,"—he interrupted.—"Thou knowest that shortly after thy departure from Petersburg, I was transferred to Nóvgorod. I spent quite a long time in Nóvgorod, and, I must confess that I was bored, although I did meet there a certain being. . . ." (He heaved a sigh) . . . . " But there 's no time to go into that now; but a couple of years ago a splendid little post fell to my lot, a trifle distant, 't is true, in the Government of Irkútsk, but what 's the harm in that! Evidently, it was written in my father's fate and in mine that we should visit Siberia. A glorious land is Siberia! Rich and fertile, as any one will tell you. I liked it very much there. The natives of foreign stock were under my authority; a peaceable folk; but to my misfortune a score of their men, no more, took it into their heads to smuggle contraband goods. I was sent to seize them. So far as seizing them is concerned, I effected that, but one of them, out of caprice, it must have been, tried to defend himself, and treated me to that arrow. . . . I came near dying, but recovered. And now here I am on my way to make a final cure. . . The authorities have given the money,—may God grant them all health! "

Pásynkoff, completely exhausted, dropped his head on the pillow, and ceased speaking. A faint flush spread over his cheeks. He closed his eyes.

" He cannot talk much,"—said Elisyéi, who had not left the room, in an undertone.

" Here now,"—he went on, opening his eyes:— " I must have caught cold. The local district doctor is attending me,—thou wilt see him; he appears to know his business. But I am glad it has happened, because, otherwise, how could I have met thee?" (And he clasped my hand. His hand, which shortly before had been as cold as ice, was now burning hot.) — "Tell me something about thyself,"—he began again, throwing his cloak off his breast:—"for God knows when we shall see each other again."

I hastened to comply with his wish, if only to prevent his talking, and began my narration. At first he listened to me with great attention, then asked for a drink, then began to close his eyes again and to throw his head about on the pillow. I advised him to take a little nap, adding that I would not proceed further until he should recover, and would establish myself in the adjoining room.

"Things are very wretched here," . . . . Pásynkoff was beginning; but I stopped his mouth and softly left the room. Elisyéi followed me out.

"What's the meaning of this, Elisyéi? Why, he is dying, is n't he?"—I asked the faithful servant.

Elisyéi merely waved his hand in despair, and turned away.

Having dismissed my postilion, and hastily established myself in the adjoining room, I went to see whether Pásynkoff had fallen asleep. At his door I collided with a tall, very fat and heavy man. His puffy, pock-marked face expressed indolence—and nothing else, his tiny eyes were all but closed, and his lips glistened as though after sleep.

"Allow me to inquire,"—I asked him, "whether you are not the doctor?"

The fat man looked at me, after having, with an effort elevated his overhanging forehead with his eyebrows.

"I am, sir," he said at last.

"Will not you do me the favour to come this way to my room, doctor? I think Yákoff Ivánitch is asleep at present. I am his friend, and I should like to have a talk with you about his malady, which causes me great anxiety."

"Very good, sir,"—replied the doctor, with an expression which seemed to say: "What in the world possesses you to talk so much? I would have gone any way," and followed me.

"Tell me, please,"—I began, as soon as he had dropped down on a chair: "is my friend's condition dangerous? What do you think?"

"Yes,"—calmly replied the fat man.

"And . . . . is it very critical?"

"Yes, it is."

"So that he may even . . . . die?"

"Yes."

I must confess that I gazed at my interlocutor almost with hatred.

"Good gracious!"—I began: "then we must resort to some measures, call a consultation, or something. . . . Why, things cannot be left in this condition. . . Good heavens!"

" A consultation?—That can be done. Why not? We might call in Iván Efrémitch. . . ."

The doctor spoke with difficulty, and sighed incessantly. His belly heaved visibly, when he spoke, as though ejecting every word with an effort.

" Who is Iván Efrémitch? "

" The town doctor."

" Would n't it be better to send to the capital of the government—what think you? There certainly must be good physicians there."

" Why not? We might do that."

" And who is considered to be the best physician there? "

" The best? There was a Dr. Kohlrabus there . . . . only, I—I rather think he has been transferred somewhere else. However, I must confess that there is no necessity for sending."

" Why not? "

" Even the governmental doctor cannot help your friend."

" Is it possible that he is as bad as that? "

" Yes, exactly that; he 's done for."

" What, in particular, is his ailment? "

" He has received a wound. . . The lungs have been injured, you know. . . Well, and then he has caught cold, and fever has set in . . . . well, and so forth. . . And he has no reserve force. A man can't recover without reserve force, as you know yourself."

We both remained silent for a while.

"We might try homeopathy,"—said the fat man, darting a sidelong glance at me.

"Homeopathy? Why, you are an allopath, are you not?"

"Well, and what if I am an allopath! Do you think I don't know about homeopathy? Just as well as anybody. Our apothecary here gives homeopathic treatment, and he has no learned degree."

"Well!"—I said to myself: "things are in a bad way! . . . . No, doctor," I said: "you had better treat him by your usual method."

"As you like, sir."

The fat man rose, and heaved a sigh.

"Are you going to him?"—I inquired.

"Yes; I must take a look at him."

And he left the room.

I did not follow him. It was more than my strength would bear to see him at the bedside of my poor friend. I called my man and ordered him to drive immediately to the capital of the government, and inquire there for the best physician, and bring him, without fail. There came a rapping in the corridor; I opened the door quickly.

The doctor had already come out of Pásynkoff's room.

" Well, how is he? "—I asked in a whisper.

" All right; I have prescribed a potion."

" I have decided, doctor, to send to the government town. I do not doubt your skill; but you know yourself that two heads are better than one."

" Very well, that 's laudable! "—returned the fat man, and began to descend the stairs. Evidently, I bored him.

I went to Pásynkoff.

" Hast thou seen the local Æsculapius? "—he asked me.

" Yes,"—I replied.

" What I like about him,"—remarked Pásynkoff,—" is his wonderful composure. A doctor ought to be phlegmatic, ought n't he? That is very encouraging for the patient."

As a matter of course, I did not attempt to persuade him to the contrary.

Toward evening, contrary to my anticipations, Pásynkoff felt more at ease. He requested Elisyéi to prepare the samovár, announced that he was going to treat me to tea, and would drink a cup himself, and he was perceptibly more cheerful. Nevertheless, I endeavoured to prevent his talking; and perceiving that he was absolutely determined not to be quiet, I asked him if he did not wish me to read something aloud to him.

" As we used to do at Winterkeller's—dost thou remember? "—he replied: " Certainly, with pleasure. What shall we read? Look over my books, yonder on the window-sill. . . ."

I went to the window and took up the first book which came to hand. . . .

" What is that? "—he asked.

" Lérmontoff."

" Ah, Lérmontoff! Very good indeed! Púshkin is higher, of course. . . . Dost thou remember: ' Again the storm-clouds over me have gathered in the gloom,' . . . . or: ' For the last time thine image dear, I dare caress in mind.' Akh, how wonderfully fine! wonderfully fine! But Lérmontoff is good also. Come here, brother, take and open the book at haphazard, and read! "

I opened the book and was disconcerted; I had hit upon " The Testament." I tried to turn over the leaf, but Pásynkoff noticed my movement, and said hastily: " No, no, no! Read where it opened."

There was no help for it; I read " The Testament."

" A splendid thing! "—remarked Pásynkoff, as soon as I had uttered the last line.—" A splendid thing! But it is strange,"—he added, after a brief pause,—" it is strange that thou shouldst have hit upon ' The Testament,' of all things. . . . Strange! "

I began to read another poem, but Pásynkoff did not listen to me, gazed to one side, and repeated " strange! " a couple of times more.

I dropped the book on my knees.

" ' They have a little neighbour,' "—he whispered, and suddenly turning to me, he asked: " Dost thou remember Sófya Zlotnítzky? "

I flushed scarlet.

" How can I help remembering? ! "

" She married, did n't she? " . . .

" Yes; she married Asánoff, long ago. I wrote thee about that."

" Exactly, exactly so, thou didst write. Did her father forgive her in the end? "

" Yes; but he would not receive Asánoff."

" The stubborn old man! Well, and what dost thou hear about it? Do they live happily? "

" I really do not know. . . . I think they do. They are living in the country, in the *** Government; I have not seen them; but I have driven past."

" And have they children? "

" I believe so. . . By the way, Pásynkoff? "—I. asked.

He glanced at me.

" Confess,—I remember that thou wouldst not answer my question at the time; thou didst tell her that I was in love with her, didst thou not? "

" I told her everything, the whole truth. . . I always spoke the truth to her. To have concealed anything from her would have been a sin! "

Pásynkoff ceased speaking.

" Come, tell me,"—he began again: " didst thou get over thy love for her promptly or not? "

" Not very promptly; but I did get over it. What 's the use of sighing in vain? "

Pásynkoff turned his face toward me.

" But I, my dear fellow,"—he began, and his lips quivered,—" am no match for thee; I have n't got over my love for her to this day."

" What! "—I exclaimed with inexpressible amazement.—" Wert thou in love with her? "

" I was,"—said Pásynkoff, slowly, raising both hands to his head.—" How I loved her God alone knows. I never spoke of it to any one in the world, and never meant to mention it to any one . . . . but it has come out! ' I have but a brief while to live in this world,' they say. . . . So it does not matter! "

Pásynkoff's unexpected confession astounded me to such a degree that I was positively unable to utter a word, and merely thought: " Is it possible? how is it that I did not suspect this? "

" Yes,"—he went on, as though talking to himself:—" I loved her. I did not cease to love her, even when I learned that her heart belonged to Asánoff. But it pained me to learn that! If she had fallen in love with thee, I would, at all events, have rejoiced on thy account; but Asánoff. . . . How could he please her? It was his luck! And she was not able to be unfaithful to her feeling, to cease to love him. An honourable soul does not change. . . ."

I recalled Asánoff's visit after the fatal dinner, Pásynkoff's intervention, and involuntarily clasped my hands.

" Thou didst learn all that from me, poor fellow! "—I exclaimed:—" and thou didst take it upon thyself to go to her, nevertheless! "

" Yes,"—said Pásynkoff:—" that explanation with her—I shall never forget it. It was then I learned, it was then I understood the meaning of the motto I had long before chosen for myself: ' Resignation.' But she still remained my constant dream, my ideal. . . . And pitiable is he who lives without an ideal! "

I glanced at Pásynkoff; his eyes seemed to be fixed on the distance, and blazed with a feverish gleam.

" I loved her,"—he went on:—" I loved her, her, quiet, honourable, inaccessible, incorruptible; when she went away, I became nearly crazed with grief. . . . I have never loved any one since. . . ."

And suddenly, turning round, he pressed his face to his pillow, and fell to weeping softly.

I sprang to my feet, bent over him, and began to comfort him. . . .

" Never mind,"—he said, raising his head, and shaking back his hair:—" I did n't mean to do it. I feel rather sad, rather sorry . . . . for myself, that is to say. . . . But it is of no consequence. The poetry is to blame for it all. Read me some other poems—something more cheerful."

I took up Lérmontoff, and began hastily to turn over the leaves; but, as though expressly, I kept hitting upon poems which might again agitate Pásynkoff. At last I read him " The Gifts of the Térek."

" Rhetorical crackling! "—remarked my poor friend, in the tone of an instructor:—" but there are good places! I tried my hand at poetry myself, my dear fellow, in thine absence, and began a poem: ' The Beaker of Life,'—but it came to nothing! my business, brother, is to sympathise, not to create. . . . But I feel tired, somehow; I believe I had better take a nap—what dost thou think? What a splendid thing sleep is, when you come to think of it! All our life is a dream, and the best thing in it is sleep."

" And poetry? "—I asked.

" Poetry is a dream also, only a dream of paradise."

Pásynkoff closed his eyes.

I stood for a while beside his bed. I did not think that he could get to sleep quickly; but his breathing became more even and prolonged. I stole out of the room on tiptoe, returned to my own chamber, and lay down on the divan. For a long time I reflected on what Pásynkoff had told me, recalled many things, marvelled, and, at last, fell asleep myself. . . .

Some one nudged me: before me stood **Elisyéi**.
" Please come to my master,"—he said.
I rose at once.
" What is the matter with him? "
" He is delirious."
" Delirious? And he has not been so before? "
" Yes; he was delirious last night also; but somehow it is dreadful to-night."

I entered Pásynkoff's room. He was not lying on his bed, but sitting up, with his whole body bent forward, softly throwing his hands apart, smiling and talking—talking incessantly in a weak, toneless voice, like the rustling of reeds. His eyes were wandering. The melancholy light of the night-taper, placed on the floor, and screened by a book, lay in a motionless patch on the ceiling; Pásynkoff's face looked paler than ever in the half gloom.

I went up to him, called him by name—he did not reply. I began to listen to his mumblings: he was raving about Siberia, about its forests. At times there was sense in his ravings.

" What trees! "—he whispered: " they reach to the very sky. How much hoar-frost there is on them! Silver. . . . Snow-drifts. . . . . And yonder are little tracks . . . . a hare has leaped along, or a white ermine. . . . No, it is my father who has run past with my papers. Yonder he is! . . . Yonder he is! I must go; the moon is shining. I must go and find my papers. . . .

Ah, a flower, a scarlet flower—Sófya is there. . . .
There, little bells are ringing, oh, it is the frost
ringing. . . Akh, no; it is the stupid bull-finches
hopping in the bushes, and whistling. . . . See
the red-breasted warblers! It is cold. . . . Ah!
there is Asánoff. . . . Akh, yes, he is a cannon,
you know—a brass cannon, and his gun-carriage
is green. That is why he pleases people. Was
that a shooting-star? No, it is an arrow flying.
. . . . Akh, how swiftly, and straight at my
heart! . . . . Who is that shooting? Thou, Sónetchka?"

He bent his head and began to whisper incoher-
ent words. I glanced at Elisyéi; he was standing with his hands clasped behind his back, and
gazing compassionately at his master.

"Well, my dear fellow, hast thou become a
practical man?"—he suddenly inquired, fixing
on me a glance so clear, so full of intelligence,
that I gave an involuntary start, and was on the
point of answering, but he immediately went on:
—"But I, brother, have not become a practical
man, I have not done that which thou wilt do!
I was born a dreamer, a dreamer! Dreams,
dreams. . . . What is a dream? Sobakévitch's
peasant,—that 's what a dream is. Okh! . . . ."

Pásynkoff raved until nearly daylight; at last,
he quieted down a little, sank back on his pillow,
and fell into a doze. I returned to my own room.

Exhausted by the cruel night, I fell into a heavy slumber.

Again Elisyéi awakened me.

"Akh, dear little father!"—he said to me in a trembling voice:—"I believe Yákoff Ivánitch is dying. . . ."

I ran to Pásynkoff. He was lying motionless. By the light of the dawning day, he already looked like a corpse. He recognised me.

"Farewell,"—he whispered:—"remember me to her, I am dying. . . ."

"Yásha!"—I cried:—"don't say that! Thou wilt live. . . ."

"No; what's the use? I am dying. . . . Here, take this in memory of me . . ." (He pointed at his breast.) . . . .

"What is this?"—he suddenly began to speak again:—"Look! the sea . . . . all golden; on it are blue islands, marble temples, palms, incense. . . ."

He fell silent . . . . dropped his eyes. . . .

Half an hour later he was dead. Elisyéi fell, weeping, on his breast. I closed his eyes.

On his neck was a small silken amulet, attached to a black cord. I took possession of it.

On the third day he was buried. . . . The noblest of hearts had vanished forever from the world! I myself flung the first handful of earth on him.

III

ANOTHER year and a half passed. Business forced me to go to Moscow. I established myself in one of the best hotels there. One day, as I was passing along the corridor, I glanced at the black-board whereon stood the names of travellers, and almost cried aloud in surprise: opposite No. 1 stood the name of Sófya Nikoláevna Asánoff. I had accidentally heard much that was evil about her husband of late; I had learned that he had become passionately addicted to liquor and cards; had ruined himself, and, altogether, was conducting himself badly. People spoke with respect of his wife. . . . Not without agitation did I return to my own room. Passion which had cooled long, long ago, seemed to begin to stir in my heart, and my heart began to beat violently. I decided to go to Sófya Nikoláevna. "What a long time has passed since the day we parted," I thought: "she has probably forgotten everything which took place between us then."

I sent to her Elisyéi, whom I had taken into my service after Pásynkoff's death, with my visiting-card, and ordered him to inquire whether she was at home, and whether I could see her. Elisyéi speedily returned, and announced that

Sófya Nikoláevna was at home, and would receive me.

I betook myself to Sófya Nikoláevna. When I entered, she was standing in the middle of the room, and taking leave of some tall, stout gentleman or other. "As you like,"—he was saying, in a thick, sibilant voice:—"he is not a harmless man, he is a useless man; and every useless man in well-regulated society is harmful, harmful!"

With these words, the tall gentleman left the room. Sófya Nikoláevna turned to me.

"What a long time it is since we met!"—said she.—"Sit down, I beg of you. . . ."

We sat down. I looked at her. . . . To behold, after a long separation, features once dear; to recognise them, yet not to recognise them, as though through the former, still unforgotten face, another face—like, yet strange—had emerged; momentarily, almost involuntarily to note the traces imposed by time,—all this is sad enough. "And I, also, must have changed," one thinks to himself. . . .

Sófya Nikoláevna had not aged greatly, however; but when I had seen her for the last time, she had just entered her seventeenth year, and nine years had elapsed since that day. Her features had become more severe and regular than ever. As of old, they expressed sincerity of feeling and firmness; but in place of their former composure, a certain hidden pain and anxiety was manifested in them. Her eyes had grown deeper and darker. She had come to resemble her mother. . . .

Sófya Nikoláevna was the first to start the conversation.

" We are both changed,"—she began.— " Where have you been all this time? "

" I have been wandering about here and there," I replied.—"And have you been living in the country all the while? "

" Chiefly in the country. And I am only passing through here now."

" How are your parents? "

" My mother is dead, but my father is still in Petersburg; my brother is in the service; Várya lives with him."

" And your husband? "

" My husband? "—she said in a somewhat hurried voice:—" He is now in southern Russia, at the fairs. He was always fond of horses, as you know, and he has set up a stud-farm of his own . . . so, for that purpose . . . he is now buying horses."

At that moment a little girl of eight entered the room, with her hair dressed in Chinese fashion, a very sharp and vivacious little face, and large, dark-grey eyes. On catching sight of me, she immediately thrust out her little foot, made a swift curtsey, and went to Sófya Nikoláevna.

" Let me introduce to you my little daughter,"
—said Sófya Nikoláevna, touching the little girl
with her finger under her chubby chin:—" she
would not consent to remain at home, but entreated me to take her with me."

The little girl swept her quick eyes over me,
and frowned slightly.

" She 's my fine, courageous girl,"—went on
Sófya Nikoláevna:—" she is not afraid of anything. And she studies well; I must praise her
for that."

" *Comment se nomme monsieur?* "—inquired
the little girl, in a low voice, bending toward her
mother.

Sófya Nikoláevna mentioned my name.
Again the little girl glanced at me.

" What is your name? "—I asked her.

" My name is Lídiya,"—replied the little girl,
looking me boldly in the eye.

" They spoil you, I suppose,"—I remarked.

" Who spoils me? "

" Who? Why, everybody, I suppose, beginning with your parents." (The little girl darted
a silent glance at her mother.) " Konstantín
Alexándrovitch, I imagine,"—I went on. . . .

" Yes, yes,"—interposed Sófya Nikoláevna,
while her little daughter did not remove her attentive gaze from her; " my husband, of course
. . . . . he is very fond of children. . . ."

A strange expression flashed over Lídiya's intelligent little face. Her lips pouted slightly; she cast down her eyes.

" Tell me,"—hastily added Sófya Nikoláevna:
—" you are here on business, I suppose? "

" Yes. . . . And you also? "

" Yes; I also. . . . In my husband's absence, you understand, I am forced to attend to business."

" *Maman!* "—began Lídiya.

" *Quoi, mon enfant?* "

" *Non—rien. . . . Je te dirai après.*"

Sófya Nikoláevna laughed, and shrugged her shoulders.

We both maintained silence for a space, while Lídiya folded her arms pompously on her breast.

" Tell me, please,"—began Sófya Nikoláevna again:—" I remember that you had a friend . . . . what in the world was his name? he had such a kind face . . . . he was always reading poetry; a very enthusiastic man. . . ."

" Was n't it Pásynkoff? "

" Yes, yes; Pásynkoff . . . . where is he now? "

" He is dead."

" Dead? "—repeated Sófya Nikoláevna:— " what a pity! . . , ."

" Have I seen him? "—asked the little girl in a hasty whisper.

" No, Lídiya, thou hast not seen him. What a pity! "—repeated Sófya Nikoláevna.

"You mourn for him . . . ." I began:—
"What would you do if you had known him as
I knew him? . . . But permit me to inquire:
why did you mention him in particular?"

"By accident; I really don't know why. . . ."
(Sófya Nikoláevna dropped her eyes.)—"Lídiya,"—she added:—"go to thy nurse."

"Wilt thou call me when I may come?"—
asked the little girl.

"I will."

The little girl left the room. Sófya Nikoláevna turned to me.

"Tell me, please, everything you know about
Pásynkoff."

I began my narration. I sketched, in brief
words, the whole life of my friend; I tried, to
the best of my ability, to depict his soul; I described his last meeting with me, his end.

"And so that was the sort of man he was!"—
I exclaimed, as I concluded my narration:—"he
is gone from us, unnoticed, almost unappreci-
ated! And that would be no great harm. What
does popular appreciation amount to? But I
feel pained, affronted, that such a man, with
so loving and devoted a heart should have died,
without having even once experienced the bliss
of mutual love, without having awakened sympathy in a single woman's heart worthy of him!
. . . What if the rest of us do not taste that
bliss? We are not worthy of it; but Pásynkoff!

. . . And, moreover, have not I in my day encountered a thousand men who were not to be compared with him in any way, and who have been beloved? Are we bound to assume that certain defects in a man,—self-confidence, for example, or frivolousness, are indispensable in order that a woman shall become attached to him? Or is love afraid of perfection, of such perfection as is possible here on earth, as of something alien and terrible to it?"

Sófya Nikoláevna listened to me to the end, without taking from me her stern and piercing eyes, or unsealing her lips; only her brows twitched from time to time.

"Why do you assume,"—she said, after a brief pause,—"that not a single woman loved your friend?"

"Because I know it, I know it for a fact."

Sófya Nikoláevna was on the point of saying something, but stopped short. She seemed to be struggling with herself.

"You are mistaken,"—she said at last:—"I know a woman who loved your dead friend fervently: she loves and remembers him to this day . . . . and the news of his death will wound her deeply."

"Who is the woman?—permit me to ask."

"My sister Várya."

"Varvára Nikoláevna!"—I exclaimed in amazement.

" Yes."

" What? Varvára Nikoláevna? "—I repeated:—" that . . . ."

" I will complete your thought,"—pursued Sófya Nikoláevna:—" that cold, indifferent, in your opinion, languid girl, loved your friend; that is the reason she has not married, and will not marry. Until to-day, I have been the only one to know this. Várya would have died, rather than betray her secret. In our family, we know how to hold our peace and endure."

For a long time I gazed intently at Sófya Nikoláevna, involuntarily meditating on the bitter significance of her last words.

" You have astounded me,"—I said at last.—" But do you know, Sófya Nikoláevna, if I were not afraid of awakening in you unpleasant memories, I also, in my turn, could astound you. . . ."

" I do not understand you,"—she returned slowly, and in some confusion.

" You really do not understand me,"—said I, rising hastily:—" and therefore, permit me, instead of a verbal explanation, to send you a certain article. . . ."

" But what is it? "—she asked.

" Be not disturbed, Sófya Nikoláevna; the question does not concern me."

I bowed and returned to my room, got out the amulet which I had taken from Pásynkoff, and sent it to Sófya Nikoláevna, with the following note:

"This amulet, my dead friend wore constantly on his breast, and died with it there. In it you will find a note of yours to him, of utterly insignificant contents; you may read it. He wore it because he loved you passionately, as he confessed to me only the night before he died. Now that he is dead, why should not you know that his heart belonged to you?"

Elisyéi soon returned, and brought me back the amulet.

"How is this?"—I asked:—"Did she send no message to me?"

"No, sir."

I said nothing for a while.

"Did she read my note?"

"She must have read it, sir; her little girl carried it to her."

"Unapproachable,"—I thought, recalling Pásynkoff's last words.—"Well, go,"—I said aloud.

Elisyéi smiled in a strange sort of way, and did not leave the room.

"A certain young girl . . . . has come to see you, sir,"—he began.

"What girl?"

Elisyéi was silent for a space.

"Did n't my late master tell you anything, sir?"

" No. . . . What dost thou mean? "

" When he was in Nóvgorod,"—went on Elisyéi, touching the jamb of the door with his hand, ... " he made acquaintance with a certain young girl, say, for example. So it is that girl who wishes to see you, sir. I met her on the street the other day. I said to her: ' Come; if the master commands, I will admit thee.' "

" Ask her in, ask her in, of course. But . . . . what sort of a girl is she? "

" A lowly girl, sir . . . . from the petty burgher class . . . . a Russian."

" Did the late Yákoff Ivánitch love her? "

" He loved her right enough, sir. Well, she . . . . when she heard that my master was dead, she was greatly afflicted. She 's a good girl, right enough, sir."

" Ask her in, ask her in."

Elisyéi went out, and immediately returned. Behind him came a girl in a gaily-coloured cotton gown, and with a dark kerchief on her head, which half covered her face. On catching sight of me, she was abashed, and turned away.

" What ails thee? "—Elisyéi said to her:— " Go along, have no fear."

I stepped up to her, and took her hand.

" What is your name? "—I asked her.

" Másha,"—she said, in a soft voice, casting a covert glance at me.

Judging from her appearance, she was twenty-two or three years of age; she had a round, rather plain but agreeable face, soft cheeks, gentle blue eyes, and small, very pretty, clean hands. She was neatly dressed.

" Did you know Yákoff Ivánitch? " — I went on.

" Yes, sir," — she said, plucking at the ends of her kerchief, and tears started out on her eyelashes.

I asked her to be seated.

She immediately sat down on the edge of a chair, without ceremony, and without putting on airs. Elisyéi left the room.

" You made his acquaintance in Nóvgorod? "

" Yes, in Nóvgorod, sir," — she replied, tucking both hands under her kerchief. " I only heard of his death day before yesterday, from Elisyéi Timoféitch, sir. Yákoff Ivánitch, when he went away to Siberia, promised to write, and he did write twice; but after that he did not write any more, sir. I would have followed him to Siberia, but he did not want me to, sir."

" Have you relatives in Nóvgorod? "

" I have."

" Did you live with them? "

" I lived with my mother and my married sister; but afterward my mother got angry with me; and it got crowded at my sister's: they had a lot of children; so I moved away. I always set my hopes on Yákoff Ivánitch, and wanted nothing except to see him, for he was always affectionate to me—ask Elisyéi Timoféitch if he was n't."

Másha ceased speaking for a little while.

"I have his letters with me,"—she went on.— "Here, look at them, sir."

She drew from her pocket several letters and gave them to me:—"Read them, sir,"—she added.

I unfolded one letter, and recognised Pásynkoff's handwriting.

"Dear Másha!" (He wrote a large, fine hand)—"yesterday thou didst lean thy dear little head against my head, and when I asked: 'why art thou doing this?' thou didst say to me: 'I want to listen to what you are thinking about.' I will tell thee what I was thinking about: I was thinking how nice it would be for Másha to learn to read and write! Then she could have deciphered this letter. . . ."

Másha glanced at the letter.

"He wrote me that while he was still in Nóvgorod,"—she said:—"when he was planning to teach me to read and write. Look at the others, sir. There is one from Siberia, sir. Here, read this one, sir."

I read the letters. They were all very affectionate, even tender. In one of them, precisely in that first letter from Siberia, Pásynkoff called Másha his best friend, and promised to send her money to come to Siberia, and wound up with

the following words: " I kiss thy pretty little
hands; the young girls here have no such hands;
and their heads are no match for thine, neither
are their hearts. . . . Read the little books which
I gave thee, and remember me, and I shall not
forget thee. Thou alone, alone hast loved me;
and so I wish to belong to thee only. . . ."

" I see that he was very much attached to thee,"
—I said, returning the letters to her.

" He loved me very much,"—returned Másha,
carefully stowing the letters away in her pocket,
and tears coursed slowly down her cheeks.—
" I always set my hopes on him; if the Lord
had prolonged his life, he would not have abandoned me. May God grant him the kingdom
of heaven! . . . ."

She wiped her eyes with a corner of her kerchief.

" Where are you living now? "—I inquired.

" I am living in Moscow now; I came with a
lady; but now I am without a place. I went to
Yákoff Ivánitch's aunt, but she is very poor herself. Yákoff Ivánitch often talked to me about
you, sir,"—she added, rising and bowing:—
" he was always very fond of you, and remembered you. I met Elisyéi Timoféitch here the
day before yesterday, and I thought: would n't
you be willing to help me, as I have no place at
present. . . ."

"With great pleasure, Márya .... allow me to inquire your patronymic?"

"Petróff,"—replied Másha, and dropped her eyes.

"I will do everything in my power for you, Márya Petróvna,"—I went on:—"I am only sorry that I am only passing through the town, and am very little acquainted in nice houses."

Másha sighed.

"I'd like to get some sort of a place, sir. . . . I don't know how to cut out, but when it comes to sewing, I can sew anything . . . . well, and I can take care of children."

"I must give her some money," I thought: "but how am I to do it?"

"Hearken, Márya Petróvna,"—I began, not without confusion:—"you must excuse me, please, but you know from Pásynkoff's words on what friendly terms I was with him. . . . Will you not permit me to offer to you . . . . for present necessities . . . . a small sum? . . ."

Másha darted a look at me.

"What, sir?"—she asked.

"Are you not in need of money?"—I said.

Másha blushed all over and bent her head.

"What should I do with money?"—she whispered. "Better get me a place, sir. . . ."

"I will try to get you a place; but I cannot answer for that with certainty; and really, it is wrong for you to feel ashamed. . . . For I am not a mere stranger to you. . . Accept this from me, in memory of your friend. . . ."

I turned away, hastily took several bank-notes from my pocket-book, and gave them to her.

Masha stood motionless, her head drooping still lower. . . .

" Take it,"—I repeated.

She softly raised her eyes to mine, looked into my face with a mournful gaze, softly liberated her pale hand from under her kerchief, and stretched it out to me. I laid the bank-notes on her cold fingers. She silently hid her hand again under her kerchief, and dropped her eyes.

" And in future, Márya Petróvna,"—I went on,—" if you are in want of anything, please appeal directly to me.—I will give you my address."

" I thank you humbly, sir,"—she said; and after a brief pause, she added: " Did n't he speak to you about me, sir? "

" I met him the day before he died, Márya Petróvna. However, I do not recollect. . . . I think he did speak of you."

Masha passed her hand over her hair, propped her cheek lightly on it, meditated, and after saying: " Farewell, sir," she left the room.

I sat down at the table, and began to think bitter thoughts. This Másha, her relations to

YÁKOFF PÁSYNKOFF

Pásynkoff, his letters, the secret love of Sófya
Nikoláevna's sister for him. . . . " Poor fellow!
Poor fellow!"—I whispered, sighing heavily.
I recalled the whole of Pásynkoff's life, his
childhood, his youth, Fräulein Frederika. . . .
" There now,"—I thought: " Fate did not give
thee much! she did not gladden thee with a great
deal!"

On the following day, I called again on Sófya
Nikoláevna. I was made to wait in the anteroom, and when I entered, Lídiya was already
sitting beside her mother. I understood that
Sófya Nikoláevna did not wish to renew the conversation of the preceding day.

We began to chat—really, I do not remember
about what,—rumours of the town, business
matters. . . . Lídiya frequently put in her little
word, and gazed slily at me. An amusing importance had suddenly made its appearance on
her mobile little face. . . . The clever little girl
must have divined that her mother had placed her
by her side of deliberate purpose.

I rose, and began to take my leave. Sófya
Nikoláevna escorted me to the door. " I made
you no reply yesterday,"—she said, halting at
the threshold:—" and what reply was there to
make? Our life does not depend on ourselves;
but we all have one anchor, from which we need
never break away, unless we so wish it ourselves:
the sense of duty."

I silently bent my head in token of assent, and bade farewell to the young Puritan.

All that evening I remained at home; but I did not think of her; I kept thinking, thinking incessantly of my dear, my never-to-be-forgotten Pásynkoff—of that last of the romanticists; and feelings now sad, now tender, surged up sweetly in my breast, and resounded on the strings of my heart, which was not yet grown utterly old. . . . Peace to thy ashes, thou unpractical man, thou kind-hearted idealist! And may God grant to all practical gentlemen, to whom thou were ever an alien, and who, perchance, will still ridicule thy shadow,—may God grant them to taste at least the hundredth part of those pure delights, wherewith, in spite of Fate and men, thy poor and submissive life was adorned!

"FAUST"

(1855)

"FAUST"

A STORY IN NINE LETTERS

Entbehren sollst du, sollst entbehren.
"FAUST." (Part I.)

FIRST LETTER

*From Pável Alexándrovitch B*** to Semyón
Nikoláevitch V***.*

VILLAGE OF M .... OE, June 6, 1850.

I ARRIVED here three days ago, my dear
friend, and, in accordance with my promise,
I take up my pen to write to thee. A fine rain
has been drizzling down ever since morning; it
is impossible to go out; and besides, I want to
have a chat with thee. Here I am again, in my
old nest, in which I have not been—dreadful to
say—for nine whole years. Really, when one
comes to think of it, I have become altogether
another man. Yes, actually, another man. Dost
thou remember in the drawing-room the small,
dark mirror of my great-grandmother, with
those queer scrolls at the corners? Thou wert
always meditating on what it had beheld a hundred years ago. As soon as I arrived, I went

129

to it, and was involuntarily disconcerted. I suddenly perceived how I had aged and changed
of late. However, I am not the only one who has
grown old. My tiny house, which was in a state
of decrepitude long since, hardly holds itself upright now, and has sagged down, and sunk into
the ground. My good Vasílievna, the housekeeper (thou hast not forgotten her, I am sure:
she used to regale thee with such splendid pre-
serves), has quite dried up and bent together.
At sight of me, she could not cry out, and she
did not fall to weeping, but merely grunted and
coughed, sat down exhausted on a chair, and
waved her hand in despair. Old Terénty is still
alert, holds himself erect as of old, and as he
walks turns out his feet clad in the same yellow
nankeen trousers, and shod with the same squeak-
ing goat's-leather shoes, with high instep and
knots of ribbon, which evoked your emotions
more than once. . . . But great heavens!—how
loose those trousers now hang on his thin legs!
how white his hair has grown! And his face has
all shrivelled up to the size of your fist; and when
he talked with me, when he began to make ar-
rangements and issue orders in the adjoining
room, I found him ridiculous, and yet I was
sorry for him. All his teeth are gone, and he
mumbles with a whistling and hissing sound.

On the other hand, the park has grown wonderfully beautiful: the little modest bushes of

lilac, acacia, and honeysuckle (you and I set them
out, dost remember?) have grown up into magnificent, dense thickets; the birches and maples,
have all spread upward and outward; the lin-
den alleys in particular, have become very fine.
I love those alleys, I love their tender grey-
green hue, and the delicate fragrance of the air
beneath their arches; I love the mottled network
of circles of light on the dark earth—I have no
sand, as thou knowest. My favourite oak-sap-
ling has already become a young oak-tree. Yesterday, in the middle of the day, I sat for more
than an hour in its shade, on a bench. I felt
greatly at my ease. Round about the grass
gleamed so merrily green; over all lay a golden
light, strong and soft; it even penetrated into
the shade . . . . and how many birds I heard!
Thou hast not forgotten, I trust, that birds are
my passion! The turtle-doves cooed incessantly,
now and then an oriole whistled, a chaffinch executed its charming song, thrushes waxed angry
and chattered, a cuckoo answered from afar;
suddenly, like a madman, a woodpecker uttered
a piercing scream. I listened, listened to all this
soft, commingled din, and did not want to move,
and in my heart was something which was not
indolence, nor yet emotion.

And the park is not the only thing that has
grown up; sturdy, robust lads, in whom I should
never have recognised the little urchins whom I

used to know, are constantly coming under my eye. And thy favourite, Timósha, has now become such a Timofyéi as thou canst not picture to thyself. Thou hadst fears for his health then, and predicted consumption for him; but thou shouldst take a look now at his huge, red hands, and the way they stick out from the tight sleeves of his nankeen coat, and what round, thick muscles stand out all over him! The nape of his neck is like that of a bull, and his head is all covered with round, blond curls,—a regular Farnese Hercules! His face has undergone less change, however, than the faces of the others have; it has not even increased greatly in size, and his cheery, " gaping " smile, as thou wert wont to express it, has remained the same as of yore. I have taken him for my valet; I discarded my Petersburg valet in Moscow: he was altogether too fond of putting me to shame, and making me feel his superiority in the usages of the capital.

I have not found a single one of my dogs; they are all dead. Néfta alone outlived the rest—and even she did not survive till my arrival, as Argos waited for Ulysses; she was not fated to behold her former master and comrade of the hunt with her dimmed eyes. But Shávka is still sound, and still barks hoarsely, and one ear is torn, as usual, and there are burrs in his tail, as is fitting.

I have established myself in thy former chamber. The sun strikes on it, it is true, and there

are a great many flies in it; but, on the other
hand, it has less of the odour of an old house about
it than the other rooms. 'T is strange! that
musty, somewhat sour and withered odour acts
powerfully on my imagination. I will not say
that it is disagreeable to me—on the contrary;
but it evokes in me sadness, and, eventually,
dejection. Like thyself, I am very fond of the
pot-bellied chests of drawers with their brass
fastenings, the white arm-chairs with oval backs
and curved legs, the glass chandeliers covered
with fly-specks, with the huge egg of purple
tinsel in the middle,—in a word, all sorts of furniture belonging to our grandfathers; but I cannot look at all this constantly: a sort of perturbed
tedium (precisely that!) takes possession of me.
In the room where I have settled myself, the furniture is of the most ordinary description, home-
made; but I have left in one corner a tall, narrow
cupboard with shelves, on which, athwart the
dust are barely visible divers old-fashioned, pot-
bellied vessels, of blue and green glass. And I
have given orders that there shall be hung on the
wall,—thou wilt recall it,—that portrait of a
woman, in the black frame, which thou wert wont
to call the portrait of Manon Lescaut. It has
grown a little darker in these nine years; but the
eyes look forth as pensively, slily, and tenderly
as ever, and the lips smile in the same frivolous
and mournful way as of old, and the half-

stripped rose dangles as softly as ever from the slender fingers. The window-shades in my room amuse me greatly. Once upon a time they used to be green, but have grown yellow in the sunlight. Upon them, in black, are painted scenes from d'Arlincourt's "Hermit." On one shade, this hermit, with the biggest sort of a beard, staringly-prominent eyes, and in sandals, is dragging off to the mountains some dishevelled young lady or other; on the other shade, a fierce combat is in progress between four knights in skull-caps, and with puffs on their shoulders; one is lying, *en raccourci,* slain—in short, all the horrors are depicted, and all around reigns such undisturbed tranquillity, and such gentle reflections are cast on the ceiling from the shades themselves. . . . A sort of spiritual quietude has descended upon me since I have established myself here. I do not want to do anything; I do not want to see any one, to meditate about anything. I am too indolent to speculate; but not too indolent to think; but thinking is not indolence; they are two separate things, as thou art well aware.

At first the memories of my childhood invaded me. . . . Wheresoever I went, whatsoever I looked at, they surged up from every direction, clear, clear to the most minute details, and motionless, as it were, in their distinct definiteness. . . . . Then those memories were succeeded by others; then . . . then I softly turned away from the past, and there remained nothing in my breast save a sort of dreamy burden. Just imagine! As I sat on the dam, under the willow, I suddenly fell to weeping, quite unexpectedly; and would have wept for a long time, in spite of my advanced age, had I not been mortified by a passing peasant-wife, who stared at me with curiosity, then, without turning her head toward me, made a straight, low obeisance, and walked past. I should have liked greatly to remain in that frame of mind (I shall not weep any more, of course) until my departure hence, that is to say, until the month of September; and I shall be very much chagrined, if any one of the neighbours should take it into his head to call on me. However, apparently, there is nothing to fear in that quarter; for I have no near neighbours. Thou wilt understand me, I am convinced; thou knowest, from thine own experience, how beneficial solitude often is. . . . I need it now, after all sorts of wanderings.

But I shall not be bored. I have brought with me several books, and I have a very fair library here. Yesterday I opened the cases, and rummaged for a long time among the musty books. I found many curious things, which I had not noticed before: " Candide," in a manuscript translation of the '70s; newspapers and journals of the same period; " The Triumphant Chame-

leon " (that is to say, Mirabeau) ; " Le Paysan
Perverti," and so forth. I came upon some children's books, my own, and those of my father,
and my grandmother, and, even—just fancy!—
of my great-grandmother. On one very, very
ancient French grammar, in a gay binding, was
written in large letters: *" Ce livre appartient à
M-lle Eudoxie de Lavrine,"* and the year was
added—1741. I saw books which I had brought
from abroad some time or other; among others,
Goethe's " Faust." Perhaps thou art not aware
that there was a time when I knew " Faust " by
heart (the first part, of course), word for word;
I could not read it enough to satisfy myself. . . .
But, other times, other dreams, and in the course
of the last nine years I don't believe I have taken
Goethe in my hand a single time. With what
an inexpressible feeling did I behold the little
book, but too familiar to me (a bad edition of
1828). I carried it off with me, lay down on
my bed, and began to read. What an effect the
whole magnificent first scene had upon me! The
appearance of the Spirit of Earth, his words;
thou rememberest: " On the billows of life, in
the whirlwind of action," aroused within me the
trepidation and chill of rapture which I have not
experienced for many a day. I recalled everything: Berlin, and my student days, and Fräulein Klara Schtik, and Zeidelmann, in the part
of Mephistopheles, and everything and every

one. . . . For a long time I could not get to
sleep; my youth came and stood before me, like
a ghost; like a fire, like a poison, it coursed
through my veins; my heart expanded and refused to contract; something swept across its
strings, and desires began to seethe. . . . .

Such were the reveries to which thy friend,
aged almost forty, surrendered himself as he sat
solitary, in his isolated little house! What if some
one had seen me? Well, what if they had? I should
not have been in the least ashamed. To feel
ashamed is also a sign of youth; but I have begun
to notice that I am growing old, and knowest thou
why? This is the reason. I now try to magnify
to myself my cheerful sensations, and to belittle
the mournful ones, while in the days of youth
I proceeded on the diametrically opposite plan.
One goes about then hoarding his sorrow as
though it were a treasure, and is ashamed of a
cheerful impulse. . . .

And nevertheless, it seems to me that, notwith-
standing all my experience of life, there is still
something more in the world, friend Horatio,
that I have not experienced, and that that "something " is about the most important of all.

Ekh, how I have run on! Farewell! until another time. What art thou doing in Petersburg?
By the way: Savély, my rustic cook, asks to be
remembered to thee. He also has grown old,
but not too much so, has waxed fat and some-

what pot-bellied. He makes just as well as of old, chicken soup with boiled onions, curd-cakes with fancy edges, and *pigus,*[1] the famous dish of the steppes, which made thy tongue turn white, gave thee indigestion, and stood like a stake through thee for four-and-twenty hours. On the other hand, he dries up the roasts, as of old, to such a point, that you might bang them against the plate—they are regular cardboard. But farewell!

Thine,

P. B.

SECOND LETTER

From the same to the same

VILLAGE OF M . . . . OE, June 12, 1850.

I HAVE a rather important bit of news to communicate to thee, my dear friend.—Listen! Yesterday, before dinner, I took a fancy for a stroll, —only not in the park; I walked along the road leading to town. It is very pleasant to walk on a long, straight road, without any object, and with long strides. One seems to be engaged in business, hastening somewhere or other.—I look: a calash is driving to meet me. " Is n't it coming to my house? " I thought with secret alarm. . . . But, no; in the calash sits a gentleman with a moustache, a stranger to me. I recover my

[1] A sour soup, with cucumbers. —TRANSLATOR.

equanimity. But suddenly this gentleman, on coming alongside of me, orders his coachman to stop the horses, courteously lifts his cap, and with still geater courtesy asks me: " Am not I so-and-so? " calling me by name. I, in turn, come to a halt, and with the animation of a criminal being conducted to his trial, reply: " I am so-and-so," and stare the while, like a sheep, at the gentleman with the moustache, thinking to myself: " Why, I certainly have seen him somewhere or other! "

" You do not recognise me? "—he enunciates, alighting in the meantime, from the calash.

" I do not in the least, sir."

" But I recognised you instantly."

One word follows another; it turns out that he is Priímkoff,—dost thou remember? Our old comrade in the university. " What important bit of news is this? " thou art thinking at this moment, my dear Semyón Nikoláitch.—" Priímkoff, so far as I recollect, was a rather frivolous fellow, although neither malicious nor stupid." —All that is so, my dear friend; but listen to the continuation of my tale.

" I was greatly delighted," says he, " when I heard that you had come to your village, to our neighbourhood. But I was not the only one who rejoiced."

" Allow me to inquire,"—I inquired:—" who else was so amiable. . . ."

" My wife."

" Your wife? "

" Yes, my wife; she is an old acquaintance of yours."

" Permit me to inquire your wife's name? "

" Her name is Vyéra Nikoláevna; she was born Éltzoff. . . . ."

" Vyéra Nikoláevna! "—I exclaimed involuntarily. . . .

So this is that same important piece of news, of which I spoke to thee at the beginning of my letter.

But perhaps thou wilt not discern anything important about it. . . . I must narrate to thee somewhat of my past . . . . of my long-past life.

When we, thou and I, came out of the university, I was twenty-two years of age. Thou didst enter the government service; I, as thou art aware, decided to betake myself to Berlin. But there was nothing to do in Berlin before October. I wanted to spend the summer in Russia, in the country, to have my fill of lounging for the last time; and then to set to work in sober earnest. As to how far this last project was executed, I will not dilate at present. . . . " But where shall I spend the summer? " I asked myself. I did not wish to go to my own country-place: my father had recently died, I had no near relatives, I dreaded solitude, tedium. . . .

And therefore, I joyfully accepted the suggestion of one of my relatives, my great-uncle, that I should visit him on his estate, in the T*** Government. He was a wealthy man, kind-hearted and simple, lived in fine style, and had a manor worthy of a nobleman. I established myself in his house. My uncle had a large family: two sons and five daughters. In addition to these, there dwelt in his house a throng of people. Guests were incessantly arriving,—and, nevertheless, things were not cheerful. The days flowed by noisily; there was no possibility of isolating one's self. Everything was done in company; everybody tried to divert themselves in some way, to devise something, and by the end of the day everybody was frightfully tired. This life had a commonplace savour. I had already begun to meditate departure, and was only waiting until my uncle's Name-day should arrive; but on that very day—the Name-day—I saw Vyéra Nikoláevna Éltzoff at the ball,—and remained.

She was then sixteen. She lived with her mother on a tiny estate, about five versts from my uncle's. Her father—a remarkable man, they say—had speedily attained to the rank of colonel, and would have risen still higher, but perished while yet a young man, accidentally shot in hunting by a comrade. Vyéra Nikoláevna was a child when he died. Her mother, also,

was a remarkable woman: she spoke several lan-
guages, she knew a great deal. She was seven
or eight years older than her husband, whom
she had married for love; he had secretly carried her off from her father's house. She barely
survived his loss, and until her own death (according to Priímkoff's statement, she died soon
after her daughter's marriage) she wore black
garments only. I vividly recall her face: expressive, dark, with thick hair sprinkled with
grey, large stern eyes which seemed extinguished, and a straight, delicate nose. Her father—his surname was Ladánoff—had lived for
fifteen years in Italy. Vyéra Nikoláevna's mother had ben born the daughter of a plain peas-
ant-woman of Albano, who had been killed on
the day after the birth of her child, by a man of
Transtevere, her betrothed, from whom Ladánoff had stolen her. . . . This story had made
a great noise in its day. On his return to Russia,
Ladánoff not only did not step out of his house,
but even out of his study, busied himself with
chemistry, anatomy, the cabalistic art; tried to
lengthen the life of mankind, and imagined that
he could enter into relations with spirits, and
call up the dead. . . . The neighbours looked
on him as a wizard. He was extremely fond of
his daughter, taught her everything himself; but
did not forgive her for her elopement with Éltzoff, would not admit her to his presence, either

her or her husband, foretold a sorrowful life for both of them, and died alone. On being left a widow, Madame Éltzoff consecrated her leisure to the education of her daughter, and received almost no one. When I made the acquaintance of Vyéra Nikoláevna,—just imagine it!—she had never been in a large town in her life, not even in her county town.

Vyéra Nikoláevna did not resemble the ordinary young Russian gentlewoman; a sort of special stamp lay upon her. What instantly impressed me in her was the wonderful repose of all her movements and remarks. Apparently, she did not worry about anything, did not get excited, answered simply and sensibly, and listened attentively. The expression of her face was sincere and upright, as that of a child, but somewhat cold and monotonous, although not pensive. She was rarely merry, and then not like other people: the clarity of an innocent soul, more delightful than merriment, glowed in all her being. She was short of stature, very well made, rather thin; she had regular and tender features, a very handsome, smooth brow, golden-chestnut hair, a straight nose, like her mother, and quite full lips; her grey eyes, with a tinge of black, looked out somewhat too directly from beneath her thick, upward-curling lashes. Her hands were small, but not very pretty; people who possess talent do not have such hands . . . . and, as a matter of fact, Vyéra Nikoláevna had no particular talents. Her voice was as ringing as that of a seven-year-old girl. At my uncle's ball I was introduced to her mother, and, a few days later, I drove to see them for the first time.

Madame Éltzoff was a very strange woman, with a great deal of character, persistent and concentrated. She exerted a strong influence on me: I both respected and feared her. With her everything was done on a system; and she had reared her daughter on a system, but did not restrain her of her liberty. Her daughter loved her and believed in her blindly. It sufficed for Madame Éltzoff to give her a book, and to say: " Here, don't read this page,"—and she would, probably, skip the preceding page, but would not even glance at the forbidden one. But Madame Éltzoff had also her *idées fixes,* her hobbies. For example, she feared everything which might act on the imagination, as she did fire; and therefore her daughter, up to the age of seventeen, had not read a single poem, while in geography, history, and even natural history, she frequently nonplussed me, a university graduate, and not one who had stood low in his class either, as thou wilt, perhaps, remember. I once undertook to argue with Madame Éltzoff about her hobby, although it was difficult to draw her into conversation: she was extremely taciturn. She merely shook her head.

"You say,"—she remarked at last,—"that it is *both* useful *and* agreeable to read poetical productions. . . . I think that one should, as early as possible, make a choice in life *either* of the useful *or* of the agreeable, and so make up one's mind once for all. I, also, once upon a time, tried to combine the two things. . . . It is impossible and leads to destruction or to insipidity."

Yes, a wonderful being was that woman, an honourable, proud being, not devoid of fanaticism and superstition of a certain sort. "I fear life,"—she said to me one day.—And, in fact, she did fear it,—she feared those secret forces upon which life is erected, and which rarely but suddenly make their way to the surface. Woe to the person over whose head they break! These forces had made themselves felt by Madame Éltzoff in a terrible manner: remember the death of her mother, her husband, her father. . . . It was enough to terrify any one. I never saw her smile. She seemed to have locked herself up, and flung the key into the water. She must have gone through a great deal of sorrow in her day, and she never shared it with any one whomsoever. She had trained herself not to give way to her feelings to such a degree, that she was even ashamed to display her passionate love for her daughter; she never once kissed her in my presence, never called her by a pet name, but always "Vyéra." I remember one remark of

hers. I happened to say to her that all we people of the present day were half-broken. . . .
"There's no use in breaking one's self so,"—she
said:—"one must subdue one's self thoroughly,
—or not touch one's self. . . ."

Very few persons called at Madame Éltzoff's; but I visited her frequently. I was secretly conscious that she felt kindly toward me;
and I liked Vyéra Nikoláevna very much. She
and I chatted and strolled together. . . . Her
mother did not interfere with us; the daughter
herself did not like to be apart from her mother,
and I, on my side, did not feel any need of solitary conversations. . . . Vyéra Nikoláevna had
a strange habit of thinking aloud; at night she
talked loudly and intelligibly in her sleep of what
had impressed her during the day.—One day,
after scanning me attentively, and, according
to her wont, softly propping her chin on her
hand, she said: "It strikes me that B*** is a
good man; but one cannot rely on him." Our
relations were of the most friendly and even
character; only one day it seemed to me that I
noticed far away, somewhere in the depths of
her bright eyes, a strange something, a sort of
softness and tenderness. . . . But perhaps I was
mistaken.

In the meanwhile, time passed on, and the day
came when I was obliged to make preparations
for departure. But still I tarried. As I recall

it, I persisted in thinking that I should not soon
see again that charming girl, to whom I had
grown so attached—and I should feel uncomfortable. . . . Berlin began to lose its power of
attraction. I did not dare to admit to myself
what had taken place in me,—and I did not understand what it was that had taken place in
me,—it was as though a mist were roving about
in my soul. At last, one morning, everything
suddenly became clear to me. " What 's the use
of seeking further? "—I thought. " Why
should I strive onward? For the truth will not
surrender itself into my hands, all the same.
Would it not be better to remain here? Ought not
I to marry? " and, just imagine, this thought of
marriage did not alarm me in the least then.
On the contrary, I was delighted at it. More
than that; that very same day, I avowed my intentions, only not to Vyéra, but to Madame Éltzoff herself. The old lady looked at me.

" No,"—said she:—" my dear fellow, go to
Berlin, and break yourself a little more. You
are good; but you are not the sort of husband
whom Vyéra needs."

I cast down my eyes, flushed scarlet, and—
what will probably amaze thee still more—I inwardly agreed with Madame Éltzoff on the spot.
A week later I took my departure, and have
never seen either her or Vyéra since that time.

I have described to thee my adventure in brief,

because I know that thou dost not like anything "long-drawn-out." On arriving in Berlin, I very promptly forgot Vyéra Nikoláevna. . . . But, I must confess, that the unexpected news of her has agitated me. I have been impressed by the thought that she is so near, that she is my neighbour, that I shall see her in a few days. The past has suddenly started up before me, as though it had sprung out of the earth, and were fairly swooping down on me. Priímkoff informed me that he had called upon me with the express purpose of renewing our ancient acquaintance, and that he hoped to see me at his house very shortly. He informed me that he had served in the cavalry, had retired with the rank of lieutenant, purchased an estate eight versts distant from mine, and was intending to occupy himself with farming; that he had had three children, but two of them had died, and only a five-year-old daughter was left.

"And does your wife remember me?"—I asked.

"Yes, she does,"—he replied with a slight hesitation.—"Of course, she was then a child, so to speak; but her mother always praised you highly, and you know how she prizes every word of the deceased."

Madame Éltzoff's words, that I was not a suitable husband for Vyéra, recurred to my memory. . . . "So thou wert suitable,"—I thought, darting a sidelong glance at Priímkoff. He spent several hours at my house. He is a very good, nice fellow, he talks very modestly, has a very good-natured gaze; one cannot help liking him . . . . but his intellectual faculties have not developed since the period of our acquaintance with him. I shall go to see him without fail, to-morrow, perhaps. I shall find it extremely interesting to see how Vyéra Nikoláevna has turned out.

Thou art, probably, laughing at me now, thou rascal, as thou sittest at thy director's table; but nevertheless, I shall write to thee what impression she makes on me. Farewell! Until the next letter. Thine,

P. B.

THIRD LETTER

From the same to the same

Village of M . . . . oe, June 16, 1850.

WELL, my dear fellow, I have been at her house, I have seen her. First of all, I must communicate to thee a remarkable circumstance: believe me or not, as thou wilt, but she has hardly changed at all, either in face or in figure. When she came out to greet me, I almost exclaimed aloud: a young girl of seventeen, and that 's all there is to be said! Only, her eyes are not like those of

a little girl; however, even in her youth she did
not have childish eyes, they were too bright.
But there is the same composure, the same seren-
ity, the same voice, not a single wrinkle on her
brow, just as though she had been lying somewhere in the snow all these years. And now
she is twenty-eight years old, and has had three
children. . . 'T is incomprehensible! Pray, do
not think that I am exaggerating out of preju-
dice; on the contrary, this immutability in her
does not please me.

A woman of eight-and-twenty, a wife and a
mother, ought not to look like a young girl; for
she has not lived in vain. She greeted me very
cordially; but my arrival simply enraptured Priímkoff; that good fellow looks as though he
would like to get attached to some one. Their
house is very comfortable and clean. Vyéra Nikoláevna was dressed like a young girl, also; all
in white, with a sky-blue sash, and a slender gold
chain on her neck. Her little daughter is very
charming, and does not resemble her in the
least; she reminds one of her grandmother. In
the drawing-room, over the divan, hangs a portrait of that strange woman, a striking likeness.
It caught my eye the moment I entered. She
seemed to be staring sternly and attentively at
me. We sat down, recalled old times, and gradually got into conversation. I kept involuntarily
glancing at the gloomy portrait of Madame

Éltzoff. Vyéra Nikoláevna was sitting directly
under it; it is her favourite place. Fancy my
amazement! To this day, Vyéra Nikoláevna has
not read a single romance, a single poem—in
short, as she expresses it, a single work of fiction!
This incredible indifference to the loftiest joys
of the mind enraged me. In a sensible woman,
and one who, so far as I can judge, possesses delicate feelings, this is simply unpardonable.

"Why,"—I said:—"have you made it a rule
never to read such books?"

"I have never happened to do it,"—she replied.—"I have not had the time."

"Not had the time! I am astonished! You
might at least have inspired your wife with a wish
to do so,"—I went on, addressing Priímkoff.

"It would have given me great pleasure . . . ."
Priímkoff began, but Vyéra Nikoláevna interrupted him.

"Don't pretend; thou art no great lover of
poetry thyself."

"Of poetry,"—he began,—"I really am not
very fond; but romances, for example. . . ."

"But what do you do, how do you occupy
yourselves evenings?"—I inquired.—"Do you
play cards?"

"Sometimes we do,"—she replied:—"but
is n't there plenty to occupy us? We read, also;
there are good books besides poetry."

"Why do you attack poetry so?"

" I don't attack it; I have been accustomed from my childhood not to read works of fiction; my mother thought that was proper, and the longer I live, the more convinced do I become that everything which my mother did, everything she said, was the truth, the sacred truth."

" Well, as you like; but I cannot agree with you. I am convinced that you do wrong in depriving yourself of the purest, the most lawful enjoyment. Surely, you do not reject music, painting; then why should you reject poetry? "

" I do not reject it. Up to the present time I have not made acquaintance with it—that is all."

" Then I shall take the matter in hand! Surely, your mother did not forbid you to acquaint yourself with the productions of elegant literature during your entire life? "

" No; when I married, my mother removed all restrictions from me; it has never entered my head to read . . . . what was it you called it? . . . well, in short, to read romances."

I listened with surprise to Vyéra Nikoláevna. I had not expected this.

She gazed at me with her tranquil look. That is the way birds gaze, when they are not afraid.

" I will bring you a book! "—I exclaimed. (The thought of " Faust," which I had recently read, flashed through my mind.)

Vyéra Nikoláevna heaved a soft sigh.

" It . . . . it is not Georges Sand? "—she inquired, not without timidity.

" Ah! so you have heard of her? Well, and
what if it were she, where 's the harm? . . . No;
I shall bring you another author. You have not
forgotten your German, I suppose? "

" No, I have not forgotten it."

" She speaks it like a German,"—interposed
Priímkoff.

" Well, that 's fine! I shall bring you . . .
but there now, you shall see what a marvellous
thing I shall bring you."

" Well, very good, I shall see. And now let
us go into the garden, for Natásha will not be
able to sit quietly otherwise."

She put on a round straw hat, a child's hat, exactly like the one which her daughter donned,
only a little larger, and we betook ourselves to the
garden. I walked by her side. In the fresh
air, in the shadow of the lofty lindens, her face
seemed to me more charming than ever, especially when she turned slightly and threw back
her head in order to look up at me from under
the brim of her hat. Had it not been for Priímkoff, had it not been for the little girl who was
skipping on in front of us, I really might have
thought that I was not thirty-five years of age,
but three-and-twenty; that I was only just making ready to set out for Berlin; the more so, as
the garden in which we were greatly resembled

the garden on Madame Éltzoff's estate. I could not refrain from communicating my impressions to Vyéra Nikoláevna.

" Everybody tells me that I have changed very little in outward appearance,"—she replied:—" moreover, I have remained the same inwardly also."

We approached a small Chinese house.

" There, we did not have such a little house at Ósinovko,"—she said:—" but you must not mind its being so rickety and faded; it is very nice and cool inside."

We entered the little house. I glanced about me.

" Do you know what, Vyéra Nikoláevna,"—I said:—" order a table and a few chairs to be brought hither before I come. It really is extraordinarily nice here. I will read aloud to you here. . . . Goethe's ' Faust ' . . . . that is the thing I mean to read to you."

" Yes; there are no flies here,"—she remarked ingenuously;—" but when shall you come? "

" Day after to-morrow."

" Very well,"—she said:—" I will give orders."

Natásha, who had entered the house in company with us, suddenly uttered a scream, and sprang back, all pale.

" What is the matter? "—asked Vyéra Nikoláevna.

" Akh, mamma,"—said the little girl, pointing

at one corner,—" look, what a dreadful spider! . . . ."

Vyéra Nikoláevna glanced at the corner; a huge, mottled spider was crawling quietly along the wall.

" What is there to be afraid of? "—she said:— " it does not bite; see here."

And before I could stop her, she took the hideous insect in her hand, let it run about on her palm, and flung it aside.

" Well, you are a brave woman! "—I exclaimed.

" Where is the bravery in that? That is not one of the poisonous spiders."

" Evidently, as of old, you are strong in natural history. I would n't have taken it in my hand."

" There 's no cause to be afraid of it,"—repeated Vyéra Nikoláevna.

Natásha gazed silently at us and smiled.

" How much like your mother she is! "—I remarked.

" Yes,"—replied Vyéra Nikoláevna, with a smile of satisfaction;—" that delights me greatly. God grant that she may resemble her not in face alone! "

We were summoned to dinner, and after dinner I took my departure. *N. B.* The dinner was very good and savoury.—I make this remark in parenthesis, for thy benefit, thou sponger! To-morrow I shall carry " Faust " to them. I 'm afraid that old Goethe and I shall suffer defeat. I will describe everything to thee in detail.

Come now, what thinkest thou about all " these events "? Probably, that she has made a powerful impression on me, that I am ready to fall in love, and so forth? Nonsense, my dear fellow! It is high time for me to exercise moderation. I have played the fool long enough; *finis!* One cannot begin life over again at my age. Moreover, even in former days, I never liked women of that sort. . . . But what women I did like! !

> I tremble—my heart is sore—
> I 'm ashamed of my idols.

In any case, I am very glad of these neighbours, I am glad of the possibility of meeting a sensible, simple, limpid being; but what happens further thou shalt know in due time.

Thine,

P. B.

FOURTH LETTER

From the same to the same

Village of M . . . . oe, June 20, 1850.
THE reading took place yesterday, my dear friend, and as to the precise manner of it, details follow. First of all, I make haste to say, it was

an unexpected success . . . . that is, " success "
is not the word for it. . . . Come, listen. I arrived for dinner. There were six of us at table:
she, Priímkoff, her little daughter, the governess (an insignificant little white figure), I, and
some old German or other, in a short, light-brown
frock-coat, neat, well-shaven, experienced, with
the most peaceable and honest of faces, a toothless smile, and an odour of chicory coffee . . . .
all old Germans smell like that. He was introduced to me; he was a certain Schimmel, a teacher
of the German language in the family of Prince
X***, a neighbour of Priímkoff. It appears that
he is a favourite of Vyéra Nikoláevna's, and she
had invited him to be present at the reading. We
dined late and did not leave the table for a long
time; then we went for a stroll. The weather
was magnificent. It had rained in the morning,
and the wind had been blowing; but toward evening everything had quieted down. She and I
emerged into an open glade. Directly above
this glade, a large, rosy cloud hung high and
light; grey streaks, like smoke, stretched across
it; on its extreme edge twinkled a tiny star, now
appearing, now disappearing, while a little further off the white sickle of the moon was visible
against the faintly crimsoned azure. I pointed
out the cloud to Vyéra Nikoláevna.

"Yes,"—she said:—"it is very beautiful; but
look yonder."—I looked. A huge, dark-blue

storm-cloud was ascending like smoke, and concealing the setting sun; in aspect, it presented the
likeness of a mountain spouting fire; its crest was
spread athwart the sky in a broad sheaf; an ominous crimson glow surrounded it with a brilliant
border, and in one spot, at the very centre of it,
forced its way through the heavy mass, as though
tearing itself free from a red-hot crater. . . .

" There is going to be a thunder-storm,"—remarked Priímkoff.

But I am getting away from the main point.—
In my last letter I forgot to tell thee that on my
return home from the Priímkoffs', I repented
of having named " Faust " in particular; Schiller
would have been much more suitable for a first
reading, if it must be a German. I was particularly alarmed by the first scene, before the acquaintance with Gretchen; I was uneasy on the
score of Mephistopheles also. But I was under
the influence of " Faust," and could not have
read anything else with good will. It was already perfectly dark when we betook ourselves
to the little Chinese house; it had been put in
order the day before. Directly opposite the door,
in front of a small divan, stood a round table,
covered with a cloth; chairs and arm-chairs were
set round about; on the table burned a lamp. I
seated myself on the divan, and got my book.
Vyéra Nikoláevna placed herself in an arm-
chair at some distance, not far from the door.

" FAUST "

Beyond the door, in the darkness, a green branch
of acacia, illuminated by the lamp, displayed
itself, swaying gently; now and then a current
of night air diffused itself through the room.
Priímkoff sat down near me, at the table, the
German by his side. The governess had remained in the house with Natásha. I made a little introductory speech; I alluded to the ancient
legend of Dr. Faustus, to the significance of
Mephistopheles, to Goethe himself, and begged
that they would stop me if anything should
seem to them unintelligible. Then I cleared my
throat. . . . Priímkoff asked me whether I did
not need some sugar and water, and, so far as I
was able to observe, was greatly pleased with
himself for having put that question to me. I
declined. Profound silence reigned. I began
to read, without raising my eyes; I felt awkward, my heart beat violently and my voice
trembled. The first exclamation of sympathy
burst from the German, and he alone, during the
course of the reading, broke the silence. . . .
" Wonderful! Sublime! "—he kept repeating,
now and then adding: " Here it is deep." Priímkoff was bored, as I could plainly see; he understood German imperfectly, and confessed
that he was not fond of poetry! . . . . It was
his own fault.—At table, I had wanted to hint
that the reading could proceed without him, but
had been ashamed to do so. Vyéra Nikoláevna

did not stir; a couple of times I shot a stealthy
glance at her; her eyes were fixed straight and
attentively on me; her face seemed to me to be
pale.   After Faust's first meeting with Gretchen, she separated herself from the back of her
chair, clasped her hands, and remained motionless in that attitude until the end.   I felt conscious that Priímkoff found it disgusting, and
at first this chilled me; but gradually I forgot
all about him, warmed up, and read with fervour,
with enthusiasm. . . . I was reading for Vyéra
Nikoláevna alone; an inward voice told me that
" Faust " was taking effect on her.   When I
had finished (I skipped the intermezzo; that bit,
by its style, belongs to the second part; and I
also omitted portions from the " Night on the
Brocken ") . . . . when I had finished, when
the last " Heinrich! " had rung out,—the German ejaculated with emotion: " Heavens! how
beautiful! "   Priímkoff sprang to his feet as
though delighted (poor fellow!), heaved a sigh,
and began to thank me for the pleasure I had
given them. . . . But I did not answer him; I
glanced at Vyéra Nikoláevna. . . . I wanted to
hear what she would say.   She rose, walked to the
door with wavering steps, stood awhile on the
threshold, and then quietly went out into the
garden.   I rushed after her.   She had already
succeeded in getting several paces away; her
white gown was barely visible in the dense
shadow.

"Well?" I cried;—"did n't you like it?"

She halted.

"Can you let me have that book?"—her voice rang out.

"I will make you a present of it, Vyéra Niko-láevna, if you care to have it."

"Thank you!"—she replied, and vanished.

Priímkoff and the German approached me.

"How wonderfully warm it is!"—remarked Priímkoff;—"even sultry. But where has my wife gone?"

"To the house, I believe,"—I replied.

"I think it will soon be supper-time,"—he responded.—"You read capitally, capitally,"—he added, after a brief pause.

"Vyéra Nikoláevna seemed to be pleased with 'Faust,'" I remarked.

"Without doubt!"—exclaimed Priímkoff.

"Oh, of course!"—chimed in Schimmel.

We entered the house.

"Where is the mistress?"—Priímkoff asked of a maid whom we encountered.

"She has been pleased to go to her bedroom."

Priímkoff directed his steps to the bedroom.

I went out on the terrace with Schimmel. The old man raised his eyes to the sky.

"How many stars there are!"—he said slowly, as he took a pinch of snuff;—"and all of them are worlds,"—he added, taking another pinch.

I did not consider it necessary to answer him, and only gazed upward in silence. A secret perplexity was weighing on my soul. . . . The stars seemed to me to be gazing seriously at us. Five minutes later, Priímkoff made his appearance and summoned us to the dining-room. Vyéra Nikoláevna soon came also. We sat down.

" Just look at Vyérotchka,"—said Priímkoff to me.

I glanced at her.

" Well? Don't you notice anything? "

I really did note a change in her face, but I know not why I answered:

" No, nothing."

" Her eyes are red,"—went on Priímkoff.

I held my peace.

" Just fancy, I went to her up-stairs, and found her; she was crying. It is a long time since that has happened with her. I can tell you the last time she cried: it was when our Sásha died. So that's what you have done with your ' Faust '! " he added with a smile.

" You must see now, Vyéra Nikoláevna,"—I began,—" that I was right when . . . ."

" I had not expected that,"—she interrupted me;—" but God knows whether you are right. Perhaps the reason my mother prohibited my reading such books was because she knew . . . ."

Vyéra Nikoláevna stopped short.

" Because she knew? "—I repeated.—" Tell me."

" What is the use? I am ashamed of myself

as it is; what was I crying about? However, you and I will discuss this further. There were many things which I did not quite understand."

" Then why did n't you stop me? "

" I understood all the words, and their sense, but . . . ."

She did not finish her phrase, and became pensive. At that moment, the noise of the foliage, suddenly stirred by the rising wind, swept through the garden. Vyéra Nikoláevna started, and turned her face toward the open window.

" I told you that there would be a thunderstorm! "—cried Priímkoff.—" But what makes thee tremble so, Vyérotchka? "

She glanced at him in silence. The lightning, flashing faintly far away, was reflected on her impassive face.

" All thanks to ' Faust,' "—went on Priímkoff.

" After supper, we must go immediately to bye-bye, ... must n't we, Herr Schimmel? "

" After moral pleasure physical repose is as beneficial as it is useful,"—replied the good German, drinking off a glass of vodka.

We parted immediately after supper. As I bade Vyéra Nikoláevna good night, I shook hands with her; her hand was cold. I reached the chamber assigned to me, and stood for a long time at the window before undressing and getting into bed.

Priímkoff's prediction was fulfilled; a thun-

der-storm gathered and broke. I listened to the
roar of the wind, the clatter and beating of the
rain, I saw how, at every flash of lightning, the
church, built close at hand, near the lake, now
suddenly was revealed in black against a white
ground, then as white against a black ground,
then again was swallowed up in the gloom. . . .
But my thoughts were far away. I was thinking
of Vyéra Nikoláevna: I was thinking of what
she would say to me when she should have read
" Faust " herself; I was thinking of her tears;
I was recalling how she had listened. . . .

The thunder-storm had long since passed off,
—the stars were beaming, everything had fallen
silent round about. Some bird with which I was
not familiar was singing in various tones, repeating the same phrase several times in succession. Its resonant, solitary voice rang out
oddly amid the profound silence; and still I did
not go to bed. . . .

On the following morning I entered the drawing-room earlier than all the rest, and halted in
front of Madame Éltzoff's portrait.—" What
didst thou make by it? "—I thought, with a secret feeling of jeering triumph,—" for here,
seest thou, I have read to thy daughter a forbidden book! " All at once, it seemed to me
. . . . probably thou hast noticed that eyes
painted *en face* always seem to be riveted
straight on the spectator? . . . But on this oc-

casion, it really did seem to me as though the old
lady had turned them on me reproachfully.

I turned away, walked to the window, and
beheld Vyéra Nikoláevna. With a parasol on
her shoulder, and a thin white kerchief on her
head, she was strolling in the garden. I immediately went out and bade her good morning. . . .

" I have not slept all night,"—she said to me;
—" I have a headache; I have come out into the
air to see if it will not pass off."

" Can it have been caused by last night's reading?"—I asked.

" Of course it was; I am not used to that.
There are things in that book of yours which I
cannot get rid of; it seems to me that they are
fairly searing my brain,"—she added, laying her
hand on her brow.

" Very good indeed,"—said I:—" but this is
the bad thing about it: I 'm afraid this sleepless-
ness and headache have destroyed your wish to
read such things."

" Do you think so?"—she returned, breaking
off a spray of wild jasmine as she passed.—
" God knows! It seems to me that any one
who has entered upon that road cannot turn
back."

She suddenly flung aside the spray.

" Let us go and sit in that arbour,"—she went
on,—" and until I speak to you of it myself,
please do not remind me . . . . of that book."

(She seemed to be afraid to pronounce the name of " Faust.")

We entered the arbour and seated ourselves.

" I will not talk to you about ' Faust,' " I be-gan;—" but you must allow me to congratulate you, and to tell you that I envy you."

" You envy me? "

" Yes; as I know you now, with your soul, how much enjoyment you have in store! There are other great poets besides Goethe: Shakspeare, Schiller . . . . yes, and our own Púshkin . . . . and you must make acquaintance with them also."

She maintained silence, and drew figures on the sand with her parasol.

Oh, my friend, Semyón Nikoláitch! if thou couldst but have seen how charming she was at that moment! Pale almost to transparency, slightly bent forward, weary, inwardly dis-traught,—and nevertheless serene as the sky! I talked, talked a long time, then fell silent—and sat there silently watching her. . . .

She did not raise her eyes, and continued now to sketch with her parasol, now to erase what she had drawn. Suddenly the sound of brisk, child-ish footsteps resounded: Natásha ran into the arbour. Vyéra Nikoláevna straightened her-self up, rose, and, to my amazement, embraced her daughter with a sort of impulsive tenderness. . . . . This was not her habit. Then Priímkoff made his appearance. That grey-haired but

166

punctual, fine fellow Schimmel had gone away
before daybreak, in order not to miss his lesson.
We went to drink tea.

But I am tired; it is time to bring this letter
to an end. It must seem silly, confused to thee.
I feel confused myself. I am out of sorts. I
don't know what ails me. There is constantly
flitting before my vision a tiny room with bare
walls, a lamp, an open door, the scent and freshness of night, and there, near the door, an attentive young face, thin, white garments. . . .
I understand now why I wanted to marry her;
evidently, I was not so stupid before my trip to
Berlin as I have hitherto thought. Yes, Semyón
Nikoláitch, your friend is in a strange frame
of mind. All this will pass off, I know . . . but
what if it should not pass off—well, what then?
I am satisfied with myself, nevertheless; in the
first place, I have spent a wonderful evening;
and in the second place, if I have awakened that
soul, who can blame me? Old Madame Éltzoff
is nailed to the wall and must hold her peace.
The old lady! . . . . I do not know all the
particulars of her life; but I do know that she
eloped from her father's house; evidently, she
was not born of an Italian mother for nothing. She wanted to insure her daughter. We
shall see.

I fling aside my pen. Thou, jeering man,
please to think of me as thou wilt, but don't

make fun of me by letter. Thou and I are old friends, and must spare each other. Farewell!

Thine,

P. B.

FIFTH LETTER

From the same to the same

VILLAGE OF M . . . . OE, July 26, 1850.

I HAVE not written to thee for a long time, my dear Semyón Nikoláitch; not for more than a month, I think. There has been plenty to write about; but I have been too lazy. To tell the truth, I have hardly thought of thee during the whole of that time. But I may deduce from thy last letter to me that thou art making assumptions about me which are unjust; that is to say, not quite just. Thou thinkest that I am carried away by Vyéra (somehow, I find it awkward to call her Vyéra Nikoláevna) ; thou art mistaken. Of course, I see her frequently; I like her extremely . . . . and who would not like her? I should just like to see thee in my place. She 's a wonderful creature! Instantaneous penetration hand in hand with the inexperience of a baby; clear, sound sense and innate feeling for beauty, a constant striving for the truth, for the lofty, and a comprehension of everything, even of the vicious, even of the ridiculous—and, over all this, like

the white wings of an angel, gentle feminine
charm. . . . But what's the use of talking! We
have read a great deal, discussed a great deal, she
and I, in the course of this month. To read with
her is a delight such as I have not hitherto experienced. It is as though one were opening
fresh pages. She never goes into raptures over
anything; everything noisy is alien to her; she
quietly beams all over when anything pleases
her, and her face assumes such a noble, good
. . . . precisely that, good expression. From
her earliest childhood Vyéra has never known
what it is to lie; she has become accustomed to
the truth, she is redolent of it, and therefore in
poetry the truth alone appears natural to her;
she immediately recognises it, without difficulty,
as a familiar face . . . . a great advantage and
happiness! It is impossible not to hold her
mother in kindly memory for that. How many
times have I thought, as I looked at Vyéra:
" Yes, Goethe is right:—' a good man in his obscure aspirations always feels where the true
road lies.' " [1] One thing is vexatious; her husband
is always hanging around. (Please don't in-
dulge in your stupid laugh, don't sully our
friendship by even so much as a thought.) He is
as capable of understanding poetry as I am of
playing the flute, and he won't leave his wife; he
wants to be enlightened also. Sometimes she

[1] " Faust," the Prologue to Part I.

herself puts me out of patience: a queer sort of mood will suddenly come over her; she will neither read nor converse; she works at her embroidery-frame, and fusses with Natásha, with the housekeeper, suddenly runs off to the kitchen, or simply sits with folded hands and stares out of the window, or sets to playing " fool "[1] with the nurse. . . . I have observed that on such occasions I must not worry her, but that it is best to wait until she herself approaches me, and starts a conversation, or takes up a book. She has a great deal of independence, and I am very glad of that. Dost thou remember how, in the days of our youth, some young girl or other would repeat to thee thy own words, to the best of her ability, and thou wouldst go into raptures over that echo and, probably, bow down before it, until thou didst get an inkling of the real state of the case? But this woman . . . no; she thinks for herself. She will accept nothing on faith; one cannot frighten her by authority; she will not dispute; but she will not give in. She and I have argued over " Faust " more than once; but—strange to say!—she never says anything about Gretchen herself, but merely listens to what I say of her. Mephistopheles alarms her, not as the devil, but as " something which may exist in every man. . . ." Those are her very words. I undertook to explain to her that

[1] A Russian card-game. — TRANSLATOR.

we called that " something " reflex action; but
she did not understand the words " reflex action "
in the German sense; she knows only the French
" *réflexion,*" and has become accustomed to consider it useful.

Our relations are remarkable! From a certain point of view I may say that I have great
influence over her, and am educating her, as it
were; but without herself being aware of the
fact, she is transforming many things in me for
the better. For example, it is solely due to her
that I have recently discovered what an immense
amount of the conventional, the rhetorical there is
in the finest, the most famous poetical productions. That to which she remains cold becomes
at once suspicious in my eyes. Yes, I have grown
better, more serene. To be intimate with her, to
meet her, and remain the same man as before is
an impossibility.

" What is to be the upshot of all this? " thou
wilt ask. Why, really, nothing, I think. I am
passing my time very agreeably until September,
and then I shall go away. Life will seem dark
and tedious to me during the first months. . . .
But I shall get used to it. I know how dangerous is any sort of a tie between a man and a
young woman, how imperceptibly one feeling
is replaced by another. . . . I would have managed to wrench myself away, had I not known
that both of us are perfectly calm. Truth to

tell, one day something strange happened with
us. I know not how, and as a result of what—
I remember that we were reading " Onyégin " [1]
—and I kissed her hand. She recoiled slightly,
riveted a glance upon me (I have never beheld such a glance in any one but her; it contains
both pensiveness and attention, and a sort of
severity) . . . . suddenly blushed, rose, and left
the room. I did not succeed in being alone with
her again that day. She avoided me, and for four
mortal hours played with her husband, the
nurse, and the governess at " Trumps." The
next morning she suggested that we should go
into the garden. We walked the whole length
of it, clear to the lake. Suddenly she whispered
softly, without turning toward me: " Please
don't do that again! "—and immediately began
to narrate something to me. . . . I was very
much abashed.

I must confess that her image never leaves my
mind, and I probably have begun to write this
letter to thee more with the object of securing
the possibility of thinking and talking about her,
than anything else. I hear the neighing and
trampling of horses: it is my calash being
brought round. I am going to their house.
My coachman no longer asks me whither he
shall drive when I take my seat in the equipage,—he drives straight to the Priímkoffs'.

[1] Púshkin's poem, " Evgény Onyégin."—TRANSLATOR.

Two versts distant from their village, at a sharp turn of the road, their manor-house suddenly peers forth from behind a birch-grove. . . . Every time my heart leaps with joy as soon as the windows of her house gleam forth. Schimmel (that harmless old man comes to them occasionally; they have seen the family of Prince X*** only once, thank God!) . . . . Schimmel says, not without cause, with the modest triumph peculiar to him, as he points to the house where Vyéra dwells: " That is the abode of peace!" The angel of peace has taken up its abode in that house. . . .

> Cover me with thy pinions,
> My heart's emotion allay, —
> And blessed shall be that shadow
> For my enchanted soul. . . .

But come, enough of this,—or God knows what thou wilt think,—until the next time. . . . What shall I write the next time?—Good-bye!—By the way, she will never say " good-bye," but always: " Well, good-bye."—I like that awfully.

Thine,

P. B.

P. S.—I don't remember whether I have told thee that she knows I proposed for her hand.

SIXTH LETTER

From the same to the same

VILLAGE OF M . . . . OE, August 10, 1850.

CONFESS that thou art expecting either a despairing or a rapturous letter from me. . . . Nothing of the sort. My letter will be like all letters. Nothing new has happened, and nothing can happen, I think. The other day we were rowing in a boat on the lake. I will describe that jaunt to thee. There were three of us: she, Schimmel and I. I cannot understand what possesses her to invite that old man so often. The X***s are put out with him, they say, because he has begun to neglect his lessons. But on this occasion he was amusing. Priímkoff did not go with us: he had a headache. The weather was magnificent, cheerful; there were huge white ragged-looking storm-clouds all over the blue sky; everywhere there was a gleam, a rustling in the trees, a plashing and rippling of the water on the shores; on the waves darting golden serpents of light, coolness and sunshine!—At first I and the German rowed; then we raised the sail and dashed headlong onward. The bow of the boat fairly dived through the waves, and the wake behind the stern hissed and foamed. She sat at the helm and steered; she had tied a kerchief over her head: a hat

174

would have blown off; her curls burst forth from
beneath it, and floated softly on the breeze.
She held the helm firmly with her sun-burned
little hand, and smiled at the splashes of water
which flew in her face from time to time. I curled
myself up in the bottom of the boat, not far from
her feet, the German pulled out his pipe, lighted
up his coarse tobacco, and—just fancy!—began
to sing in a fairly agreeable bass voice. First he
sang the old ballad: *"Freut' euch des Lebens,"*
then an aria from " The Magic Flute," then a
romance entitled " Love's Alphabet "—*"Das
A-B-C der Liebe."* In this romance the whole
alphabet is recited,—with appropriate quaint
sayings, of course,—beginning with: *"Ah, Bay,
Say, Day,—Wenn ich dich seh!"* and ending
with *"Oo, Fau, Vay, Eeks,—Mach einen Knicks!"*
He sang all the couplets through with tender
expression; but thou shouldst have seen how
roguishly he screwed up his left eye at the word
" Knicks "!—Vyéra burst out laughing and
shook her finger at him. I remarked that it struck
me Herr Schimmel had been no fool in his day.
" Oh, yes, I could stand up for myself! " he replied pompously, knocking the ashes out of his
pipe into his palm; and thrusting his fingers into
his tobacco-pouch, he gripped the mouthpiece of
his pipe swaggeringly, on one side, with his teeth.
" When I was a student,"—he added,—" o-ho-
ho! " He said no more. But what an " o-ho-ho!"

that was!—Vyéra requested him to sing some
student song, and he sang to her: " *Knaster, den
gelben,*" but got out of tune on the last note.

In the meantime, the wind had increased, the
waves had begun to run rather high, the boat
careened over somewhat; swallows were darting
low around us. We put the sail over and began
to jibe. The wind suddenly veered about; we had
not succeeded in completing the manœuvre, when
a wave dashed over the side, and the boat took in
a quantity of water. Here, also, the German
showed himself to be a fine fellow; he snatched
the sheet-rope from my hand, and jibed in proper
fashion, remarking, as he did so: " That 's the
way they do at Kuxhafen! "—" *So macht man's
in Kuxhafen!*"

Vyéra was probably frightened, for she turned
pale; but, according to her wont, she did not
utter a word, but gathered up her gown and
placed her feet on the thwart of the boat. Suddenly there flashed across my mind Goethe's
poem (I have been thoroughly infected by him
for some time past) . . . . dost thou remember
it? " On the waves twinkle thousands of quivering stars "; and I recited it aloud. When I
reached the line: " Mine eyes, why do ye droop? "
she raised her eyes a little (I was sitting lower
than she: her glance fell upon me from above)
and gazed for a long time into the far distance,
narrowing her eyes to protect them from the

wind. . . . A light rain came up in an instant, and pattered in bubbles on the water. I offered her my overcoat; she threw it over her shoulders. We landed on the shore,—not at the wharf,— and went to the house on foot. I walked arm in arm with her. All the time I felt like saying something to her; but I held my peace. But I remember asking her why, when she was at home, she always sat under the portrait of Madame Éltzoff, just like a birdling under its mother's wing.—" Your comparison is very accurate,"— she replied:—" I should never wish to emerge from beneath her wing."—" Would n't you like to emerge into freedom? "—I asked another question. She made no reply.

I do not know why I have told thee about this expedition,—perhaps because it has lingered in my memory as one of the brightest events of recent days, although, in reality, how can it be called an event? I was so delighted and speechlessly happy, and tears—light, happy tears— fairly gushed from my eyes.

Yes; just fancy! On the following day, as I was strolling through the garden, past the arbour, I suddenly heard an agreeable, ringing, feminine voice singing, *" Freut' euch des Lebens."* . . . I glanced into the arbour:—it was Vyéra.

" Bravo! "—I exclaimed;—" I was not aware that you had such a fine voice! "—She was abashed, and stopped singing. Seriously, she has

an excellent, strong soprano voice. But I don't
believe she even suspected that she had a good
voice. How many untouched treasures are still
concealed in her! She does not know herself. But
such a woman is a rarity in our day, is she not?

August 12.

WE had a very strange conversation yesterday.
First we talked about visions. Just imagine; she
believes in them, and says that she has her rea-
sons for so doing. Priímkoff, who was sitting
with us, dropped his eyes and shook his head, as
though in confirmation of her words. I tried to
interrogate her; but speedily perceived that the
conversation was disagreeable to her. We began to talk about imagination, about the force
of imagination. I narrated how, in my youth,
being in the habit of dreaming a great deal about
happiness (the customary occupation of people
who have not had, or will not have luck in life),
I had, among other things, dreamed of what
bliss it would be to pass a few weeks in Venice
with the woman I loved. I thought of this so
often, especially at night, that I gradually formed
in my mind a complete picture, which I could
summon up before me at will: all I had to do
was to shut my eyes. This is what presented
itself to me:—Night, the moon, white and tender
moonlight, fragrance . . . . the fragrance of the
orange-flower, thinkest thou? No, of vanilla,

the fragrance of the cactus, a broad watery expanse, a flat island overgrown with olive-trees; on the island, on the very shore, a small marble house, with wide-open windows; music is audible—whence, God knows; in the house are trees with dark foliage, and the light of a half-veiled lamp; a heavy velvet mantle with golden fringe has been thrown over one window-sill, and one end of it is trailing in the water; while, side by side, with their arms resting on the mantle, sit *he* and *she,* gazing far away to the spot where Venice is visible.—All this presented itself to me as plainly as though I had beheld it all with my own eyes.

She listened to my nonsense, and said that she also often indulged in reverie, but that her dreams were of a different nature: she either imagined herself on the plains of Africa, with some traveller or other, or hunting for the traces of Franklin in the Arctic Ocean; she vividly pictured to herself all the hardships which she must undergo, all the difficulties with which she must contend. . . .

" Thou hast read a quantity of travels,"—remarked her husband.

" Perhaps so,"—she rejoined. " But if one is to dream, what possesses one to dream of the impossible? "

" But why not? "—I interposed.—" How is the poor impossible to blame? "

" I did not express myself correctly,"—said she:—" I meant to say, what possesses a person to dream of himself, of his own happiness? There is no use in thinking about it; if it does not come,—why pursue it? It is like health: when one does not notice it, it means that one possesses it."

These words amazed me. That woman has a great soul, believe me. . . . From Venice the conversation passed to Italy, to the Italians. Priímkoff left the room, and Vyéra and I were left alone.

" There is Italian blood in your veins also,"— I remarked.

" Yes,"—she responded:—" I will show you the portrait of my grandmother, if you wish."

" Pray do."

She went into her boudoir and brought thence a rather large gold locket. On opening this locket, I beheld a splendidly-painted miniature portrait of Madame Éltzoff's father and his wife, —that peasant from Albano. Vyéra's grandfather surprised me by his likeness to his daughter. Only his features, rimmed with a white cloud of powder, appeared still more severe, still more sharp and pointed, and in his little, yellow eyes gleamed a sort of surly stubbornness. But what a face the Italian girl had! sensual, open like a full-blown rose, with big, prominent, humid eyes, and conceitedly-smiling, rosy lips! The thin, sensitive nostrils seemed to be quivering, and inflating, as after recent kisses; from her dark-skinned cheeks sultry heat and health seemed to emanate, and the splendour of youth, and feminine force. . . . That brow had never thought, and God be thanked for that! She was depicted in her Albanian costume; the artist (a master) had placed a spray of vine-leaves in her hair, which was black as pitch, with bright-grey reflections. Nothing could have been better suited to the expression of her face than that bacchantic decoration. And knowest thou, of whom that face reminded me? Of my Manon Lescaut in the black frame. And, what is most astonishing of all: as I gazed at that portrait, I recalled the fact that something resembling that smile, that glance, sometimes flits over Vyéra's face, despite the utter dissimilarity of the outlines. . . .

Yes, I repeat it: neither she herself nor any one else in all the world knows what lies hidden within her. . . .

By the way! Madame Éltzoff, before her daughter's marriage, related to her the story of her whole life, the death of her mother, and so forth, probably with the object of edification. That which had a particular effect upon Vyéra, was what she heard about her grandfather, about that mysterious Ladánoff. Is it not from him that she inherits her faith in visions? Strange! she herself is so pure and bright, yet she is afraid of everything gloomy, subterranean, and believes in it. . . .

But enough. Why write all this? However, since it is already written, I 'll just send it off to thee.   Thine,

P. B.

SEVENTH LETTER

From the same to the same

VILLAGE OF M . . . . OE, August 22.

I TAKE up my pen ten days after the date of my last letter. . . . Oh, my friend, I can no longer dissimulate. . . . How painful it is to me! How I love her! Thou canst imagine with what a bitter shudder I write this fateful word. I am no boy, not even a stripling; I am no longer at the age when it is almost impossible to deceive another person, while it costs no effort at all to deceive one's self. I know everything, and I see clearly. I know that I am close on forty years of age, that she is the wife of another, that she loves her husband; I know very well that I have nothing to expect from the unfortunate sentiment which has taken possession of me, save secret torments and definitive waste of my vital forces,—I know all this, I hope for nothing and I desire nothing. But I am no more at my ease for all that.

A month ago I began to notice that my attachment for her was becoming stronger and stronger. That partly disconcerted me, partly delighted me. . . . But could I have expected that all that would be repeated in me from which, as in youth, there is no return? But what am I saying! I never have loved thus, no, never! Manon Lescaut, the Frétillons—those were my idols. It is easy to shatter such idols; but now . . . . and only now have I learned what it means to love a woman. I am ashamed even to speak of it; but so it is. I am ashamed. . . . Love is egoism, nevertheless; but at my age, egoism would be unpardonable: one cannot live for himself at seven-and-thirty; one must live usefully, with the object of fulfilling one's duty, doing one's business. And I have tried to set to work. . . . And lo, everything has been dissipated again, as by a hurricane! Now I understand what I wrote to thee in my first letter; I understand what trial I lacked. How suddenly this blow has descended upon my head! I stand and gaze irrationally ahead: a black curtain hangs just in front of my eyes; my soul aches and is affrighted! I can restrain myself, I am outwardly calm, not only in the presence of others, but even when I am alone; really, I cannot go into a rage, like a boy! But the worm has crawled into my heart, and is gnawing it day and night. How is this thing going to end? Hitherto I have languished and been agitated in her absence, while in her presence I have instantly calmed down. . . . Now I am uneasy in her presence—that is what alarms me. Oh, my friend, how painful a thing it is to be ashamed of one's tears, to conceal them! . . . . Only youth is permitted to weep; tears become it alone. . . .

I cannot read over this letter; it has burst from me like a groan. I can add nothing, narrate nothing. . . . Give me time: I shall come to myself. I shall regain control of my soul, I shall talk with thee like a man, but now I should like to lean my head on thy breast and . . . .

O Mephistopheles! Even thou wilt not help me! I have intentionally lingered over, I have intentionally irritated the ironical vein in myself; I have reminded myself how ridiculous and hypocritical these complaints, these effusions, will appear to me a year, half a year hence. . . . No, Mephistopheles is powerless, and his teeth have grown blunt. . . . Farewell.

Thine,

P. B.

EIGHTH LETTER

From the same to the same

VILLAGE OF M . . . . OE, September 8, 1850.
MY DEAR FRIEND, SEMYÓN NIKOLÁITCH:

Thou hast taken my last letter too much to heart. Thou knowest how much inclined I have always been to exaggerate my feelings; I do it quite involuntarily: a feminine nature! That will pass off, with years, it is true; but I must admit, with a sigh, that up to the present time, I have not corrected myself. And, therefore, reassure thyself. I will not deny the impression which Vyéra has made upon me; but, nevertheless, I will say: there was nothing remarkable in all that. It is not in the least necessary that thou shouldst come hither, as thou writest that thou art intending to do. To gallop more than a thousand miles, God knows for what—why, that would be madness! But I am very grateful to thee for this new proof of thy friendship, and, believe me, I shall never forget it. Thy journey hither is ill-judged also because I myself intend soon to set off for Petersburg. Seated on thy divan, I will relate to thee many things; but now, really, I do not feel like it: the first thing you know, I shall get to chattering too much, and become entangled again. I will write to thee again before my departure.   So then, farewell until we meet shortly.   May health be thine, and cheerfulness, and do not worry too much over the fate of —thine sincerely,

P. B.

NINTH LETTER

From the same to the same

VILLAGE OF M . . . . OE, March 10, 1853.

I HAVE not answered thy letter for a long time; I have been thinking of thee all these days.   I have felt that thou wert prompted not by idle curiosity, but by genuine friendly sympathy; but still I have hesitated: whether I ought to follow thy advice, whether I ought to comply with thy wish.   At last I have reached a decision; I will tell thee all.   Whether my confession will relieve me, as thou assumest, I do not know; but it seems to me that I should remain culpable even if . . . . alas! still more culpable toward that unforgettable, charming spirit, if I did not confide our sad secret to the only heart which I still prize.   Thou alone, possibly, on earth dost remember Vyéra, and that thou shouldst judge of her light-mindedly and falsely, is what I cannot permit.   Then know all!   Alas! it can all be imparted in two words; that which existed between us flashed for a moment, like the lightning, and,

186

like the lightning, carried death and destruction with it. . . .

Since her death, since I settled down in this remote nook, which I shall never leave again to the end of my days, more than two years have passed, and everything is as clear in my memory, my wounds are still as fresh, my grief is as bitter as ever. . . .

I will not complain. Complaints, by irritating, alleviate sorrow, but not mine. I will begin my narration.

Dost thou remember my last letter—that letter in which I undertook to dissipate thy fears and dissuade thee from leaving Petersburg? Thou wert suspicious of its constrained ease, thou hadst no faith that we should soon see each other: thou wert right. On the eve of the day when I wrote to thee, I had learned that I was beloved.

As I trace these words I discover how difficult it will be for me to pursue my narration to the end. The importunate thought of her death will torture me with redoubled force, these memories will sear me. . . . But I shall try to control myself, and I will either discard my pen, or I will not utter a superfluous word.

This is how I learned that Vyéra loved me. First of all, I must tell thee (and thou wilt believe me), that up to that day I positively had not had a suspicion. She had, it is true, begun to be pensive at times, which had never been the case

with her previously; but I did not understand
why this happened to her. At last, one day, the
seventh of September,—a memorable day for me,
—this is what occurred. Thou knowest how I
loved her, how I was suffering. I wandered like
a ghost, I could find no place of rest. I tried
to remain at home, but could not endure it, and
went to her. I found her alone in her boudoir.
Priímkoff was not at home: he had gone off
hunting. When I entered Vyéra's room, she
looked intently at me, and did not respond to my
greeting. She was sitting by the window; on her
lap lay a book: it was my " Faust." Her face
expressed weariness. She requested me to read
aloud the scene between Faust and Gretchen,
where she asks him whether he believes in God.
I took the book and began to read. With her
head leaning against the back of her chair,
and her hands clasped on her breast, she continued to gaze at me in the same intent manner as
before.

I do not know why my heart suddenly began
to beat violently.

" What have you done to me? "—she said in a
lingering voice.

" What? "—I ejaculated in confusion.

" Yes; what have you done to me? "—she repeated.

" Do you mean to ask,"—I began:—" why
have I persuaded you to read such books? "

She rose in silence, and left the room. I stared after her.

On the threshold she halted and turned toward me.

" I love you,"—said she:—" that is what you have done to me."

The blood flew to my head. . . .

" I love you, I am in love with you,"—repeated Vyéra.

She went away, and shut the door behind her. I will not describe to thee what went on in me then. I remember that I went out into the garden, made my way into its thickets, and leaned against a tree. How long I stood there I know not. It was as though I had swooned; the feeling of bliss surged across my heart in a billow, from time to time. . . . No, I will not talk about that. Priímkoff's voice aroused me from my stupor; they had sent to tell him that I had arrived. He had returned from the chase, and had hunted me up. He was surprised at finding me in the garden alone, without a hat, and he led me to the house. " My wife is in the drawing-room,"— he said:—" let us go to her." Thou canst conjecture with what emotions I crossed the threshold of the drawing-room. Vyéra was sitting in one corner, at her embroidery-frame. I darted a covert glance at her, and for a long time thereafter, did not raise my eyes. To my amazement, she appeared to be calm; there was no tremor per-

ceptible in what she said, in the sound of her
voice. At last, I brought myself to look at her.
Our glances met. . . . She blushed almost imperceptibly, and bent over her canvas. I began
to watch her. She seemed perplexed, somehow;
a cheerless smile now and then flitted across her
lips.

Priímkoff left the room. She suddenly raised
her head and asked me in quite a loud tone:

" What dost thou intend to do now? "

I was disconcerted, and hastily, in a dull voice,
I replied that I intended to fulfil the duty of an
honourable man—to go away, " because,"—I
added,—" I love you, Vyéra Nikoláevna, as you
have, probably, long since perceived."

" I must have a talk with you,"—said she:—
" come to-morrow evening, after tea, to our little
house . . . you know, where you read ' Faust.' "

She said this so distinctly that even now I cannot understand how Priímkoff, who entered the
room at that moment, failed to hear anything.
Slowly, with painful slowness did that day pass.
Vyéra gazed about her from time to time, with
an expression as though she were asking herself:
" Was not she dreaming? " And, at the same
time, decision was written on her countenance.
While I . . . . I could not recover my composure. Vyéra loves me! These words gyrated
incessantly in my mind; but I did not understand
them,—I understood neither myself nor her. I

did not believe in such unexpected, such soul-disturbing happiness; with an effort I recalled the past, and I also looked and talked as in a dream. . . .

After tea, when I had already begun to meditate how I might slip unperceived out of the house, she herself suddenly announced that she wished to take a stroll, and proposed to me that I should accompany her. I dared not begin the conversation, I could barely draw my breath, I waited for her first word, I waited for an explanation; but she maintained silence. In silence we reached the little Chinese house, in silence we entered it, and there—to this day I do not know, I cannot comprehend how it came about—but we suddenly found ourselves in each other's arms. Some invisible force dashed me to her, and her to me. By the dying light of day, her face, with its curls tossed back, was illuminated for a moment by a smile of self-forgetfulness and tenderness, and our lips melted together in a kiss. . . .

This kiss was the first and the last.

Vyéra suddenly tore herself from my arms, and, with an expression of horror in her widely-opened eyes, staggered back. . . .

" Look round,"—she said to me in a quivering voice:—" do you see nothing? "

I wheeled swiftly round.

" No, nothing. But do you see any one? "

" I don't now, but I did."

She was breathing deeply and slowly.

" Whom?   What? "

" My mother,"—she said slowly, trembling all over.

I also shivered, as though a chill had seized me. I suddenly felt alarmed, like a criminal. And was not I a criminal at that moment?

" Enough! "—I began.—" What ails you? Tell me rather . . . ."

" No, for God's sake, no! "—she interrupted, clutching her head.—" This is madness. . . . I shall go out of my mind. . . . This is not to be trifled with—this is death. . . . Farewell. . . ."

I stretched out my arms toward her.

" Stay one moment, for God's sake,"—I cried in an involuntary transport. I did not know what to say, and could hardly stand on my feet.— " For God's sake . . . . why, this is cruel. . . ."

She glanced at me.

" To-morrow, to-morrow evening,"—she said: —" not to-day, I beg of you. . . . Go away to-day . . . . Come to-morrow evening to the wicket-gate in the garden, near the lake. I shall be there, I will come. . . . I swear to thee that I will come,"—she added, with an effort, and her eyes flashed.—" No matter who may seek to stop me, I swear it! I will tell thee all, only let me go to-day."

And before I could utter a word, she vanished.

Shaken to the very foundations, I remained rooted to the spot. My head was reeling. A feeling of anguish crept through the mad joy which filled my being. I glanced about me. The chamber in which I was standing, with its low vault and dark walls, seemed horrible to me.

I went out and betook myself with hasty steps to the house. Vyéra was waiting for me on the terrace; she went into the house as soon as I approached, and immediately retired to her bedroom.

I went away.

How I spent that night and the following day until the evening, I cannot describe. I remember only that I lay prone, with my face hidden in my hands, recalling her smile which had preceded the kiss, and whispering: " Here she is, at last. . . ."

I recalled also Madame Éltzoff's words, which Vyéra had repeated to me. She had said to her one day: " Thou art like ice; until thou shalt melt, thou art strong as a rock, but when thou meltest, there will not remain a trace of thee."

And here is another thing which recurred to my memory: Vyéra and I had, somehow, got into a discussion as to what are knowledge and talent.

" I know only one thing,"—she said:—" how to hold my peace until the last minute."

I had understood nothing at the time.

"But what is the meaning of her fright?"—I asked myself. . . . "Did she really see Madame Éltzoff? Imagination!"—I thought, and again surrendered myself to the emotions of anticipation.

That same day I wrote to thee—with what thoughts I shudder to recall—that artful letter.

In the evening, before the sun had set, I was standing at a distance of fifty paces from the garden gate, in a tall, thick mass of vines, on the shore of the lake. I had come from home on foot. I confess it, to my shame: terror, the most pusillanimous terror filled my breast, I kept trembling incessantly . . . . but I felt no remorse. Concealing myself among the branches, I stared fixedly at the gate. It did not open. The sun set, darkness descended: the stars had already come out, and the sky had grown black. No one appeared. Fever seized upon me. Night came. I could endure it no longer, and cautiously emerging from the vines, I crept up to the gate. Everything was quiet in the garden. I called Vyéra in a whisper, I called a second time, a third. . . . No voice responded. Another half hour, an hour elapsed; it had grown perfectly dark. Anticipation had exhausted me; I pulled the gate toward me, opened it at one movement and directed my way on tiptoe, like a thief, toward the house. I halted in the shadow of the lindens.

Almost all the windows in the house were

lighted: people were moving to and fro in the rooms. This astonished me: my watch, so far as I could make out by the dim light of the stars, indicated half-past eleven. Suddenly a rumbling resounded on the other side of the house: an equipage had driven into the courtyard.

" Evidently, there are visitors,"—I thought. Abandoning all hope of seeing Vyéra, I made my way out of the garden, and strode homeward with hasty steps. It was a dark September night, warm but starless. A feeling not so much of vex-ation as of grief, which was on the point of tak-ing possession of me, was dissipated to a certain degree, and I arrived at my own house somewhat fatigued from my brisk walk, but soothed by the tranquillity of the night, happy and almost merry. I entered my bedroom, dismissed Timofyéi, threw myself on the bed without undressing, and plunged into reverie.

At first my musings were cheerful; but I speed-ily noticed a strange change in myself. I began to feel a sort of mysterious, gnawing grief, a sort of profound, inward uneasiness. I could not un-derstand whence it proceeded; but I became alarmed, and oppressed, as though an impending misfortune were menacing me, as though some one dear to me were suffering at that moment, and were appealing to me for help. On the table a wax taper was burning with a small, motionless flame, the pendulum of the clock was ticking heavily and regularly. I leaned my head on my hand, and sat to staring into the empty, semi-darkness of my solitary chamber. I thought of Vyéra, and my soul ached within me: everything in which I had delighted appeared to me in its proper light, as a calamity, as ruin from which there was no escape. The feeling of anguish kept augmenting within me; I could no longer lie down; again it suddenly seemed to me as though some one were calling me with an appealing voice. . . . . I raised my head and shuddered. I was not mistaken: a wailing shriek swept from afar, and clung, faintly quivering, to the window-panes. I was terrified: I sprang from the bed, and threw open the window. A plainly-audible groan burst into the room, and seemed to hover over me. It seemed as though some one's throat were being cut at a distance, and the unhappy person were entreating, in vain, for mercy. I did not stop, at the time, to consider whether it might not be an owl hooting in the grove, or whether some other creature had emitted that groan, but as Mazeppa answered Kotchubéy, I replied with a shriek to that sound of ill-omen.

" Vyéra, Vyéra! "—I cried:—" is it thou who art calling me? "—Timofyéi, sleepy and dumb-founded, appeared before me.

I came to my senses, drank a glass of water, and went into another room; but sleep did not visit me. My heart beat painfully, although not

frequently. I could no longer give myself up to
dreams, to happiness. I no longer dared to believe in it.

On the following day, before dinner, I set off
to see Priímkoff. He greeted me with a care-
worn face.

" My wife is ill,"—he began:—" she is in bed.
I have sent for the doctor."

" What is the matter with her? "

" I don't understand. Yesterday evening she
started to go into the garden, but suddenly came
back, beside herself, thoroughly frightened. Her
maid ran for me. I came, and asked my wife,
' What ails thee? ' She made no reply, and instantly took to her bed; during the night, delirium
set in. God knows what she said in her delirium;
she mentioned you. The maid told me an astonishing thing: it seems that Vyérotchka saw her
dead mother in the garden; her mother seemed to
be coming toward her with open arms."

Thou canst imagine my sensations at these
words!

" Of course, it is nonsense,"—pursued Priímkoff:—" but I must confess that remarkable
things have happened to my wife in that line."

" And is Vyéra Nikoláevna very ill, pray tell
me? "

" Yes, very; she was very bad during the night;
now she is unconscious."

" But what did the doctor say? "

" He said that the malady had not yet declared itself. . . ."

March 12.

I CANNOT continue as I have begun, my dear friend: it costs me too much effort and irritates my wounds too greatly. The malady declared itself, to use the doctor's words, and Vyéra died of it. She did not survive a fortnight after that fatal day of our momentary tryst. I saw her once more before her end. I possess no more cruel memory. I had already learned from the doctor that there was no hope. Late at night, when every one in the house was in bed, I crept to the door of her chamber and looked at her. Vyéra was lying in bed, with closed eyes, emaciated, tiny, with the glow of fever on her cheeks. I stared at her as though I had been petrified. Suddenly she opened her eyes, fixed them on me, took a closer look, and stretching out her emaciated hand—

> "What does he want on that holy spot,
> That man . . . that man yonder. . . ."[1]

she articulated in a voice so terrible, that I fled at full speed. She raved of " Faust " almost continuously during her illness, and of her mother, whom she called now Martha, now Gretchen's mother.

[1] " *Was will er an dem heiligen Ort,*
Der da . . . . der dort. . . ."
" Faust," Part I, Last Scene.

Vyéra died. I was at her funeral. Since that day I have abandoned everything, and have settled down here forever.

Reflect now on what I have told thee; think of her, of that being who perished so early. How this came about, how that incomprehensible interposition of the dead in the affairs of the living is to be explained, I know not, and I shall never know; but thou must agree with me that it is no fit of capricious hypochondria, as thou expressest it, which has made me withdraw from society. All this time I have thought so much about that unhappy woman (I came near saying, " young girl "), about her origin, the mysterious play of Fate which we, blind that we are, designate as blind chance. Who knows how much seed is left by each person who lives on the earth, which is destined to spring up only after his death? Who can say to what mysterious end the fate of a man is bound up with the fate of his children, his posterity, and how his aspirations will be reflected in them, his mistakes visited on them? We must all submit and bow our heads before the Unknowable.

Yes, Vyéra perished, and I have remained whole. I remember,.when I was still a child, there was in our house a beautiful vase of transparent alabaster. Not a fleck sullied its virgin whiteness. One day, when I was left alone, I began to rock the pedestal on which it stood . . . . The vase suddenly fell to the floor, and was shattered to atoms. I nearly swooned with fright, and stood motionless before the fragments. My father entered the room, saw me, and said: " Just see what thou hast done! We shall never have our beautiful vase again; there is no way to mend it now." I burst out sobbing. It seemed to me that I had committed a crime.

I have become a man—and have heedlessly shattered a vessel which was a thousand times more precious. . . .

In vain do I tell myself that I could not have anticipated this instantaneous catastrophe, that it startled even me by its unexpectedness, that I had no suspicion as to the sort of woman Vyéra was. She really did know how to hold her peace to the last minute. I ought to have fled as soon as I felt that I loved her,—loved a married woman; but I remained,—and have shattered in fragments a very beautiful creature, and with dumb despair I now gaze upon the work of my hands.

Yes; Madame Éltzoff jealously guarded her daughter. She guarded her to the end, and at her first unwary step, she bore her off with her into the tomb.

It is time for me to make an end. . . . I have not told thee the hundredth part of what I should: but this has been quite enough for me. Let everything which has flashed up in my soul sink once more into its depths. . . . In ending, I will tell thee: I have brought one conviction out of the experiences of the recent years; life is not even enjoyment, ... life is a heavy toil. Renunciation, constant renunciation,—that is its secret meaning, its solution; not the fulfilment of cherished ideas and dreams, no matter how lofty they may be,—but the fulfilment of duty,—that is what man must take heed to; not unless he imposes upon himself chains, the iron chains of duty, can he attain to the end of his course without falling; but in youth we think: " The freer the better; the further one can go." It is permissible for youth to think thus; but it is disgraceful to console one's self with an illusion, when the stern face of the truth has at last looked thee full in the eye.

Farewell! Formerly I would have added: " Be happy." Now I say to thee: Endeavour to live, it is not as easy as it seems. Remember me, not in hours of sadness, but in hours of thoughtfulness, and preserve in thy soul the image of Vyéra in all its unsullied purity. . . . Once more, farewell!   Thine,

                                                          P. B.

AN EXCURSION TO THE FOREST BELT

(1857)

AN EXCURSION TO THE FOREST BELT[1]

THE FIRST DAY

THE aspect of the huge pine woods which embrace the whole horizon, the aspect of the " Forest Belt," reminds one of the aspect of the sea. And the impressions evoked by both are the same: the same primeval, untouched strength lies in vast and regal expanse before the spectator. From the bosom of the eternal forests, from the deathless lap of the waters the selfsame voice arises: " I care nothing for thee,"—Nature says to man:—" I reign, but do thou bestir thyself as to the means of escaping death." But the forest is more monotonous and melancholy than the sea, especially a pine forest, which is forever the same, and almost noiseless. The sea menaces and caresses, it has a shifting play of all hues, it speaks with all voices; it reflects the sky, which also exhales eternity, but an eternity which does not seem alien to us. . . . The unchanging, gloomy pine forest maintains a surly silence, or roars dully,— and at the sight of it the consciousness of our in-

[1] A district in southwest Russia—TRANSLATOR.

significance penetrates still more deeply and irresistibly into the heart of man.

It is difficult for a man, the creature of a single day, yesterday born and to-day doomed to death, —it is difficult for him to endure the cold gaze of the eternal Isis riveted impassibly upon him; not his bold hopes and dreams alone quiet down and become extinguished within him, encompassed by the icy breath of the elements; no—his whole soul chirps feebly and expires; and he feels that the last of his fellows may vanish from the face of the earth—and not a single needle on those branches will quiver; he feels his isolation, his impotence, his fortuitousness and with hurried, secret terror he turns his attention to the petty cares and toils of life; he is more at his ease in that world, created by himself; there he is at home, there he still dares to believe in his own importance, in his own power.

Such were the thoughts which occurred to me several years ago, when, as I stood on the porch of a tiny posting-station, erected on the bank of the marshy little Reséta, I beheld the Forest Belt for the first time. The blue masses of the evergreen forest retreated in front of me in long, serried ranks of terraces; here and there, small birch groves glimmered only as green spots; the entire field of vision was encompassed by the pine forest; no church gleamed white, no fields shone light in any direction—there was nothing but trees, trees, nothing but jagged crests; and a thin, dull mist, the eternal mist of the Forest Belt, hung high above them. It was not indolence, that impassivity of life, no—it was absence of life, something dead, though majestic, which breathed forth upon me from all points of the horizon. I remember that huge, white clouds sailed past, softly, and high in air, and the hot summer day lay motionless and silent on the earth. The reddish water of the little stream slipped by without a plash between the dense growth of reeds; at its bottom round hillocks of prickly moss were dimly visible, and the banks now disappeared in the swampy ooze, now shone forth with the sharp whiteness of fine, friable sand. Past the posting-station itself ran the well-beaten county highway.

On this highway, directly opposite the porch, stood a peasant-cart, laden with boxes and chests. Its owner, a gaunt petty burgher, with a hawk's-bill nose and tiny, mouse-like eyes, round-shouldered and lame, was harnessing to it his wretched nag, which was lame, like himself; he was a gingerbread pedlar, who was on his way to the Karatchyóff fair. Several persons suddenly made their appearance on the threshold; others straggled after them . . . . at last, a whole throng poured forth; all of them had staves in their hands, and wallets on their backs. From their walk, which was weary and shambling, from their sunburned faces, it was evident that they came from afar: they were day-labourers, diggers, who were returning from a trip to earn money by harvest labour.   An old man of seventy, with perfectly white hair, seemed to be acting as their leader; he turned round from time to time, and spurred on the laggards with a tranquil voice. " Come, come, come, my lads,"—he said,— " co-ome on." They all advanced in silence, in a sort of impressive tranquillity.   Only one, a man of low stature, and with an angry aspect, in a sheep-pelt coat open on the breast, and a sheep-skin cap, pulled down over his very eyes, suddenly asked the gingerbread pedlar, as he came on a level with him:

" How much is gingerbread, fool? "

" That depends on the sort of gingerbread, my dear man,"—replied the astounded dealer in a shrill voice.—" I have some for a kopék—while other sorts cost two kopéks.   But hast thou two kopéks in thy purse? "

" I guess it ferments in the belly,"—retorted the man in the sheepskin coat, and strode away from the cart.

" Hurry up, my lads, hurry up! "—the old man's voice made itself heard:—" It is a long way to our halting-place for the night."

" A rough lot,"—said the gingerbread pedlar, darting a sidelong glance at me, as soon as the whole throng had straggled past him; " is that the food for them? "

TO THE FOREST BELT

And harnessing his nag with all speed, he drove down to the river, on which a small ferry-boat of planks was visible. A peasant in a white felt " shlyk " (the tall, pointed cap usual in the Forest Belt), emerged from a low earth-hut to meet him, and ferried him over to the opposite shore. The cart crawled along the rutted and gullied road, now and then emitting a squeak from one of the wheels.

I fed my horses and crossed the stream also. After crawling along for about two versts[1] through a swampy meadow, I drove, at last, on to a narrow dam at a clearing in the forest. My tarantás jolted unevenly over the round logs; I alighted and went on foot. The horses advanced at an energetic pace, snorting and tossing their heads to rid themselves of the gnats and small flies. The Forest Belt had received us into its bosom. At its border, nearest to the meadow, grew birches, aspens, lindens, maples, and oaks; then these began to occur more rarely, the thick fir woods moved up in a dense wall; further away the bare trunks of a pine wood shone red, and then again a mixed forest stretched out, over-grown below with hazel-bushes, bird-cherry, mountain-ash, and large, juicy grass. The sun's rays brilliantly illuminated the crests of the trees, and, sifting over the branches, only here and there reached the ground in pale streaks and patches.

[1] A verst is two-thirds of a mile. —TRANSLATOR.

Hardly any birds were to be heard—they are not fond of the great forests; only the mournful, thrice-repeated cry of a hoopoe, and the angry scream of a nut-bird, or a jay rang out from time to time; a reticent, always solitary rook flew across the clearing, the golden-blue of its beautiful feathers gleaming brightly. Sometimes the trees thinned out, stood further apart, there was more light ahead, the tarantás came out on a clear, sandy glade; sparse rye grew thereon in beds, noiselessly waving its pale little ears; on one side a small, ancient chapel stood out darkly with its sagging cross above a well; an invisible brook babbled peaceably, with varying and resonant sounds, as though it were flowing into an empty bottle; and then, suddenly, the road was barred by a recently-fallen birch-tree, and the forest stood round about, so aged, so lofty, so dreamy, that even the air seemed stifling. In places the clearing was all inundated with water; on both sides extended a forest morass, all green and dark, all covered with reeds and a growth of young alder-bushes; ducks kept flying upward in pairs—and strange it was to see these water-fowl flitting swiftly between the pines.—" Ga, ga, ga, ga," a prolonged cry suddenly arose; it was a shepherd driving his flock through the smaller growth of trees; a dark-brown cow with short, sharp horns butted her way noisily through the bushes, with her big, dark eyes riveted on the hound which was running on in front of me; a gentle breeze wafted to me the delicate yet strong odour of burnt wood; a tiny wreath of white smoke crawled up and down far away in circular streams against the pale-blue forest air; evidently, some peasant furnished charcoal to the glass-works or a factory. The further we advanced the more dull and quiet did it grow around us. It is always silent in a pine forest, only far away, high overhead, a sort of long murmur and suppressed roar passes through the branches. . . . One drives on and on, that everlasting murmur of the forest never ceases, and his heart gradually begins to ache, and he wants to get out as speedily as possible, into a spacious place, into the light; he wants to inhale with full lungs—and that fragrant dampness and rotting oppress his breast. . . .

We drove for fifteen versts at a foot-pace, now and then breaking into a trot. I wanted to reach the village of Svyátoe, which lay in the very heart of the forest, by daylight. Twice we encountered peasants with long logs, or linden-bark, which they had stripped from the trees, in their carts.

"Is it far to Svyátoe?"—I inquired of one of them.

"No, not far."

"How far?"

"Why, it must be about three versts."

An hour and a half passed. We were still

driving on and on. Now again a loaded cart creaked. A peasant was walking beside it.

" How much further is it to Svyátoe, brother? "

" What? "

" How far it is to Svyátoe? "

" Eight versts."

The sun had already set when, at last, I emerged from the forest and beheld before me a small village. About twenty homesteads clung closely around an ancient church, with a single, green dome, and tiny windows, which gleamed crimson in the evening glow. It was Svyátoe. I drove into the enclosure.[1] The herd on its homeward way overtook my tarantás, and ran past, lowing, grunting, and bleating. The young girls and care-worn housewives welcomed their beasts; tow-headed little urchins chased the unruly sucking pigs with merry shouts; the dust whirled along the streets, in light clouds, and turned crimson as it rose higher in the air.

I stopped at the house of the Elder, a crafty and intelligent " forest-dweller," one of those concerning whom it is said that they can see what is going on two yards under the ground. Early on the following day, I set off, in a light cart, drawn by a pair of pot-bellied horses belonging to the peasants, with the Elder's son, and another young peasant, named Egór, on a hunt

---

[1] Russian villages are enclosed with a hedge, a fence, or wattled branches.—TRANSLATOR.

for moor-cock and hazel-hens. The forest stood
in a dense-blue ring along the entire rim of the
sky—the cultivated fields around Svyátoe were
reckoned at two hundred desyatínas,[1] no more;
but we were obliged to drive for seven versts
to reach the good places. The Elder's son was
named Kondrát. He was a chestnut-haired, red-
cheeked young lad, with a kindly and pacific expression of countenance, obliging and loquacious.
He drove the horses. Egór sat beside me. I
wish to say a couple of words concerning him.

He was considered the best hunter in the entire
county. He had traversed all the localities for
fifty versts round about, in their entire length
and breadth. He rarely fired at a bird, because
of scarcity of powder and shot; but it was enough
for him that he had lured up a hazel-hen, and had
noted the crest of a wood-snipe. Egór bore the
reputation of being an upright man and a " close-
mouthed fellow." He was not fond of talking,
and never exaggerated the number of the game
he had found—a rare trait in a hunter. He was
of medium height, and gaunt; and had a pale,
elongated face and large, honest eyes. All his
features, especially his lips, were regular, and
were permanently impassive; they breathed forth
imperturbable composure. He smiled slightly,
and inwardly, as it were, when he uttered his
words, and that quiet smile was very charming.

[1] A desyatína is equal to 2.70 acres.—TRANSLATOR.

He did not drink liquor, and worked industriously, but had no luck: his wife was constantly ailing, his children died one after the other; he had been " reduced to poverty," and was absolutely unable to get on his feet again. And it must be said, that a passion for hunting is not befitting a peasant, and he who " indulges himself with a gun " is a bad farmer.

Whether it arose from dwelling constantly in the forest, face to face with the mournful and rigorous nature of that unpopulated region, or in consequence of a special turn and type of mind, at any rate, a certain modest dignity, precisely that, dignity and not thoughtfulness,—the dignity of a stately deer,—was perceptible in all Egór's movements. In the course of his career, he had killed seven bears, after having laid in wait for them in the fields of oats. It was only on the fourth night that he made up his mind to fire on the last: the bear persisted in not standing sideways to him, and he had but one bullet. Egór had killed him just before my arrival. When Kondrát conducted me to him, I found him in his little back yard: squatted on his heels in front of the huge beast, he was cutting out the fat with a short, dull knife.

" What a fine fellow thou hast laid low! "— I remarked.

Egór raised his head and gazed first at me, then at the hound which had come with me.

" If you have come to hunt, there are moor-cock at Móshnoe—three broods of them, and five of hazel-hens,"—he said, and turned again to his task.

It was with this Egór and with Kondrát that I set off on the following day on my hunting expedition. We drove briskly across the glade which surrounded Svyátoe, but on entering the forest, dragged along again at a walk.

" Yonder sits a wood-pigeon," said Kondrát, suddenly turning to me:—" 't would be a good thing to knock it over."

Egór glanced in the direction whither Kondrát was pointing, and said nothing. It was a distance of over one hundred paces to the wood-pigeon, and one cannot kill it at forty paces, such is the firmness of its feathers.

The loquacious Kondrát made a few more remarks; but not without effect did the forest stillness embrace him also: he fell silent. Only now and then exchanging words, but keeping our eyes fixed ahead, and listening to the panting and snorting of the horses, we finally reached " Móshnoe." [1] This appellation was applied to a mighty pine forest, with a sprinkling of spruce-trees here and there. We alighted. Kondrát pushed the cart into the bushes, so that the mosquitoes might not bite the horses. Egór inspected the trigger of his gun, and crossed himself: he

[1] An adjective meaning *mighty*. —TRANSLATOR.

never began anything without the sign of the cross.

The forest which we had entered was extremely aged. I do not know whether the Tatárs roved therein,[1] but the Russian bandits and the Lithuanians of the Troublous Time [2] certainly might have concealed themselves in its remote fastnesses. At a respectful distance from one another rose the mighty pines with huge, slightly-gnarled trunks of a pale-yellow hue; between them, drawn up in military array, stood others, of lesser growth. Greenish moss, all besprinkled with dead pine-needles, covered the ground; the bog-bilberry grew in dense bushes; the strong odour of its berries, resembling the perfume of musk, oppressed the breath. The sun could not penetrate through the lofty canopy of the pine-branches; but it was stifling hot and not dark in the forest, nevertheless; like huge drops of sweat, the heavy, transparent pitch oozed out and quietly trickled down the coarse bark of the trees. The motionless air, devoid of shadow and devoid of light, burned the face. All was silent; even our footsteps were not audible. We trod on the moss, as on a carpet; Egór, in particular, moved noiselessly, as though he had been a shadow; beneath his feet not even the dead

[1] During the period of the "Tatár Yoke," in the thirteenth and fourteenth centuries. — TRANSLATOR.

[2] In the beginning of the seventeenth century, which ended in the election of the first Románoff Tzar. — TRANSLATOR.

branches crackled. He walked without haste, now and then blowing his decoy-whistle; a hazel-hen soon answered, and before my very eyes dived into a thick spruce-tree; but in vain did Egór point it out to me: strain my vision as I would, I could not possibly descry it; Egór was compelled to fire at it. We also found two coveys of moor-cocks; the cautious birds rose far away, with a heavy, sharp clatter; but we succeeded in shooting three young ones.

At one *maidán*,[1] Egor suddenly came to a halt and called to me. "A bear has been trying to get water,"—he said, pointing at a broad, fresh scratch in the very centre of the pit, lined with fine moss.

"Is that a trace of his paws?"—I inquired.

"Yes; but the water had dried up. He has left his traces on that pine-tree also; he climbed it for honey. He has cut it with his claws as with a knife."

We continued to make our way into the very densest part of the forest. Egór only rarely cast a glance upward, and walked on in front calmly and confidently. I espied a tall, circular embankment, surrounded by a trench half-filled with earth.

"What is that,—a tar-pit also?"—I asked.

"No,"—replied Egór:—"a fortress of brigands used to stand here."

[1] A place where tar is distilled is called a *maidán*.

" Long ago? "

" Yes, long ago; beyond the memories of our grandfathers. And a treasure is buried here, too. But a strong malediction is placed upon it; an oath sworn on human blood."

We proceeded about a couple of versts further. I was thirsty.

" Sit down a bit,"—said Egór:—" I will go for water; there is a spring hard by."

He departed; I remained alone.

I seated myself on the stump of a felled tree, propped my elbow on my knees, and after a long silence, slowly raised my head and gazed about me. Oh, how quiet and grimly-melancholy was everything around—no, not even melancholy, but dumb, cold, and menacing at one and the same time! My heart contracted within me. At that moment, on that spot, I became conscious of the breath of death, I felt it; its proximity was almost tangible. Not a single sound quivered, not a momentary rustle arose in the motionless jaws of the pine forest which surrounded me! Again, almost in terror, I dropped my head; I seemed to have been gazing into something at which a man should not look. . . . I covered my eyes with my hand—and suddenly, as though in obedience to a mysterious command, I began to recall my whole life. . . .

Now my childhood flitted before me,—noisy and quiet, irritable and good, with hurried joys and swift griefs; then my youth rose up, troubled, strange, vain-glorious, with all its errors and enterprises, with disordered labour, and agitated inactivity. . . . Then also recurred to my mind the comrades of my aspirations . . . . then, like a flash of lightning by night, several bright memories gleamed . . . . then the shadows began to grow and move forward; it became darker and darker around me; the monotonous years flew past more dully and quietly—and sadness descended like a stone upon my heart. I sat motionless gazing with surprise and effort, as though I beheld my whole life before me, as though a scroll were being unrolled before my eyes. "Oh, what have I done?" my lips involuntarily uttered in a bitter whisper. "Oh, life, life, how art thou gone without a trace? How hast thou slipped out of my tightly-clenched hands? Hast thou deceived me, or have I failed to make use of thy gifts? Is it possible? This trifle, this poor handful of dusty ashes—is that all that is left of thee? This cold, impassive, useless something—is it I, the I of days gone by? What? My soul has thirsted for such full happiness, it has rejected with scorn everything petty, everything defective, it has waited: in another moment happiness will gush forth in a flood—and not a single drop has moistened the longing lips? Oh, my golden chords, ye, who quivered so sensitively, so sweetly once on a time,—I hardly heard your song . . . . ye had only just begun to sound, when ye broke. Or, perchance, happiness, the direct happiness of my whole life has gone by close to me, has passed me, smiling with a radiant smile—and I have failed to recognise its divine countenance? Or has it really visited me and sat on my pillow, but I have forgotten it, as though it had been a dream? As though it had been a dream,"—I repeated dejectedly. Intangible images wandered through my soul, evoking in me not precisely pity, nor yet precisely perplexity. . . . " And you,"—I thought,—" dear, familiar, vanished faces, you who have encircled me in this dead solitude, why are you so profoundly and sadly silent? From what depths have ye risen? How am I to understand your enigmatical glances? Are ye bidding me farewell, or are ye welcoming me? Oh, can it be that there is no hope, no return? Why have ye flowed from my eyes, ye scanty, belated drops? Oh, heart, to what end, wherefore, still feel pity? Strive to forget if thou desirest repose; train thyself to the submission of the last parting, to the bitter words: ' farewell ' and ' forever.' Do not look back, do not remember, do not aspire thither where it is bright, where youth smiles, where joy profound flutters its azure pinions, where love, like the dew in the crimson dawn, beams with tears of rapture; look not thither where bliss dwells and faith and power—that is no place for us! "

"Here 's your water for you,"—rang out Egór's resonant voice behind me:—"drink, with God's blessing!"

I gave an involuntary start: this living speech administered a shock to me, joyously agitated my whole being. It was as though I had fallen into an unexplored, gloomy depth, where everything round about had grown still, and nothing was audible save the quiet incessant moaning of some eternal grief . . . . as though I were dying, but could not offer resistance; and suddenly a friendly call had reached my ear, and some one's mighty hand had brought me forth, with one upward sweep, into God's daylight. I glanced round, and, with unspeakable delight, perceived the honest and composed face of my guide. He was standing before me in a light and stately pose, with his wonted smile, reaching out to me a small, damp bottle, all filled with fresh water. . . . I rose.

"Let us go on, guide me,"—I said with enthusiasm.

We set out and roved about for a long time, until evening. As soon as the midday heat " held up," it began to grow cold and dark in the forest so swiftly that one no longer felt any inclination to remain in it. " Begone, ye uneasy mortals," it seemed to be whispering to us in surly wise from behind every pine. We made our way out, but did not soon find Kondrát. We shouted, called him by name, but he did not respond. Suddenly, in the midst of the wonderful stillness of the air, we heard his " whoa! whoa! "—ring out in a ravine close at hand. . . . He had not heard our shouts because of the wind which had suddenly sprung up, and as suddenly completely died away. Only on trees which stood apart could the traces of its gusts be seen: it had turned many leaves wrong side out, and so they remained, imparting a motley appearance to the motionless foliage.

We climbed into the cart and rolled off homeward. I sat swaying to and fro and quietly inhaling the damp, rather keen air, and all my recent visions and regrets were engulfed in one sensation of dreaminess and fatigue, in one desire to return as promptly as possible under the roof of a warm house; to drink tea with thick cream; to burrow into the soft, porous hay and sleep, sleep, sleep. . . .

THE SECOND DAY

On the following morning, we three again betook ourselves to the Burnt District. Ten years previously, several thousand desyatínas had been burned over in the Forest Belt, and up to the present time it had not been covered with a new growth of trees; here and there young firs and pines are springing up, but with that exception, there is nothing but moss and ashes rendered worthless by long lying. On this Burnt District, which is reckoned as lying twelve versts from Svyátoe, grow all sorts of berries in great quantities, and woodcock, which are extremely fond of strawberries and red bilberries, breed there.

We were driving along in silence, when suddenly Kondrát raised his head.

" Eh!"—he exclaimed:—" why, I do believe 't is Efrém standing yonder. Morning, Alexándritch,"—he added, raising his voice, and lifting his cap.

A peasant of short stature, in a short, black peasant-coat girt with a rope, stepped out from under a tree and approached the cart.

" Did they release thee?"—inquired Kondrát.

" I should think they did!"—returned the peasant, displaying his teeth in a grin.—" It is n't convenient to hold fellows like me."

" And is Piótr Philíppitch all right?"

" Philíppoff is it? We know our business, he 's all right."

" You don't say so! Why, Alexándritch, I was thinking; ' come, brother,' I was thinking, ' now lie down on the frying-pan, goose!' "

" About Piótr Philíppoff is it? Not much! We 've seen his like before. He tries to play the wolf, but he has a dog's tail.—Art thou going a-hunting, master?"—the little peasant suddenly inquired, swiftly turning up to me his little, puckered-up eyes, and immediately dropping them again.

" Yes."

" And where, for example? "

" To the Burnt District,"—said Kondrát.

" You 're going to the Burnt District; look out that you don't drive into a conflagration."

" Why, what dost thou mean? "

" I have seen a lot of moor-cock,"—went on the little peasant, as though jeering and without re- plying to Kondrát,—" but you won't hit on the place; it is a good twenty versts off in a bee-line. And there 's Egór—there 's no denying it! he 's as much at home in the pine forest as in his own yard, but even he won't make his way thither. Morning, Egór, thou God's soul worth one ko- pék,"—he suddenly bellowed.

" Morning, Efrém,"—returned Egór deliber- ately.

I stared with curiosity at this Efrém. It was a long time since I had seen so strange a face. He had a long, sharp nose, big lips, and a scanty beard. His blue eyes fairly darted about like fireworks. He stood in a free-and-easy attitude, with his arms set lightly akimbo, and did not doff his cap.

" Art on a visit home, pray? "—Kondrát asked him.

" Exh-sta! on a visit! 'T is not the weather now for that, brother. I 've been on a spree.

I' ve been cutting a dash, brother, that 's what. Thou mayest lie on the stove until winter, and not a single dog will sneeze. That superintendent yonder in the town said to me: ' Leave us, Alexándritch,' says he, ' go away out of the country; we 'll give thee a first-class passport . . . . but I 'm sorry for thy Svyátoe folks: they can't produce another such thief as thou.' "

Kondrát broke out laughing.

" Thou art a jester, little uncle, a regular jester,"—he said, giving the reins a shake. The horses started on.

" Whoa!"—said Efrém. The horses came to a standstill. Kondrát did not like this sally.

" Stop thy insolence, Alexándritch,"—he remarked in an undertone. " Dost thou not see that we are driving a gentleman? He 'll get angry, the first thou knowest."

" Ekh, thou sea-drake! What is there for him to get angry about? He 's a kind gentleman. Just see now, he 'll give me some money for vodka. Ekh, master, give the wayfarer the price of a dram! I 'll dispose of it,"—he caught himself up, elevating his shoulder to his ear, and gnashing his teeth.

I involuntarily smiled, gave him a ten-kopék piece, and ordered Kondrát to drive on.

" Much obliged, Your Well-born,"—shouted Efrém after us, in military fashion.[1] " And do

---

[1] "Much satisfied " (in the plural), literally.—TRANSLATOR.

thou, Kondrát, henceforth know from whom thou shouldst take lessons; the timid man is done for, the bold man succeeds. When thou returnest drop in to see me, dost hear? I shall have liquor on hand for three days; we 'll polish off a couple of bottles; my wife 's a shrew, the housekeeping goes as on runners. . . . Hey, white-sided magpie, carouse while thy tail is whole! "

And whistling shrilly, Efrém dived into the bushes.

" What sort of a man is he? "—I inquired of Kondrát, who, as he sat on the box, kept shaking his head as though engaged in argument with himself.

" That one, you mean? "—returned Kondrát, dropping his eyes.—" That one, you mean? " he repeated.

" Yes. Is he one of your villagers? "

" Yes; he belongs in Svyátoe. He 's the sort of a man . . . . Such another is n't to be found for a hundred versts. Such a thief and rascal—and, oh, my God! his eye fairly warps at other folks' goods. You can't get away from him even by burrowing in the earth; and as for money, for example, why, he 'll drag it out from underneath your very backbone without your noticing it."

" What a daring fellow he is! "

" Daring? Yes; he is n't afraid of anybody. Just you take a good look at him: from his phynasomy he 's a knave; you can fairly detect that from his nose." (Kondrát frequently drove with gentlemen, and was in the habit of visiting the county town; consequently, he was fond, on occasion, of showing off.) "And you can't do anything to him. Many a time they 've haled him to town and put him in prison,—and only loss came of it. They will begin to bind him, and he 'll say: ' Come now, are n't you going to fetter that leg? Fetter it also, and as strongly as you can, and I 'll take a nap in the meantime; but I 'll reach home quicker than your guards.' You look: and he really has got back, he 's there again, akh! oh, thou my God! All of us hereabouts know the forest; we 've been used to it from our infancy, but we can't compete with him. Last summer, he came by night in a bee-line from Altúkhin to Syyátoe, which must be forty versts. And as for stealing honey, he 's a master-hand at that; and not a bee stings him. He has devastated all the bee-farms."

"I suppose he shows no quarter to the wild hives either?"

"Well, no; why accuse him without cause? That sin has not been noticed in him. A wild hive is a sacred thing with us. A bee-farm is fenced in; there is a guard; if he purloins that,—that 's according to luck; but a wild bee is God's affair, not guarded; only a bear touches it."

"That 's because he is a bear,"—remarked Egór.

" Is he married? "

" Certainly. And he has a son. And his son will turn out a thief also! He takes after his father completely. And he 's teaching him now. A little while ago he brought home a pot full of old five-kopék pieces,—he had stolen it somewhere, of course; he went and buried it in a glade in the forest, but returned home himself and sent his son to the glade. ' I won't give thee anything to eat until thou findest the pot,' says he; ' and I won't let thee into the house.'—The son sat a whole day in the forest, and spent the night in the forest; but he found the pot. Yes, he 's clever, that Efrém. So long as he 's at home, he 's an amiable man, he treats everybody: drink, eat, as much as thou wilt; and folks set up dancing at his house, and all sorts of drollery; but if he 's at the assembly,—we have such an assembly in our village,—the best thing a man can do is not to condemn him; he 'll come up from behind, listen, say a word, as though he were chopping something, and off he 'll go; and 't is a weighty word. And if he goes off into the forest, well, then look out for a catastrophe! Expect ruin. But I must say one thing, that he won't touch his own fellow-villagers unless he 's in a tight place himself. If he meets a Svyátoe man,—' Turn out, and get past me, brother,'—he 'll shout from afar: —' The forest spirit has come over me: I 'm in murderous mood!'—Calamity! "

" But why do you pay any heed to that? Cannot the whole countryside get the better of one man? "

" Why, apparently they can't."

" Is he a wizard, pray? "

" Who knows? A while ago, he got into the bee-farm of the neighbouring chanter, by night; yet the chanter was on guard himself. Well, he caught him, and gave him a good thrashing in the darkness. When he got through, Efrém says to him: ' And dost thou know whom thou hast thrashed? '   And when the chanter recognised him by his voice, he was fairly dumfounded. ' Well, brother,' says Efrém, ' thou shalt pay for this.'   The chanter fell at his feet: ' Take what thou wilt,' says he.—' No,' says the other, ' I 'll take from thee at my own time, and what I choose.'—And what think you? From that very day, the chanter began to wander about like a shadow, just as though he had been scalded. ' My heart is pining away within me,' says he: ' evidently, the brigand has fastened on me an awfully strong spell.'—And that 's what happened to him, to that chanter."

" That chanter must be stupid,"—I remarked.

" Stupid? And is that the way you judge? Once an order was issued to capture that same Efrém. We 've got such a sharp commissary of police! So ten men set out to capture Efrém. They see him coming toward them. . . . One of

them begins to shout: ' There he is, hold him, bind
him!' But Efrém goes into the forest, and cuts
himself a cudgel, about two fingers thick, and
leaps out again on the road, so hideous, so terrible,
and commands, like a general on parade: ' On
your knees!'—and down they all fall.—' And
who was it,'—says he,—' that shouted,—" Hold
him, bind him?" Thou, Seryóga?' And the lat-
ter just springs to his feet, and makes off. . .
But Efrém follows him and whacks him on the
heels with his cudgel. . . . He stroked him for
about a verst. And afterward he was always complaining: ' Ekh, I 'm vexed,' says he, ' that I
did n't prevent his eating flesh for the last time
before the fast.' This happened just before the
fast of St. Philip. Well, and the commissary of
police was soon superseded,—and that was the
end of the whole matter."

" But why did they all submit to him?"

" Why! because they just did. . . ."

" He has scared all of you, and now he does
what he pleases with you."

" He has scared us. . . . But he 'll scare any
one you like. And he 's clever at inventions.
O thou, my God!—Once I stumbled upon him in
the forest, and such a healthy rain was coming
down that I was about to turn aside. . . . But
he looked at me, and beckoned me up so, with his
hand. ' Come hither, Kondrát,' says he, ' don't
be afraid. Learn from me how to live in the

forest, and what to do in a rain.' I approached him, and he was sitting under a spruce-tree and had lighted a small fire of damp branches; the smoke had caught in the spruce, and prevented the rain from dripping down. I was astonished at him. And then, here 's another thing he invented, once on a time " (and Kondrát broke into a laugh), " and amused us. Our oats were being threshed on the threshing-floor, but the men had not finished; they had not managed to rake together the last pile. Well, and so they stationed two sentries for the night; but the lads were not of the brave sort. So, they were sitting and chattering, when Efrém took and filled the sleeves of his shirt with straw, and tied the ends, and put the shirt on his head. So he crept up to the kiln in that guise, and began to show himself a little from round the corner, and thrust forth his horns. One young fellow says to the other: ' Dost see? ' —' I see,' says the other, and suddenly uttered an exclamation . . . . only the cords of their bast-slippers burst. But Efrém gathered the oats into a sack and dragged it off to his house. He told all about it himself afterward. How he did shame them, shame those lads. . . . Truly! "

Again Kondrát burst out laughing. And Egór smiled. " Only the cords of their bast-slippers burst? " said he.

Again we all relapsed into silence. Suddenly Kondrát gave a start of alarm and sat up straight.

"Hey, good heavens!"—he exclaimed;—
"why, I do believe there's a fire!"

"Where? Where?"—we asked.

"Yonder, look, straight ahead in the direction
we're driving. . . . A fire it is. That Efrém,
—Efrém predicted it. Can it be his doing, the
accursed soul? . . . ."

I glanced in the direction indicated by Kondrát. In fact, two or three versts in front of us,
behind a green band of low spruce-trees, a thick
pillar of blue smoke was slowly rising from the
earth, gradually curving and assuming the form
of a cap; to the right and left of it others, smaller
and whiter, were visible.

A peasant, all red in the face and perspiring,
clad in nothing but his shirt, with his hair dishevelled above his frightened face, was galloping
straight toward us, and with difficulty drew up his
hastily-bridled horse.

"Brothers,"—he asked in a panting voice,—
"have n't you seen any of the forest guards?"

"No; we have n't. What is it—is the forest
on fire?"

"Yes. The people must be assembled; otherwise, it will take the direction of Trósnoe. . . ."

The peasant jerked his elbows, as he kicked the
flanks of his horse with his heels. . . . It galloped
off.

Kondrát also urged on his pair. We drove
straight at the smoke, which spread out more and

more widely; in places it suddenly turned black and spurted up aloft. The nearer we came, the less clear became its outlines; soon the air was all dimmed, there was a strong odour of burning, and the first pale-red tongues of flame flashed out, moving strangely and terribly among the trees.

"Well, God be thanked,"—said Kondrát:— "it appears to be a ground fire."

" A what?"

" A ground fire; the sort which runs along the ground. 'T is difficult to get control of an underground fire. What is one to do when the earth is burning for a whole arshin [1] down? There is but one salvation: dig trenches—and is that easy? But a ground fire is nothing. It will only shave off the grass, and burn up the dead leaves. The forest is all the better for it. But good heavens, just see, how it has struck out!"

We drove almost to the very verge of the conflagration. I alighted and walked toward it. This was neither difficult nor dangerous. The fire was running through the sparse pine forest *against* the wind; it was moving with an uneven line, or, to speak more accurately, in a dense, serrated wall of reflexed tongues. The smoke was carried away by the wind. Kondrát had told the truth; it really was a ground fire, which was merely shaving off the grass, and without flam-

[1] Twenty-eight inches—the Russian yard-measure.—TRANSLATOR.

ing up was proceeding onward, leaving behind it a black and smoking, but not even smouldering, track. Sometimes, it is true, in places where the fire encountered a depression filled with a thicket and dried branches, it suddenly reared itself aloft with a certain peculiar, decidedly ominous roar, in long, billowy tufts; but it speedily subsided, and ran onward as before, lightly crackling and hissing. I even noticed more than once, how an oak-bush with dry, pendent leaves, though surrounded by the flame remained untouched; it merely got a little singed below. I must confess that I could not understand why the dry leaves did not catch fire. Kondrát explained to me that this arose from the fact that it was a ground fire, " that is to say, not an angry one."

" But it is a fire, nevertheless," I retorted. —" 'T is a ground fire,"—repeated Kondrát. But although it was a ground fire, yet the conflagration produced its effect: the hares were scurrying back and forth in a disorderly sort of way, quite unnecessarily returning to the vicinity of the fire; birds got caught in the smoke, and circled about; the horses glanced about them, and snorted; the very forest seemed to be booming, —and man felt uncomfortable with the heat which suddenly struck him in the face. . . .

" What 's the use of looking at it? "—said Egór suddenly behind my back.—" Let 's go on."

" But where are we to pass through? "

" Turn to the left, over the dry marsh,—we can drive across."

We turned to the left and drove over, although sometimes it was rather hard on the horses and the cart.

All day long we dragged on through the Burnt District. Just before evening (the sunset glow had not yet kindled in the sky, but the shadows of the trees already lay motionless and long; and in the grass that chill was perceptible which precedes the dew) I lay down on the road near the cart,—to which Kondrát was engaged, without haste, in harnessing the horses which had eaten their fill,—and recalled my cheerless visions of the day before. Everything round about was as still as on the preceding day; but the soul-oppressing and crowding pine forest was not there; on the tall moss, the lilac steppe-grass, the soft dust of the road, the slender boles and clean little leaves of the young birches, lay the clear and gentle light of the low-hanging, no longer sultry, sun. Everything was resting, immersed in a soothing coolness; nothing had yet fallen asleep, but everything was already preparing for the healing slumber of the evening and the night. Everything seemed to be saying to man: " Rest, our brother; breathe lightly and do not grieve before sleep, which is near at hand." I raised my head and beheld, at the very tip of a slender branch, one of those large flies with an emerald head, a long body, and four transparent wings, which the French coquettishly designate as " demoiselles," and our guileless folk call " yokes." For a long time, more than an hour, I did not take my eyes off it. Baked through and through by the sun, it did not stir, but only now and then turned its head from side to side, and let its raised wings palpitate . . . . that is all. As I gazed at it, it suddenly seemed to me that I understood the life of nature,—understood its clear and indubitable, though for many still mysterious meaning. The slow and quiet inspiration, leisureliness and reserve of sensations and of forces, the equilibrium of health in each separate individual—that is its very basis, its irrevocable law; that is the thing on which it stands and is upheld. Everything which deviates from this level —either above or below, it makes no difference— is cast forth by it as worthless. Many insects die as soon as they know the equilibrium-destroying joy of love; an ailing wild beast plunges into the dense thickets, and expires there alone: it seems to feel that it no longer has a right to behold the sun, which is common to all, or to breathe the free air; it has not the right to live; but man, whose lot is evil in the world, whether by his own fault or through that of others, must at least know how to hold his peace.

" Come, what art thou about, Egór?"—suddenly exclaimed Kondrát, who had already managed to mount the box of the cart, and was playing with and disentangling the reins.—" Come, take thy seat. What hast thou fallen to musing about? Still about the cow? "

"About the cow? About what cow? "—I asked, glancing at Egór. Calm and dignified as ever, he really had fallen to musing, apparently, and was gazing off somewhere into the distance, at the fields which were already beginning to grow dark.

" Why, don't you know? "—retorted Kondrát: —" his last cow died last night. He has no luck— what 's to be done? "

Egór took his seat in silence on the box, and we drove off. " That man knows how to refrain from complaining," I thought.

ÁSYA

(1857)

ÁSYA

I

I WAS five-and-twenty years of age at the time [began N. N.].—'T is an affair of days long past, as you see. I had just acquired my freedom and had gone abroad; not in order to "finish my education," as people expressed it then, but simply because I wanted to see God's world. I was healthy, young, cheerful; my money was not exhausted; cares had not yet succeeded in accumulating; I lived without looking back, I did what I wished: in one word, I flourished. It never entered my head that man is not a plant, and that he cannot flourish long. Youth eats gilded gingerbread cakes and thinks they are its daily bread; but a time will come when one will beg for bread. But there is no use in discussing that.

I was travelling utterly without an aim, without a plan; I was halting everywhere where things pleased me, and immediately proceeded onward, as soon as I felt a desire to see new faces—precisely that, faces. People alone and exclusively

interested me; I hated curious monuments, noteworthy collections; the mere sight of a local guide
aroused in me a sensation of melancholy and
wrath. I nearly went out of my mind in the
Grüne Gewölbe in Dresden. Nature had a very
great effect on me, but I did not love its so-
called beauties, remarkable mountains, cliffs, and
waterfalls; I did not like to have it force itself
upon me, interfere with me. On the other hand,
faces,—living, human faces,—people's speech,
their movements, their laughter, were what I
could not dispense with. I had always felt peculiarly gay and at my ease in a crowd; I found it
cheerful to go where other people went, to shout
when others shouted; and, at the same time, I
liked to watch those others shout. It amused me
to watch people. . . . yes, and I did not even watch
them—I contemplated them with a sort of joyous
and insatiable curiosity. But I am digressing
again.

So then, twenty years ago, I was residing in the
small German town of Z., on the left bank of the
Rhine. I was seeking solitude; I had just been
wounded in the heart by a young widow, with
whom I had become acquainted at the baths. She
was very pretty and clever; she coquetted with
every one—including sinful me; and at first she
even encouraged me, but afterward wounded me
cruelly, sacrificing me to a red-cheeked Bavarian
lieutenant. I am bound to say that the wound
in my heart was not very deep; but I regarded

it as my duty to surrender myself to grief and solitude for a certain time,—with what will not youth divert itself!—and I settled in Z.

This little town pleased me by its site at the foot of two lofty hills; by its decrepit walls and towers, its aged lindens, and the steep bridge over the bright little river, which fell into the Rhine; but chiefly by its good wine. Through its narrow streets there strolled in the evening, immediately after sunset (this was in July), extremely pretty, fair-haired German maidens, and on meeting a stranger they articulated with a pleasant voice: "*Guten Abend!*"—and some of them did not depart even when the moon rose from behind the steep roofs of the ancient houses, and the tiny stones of the pavement were clearly outlined in its motionless rays. I loved to wander then through the town; the moon seemed to be gazing intently at it from the clear sky; and the town felt that gaze, and stood sensitive and peaceful, all bathed in its light,—that tranquil and, at the same time, soul-agitating light. The cock on the tall Gothic belfry glittered like pale gold; the same gold was diffused in streams over the shining black expanse of the little river; slender candles (the German is economical!) burned modestly in the narrow windows under the slate-covered roofs; grape-vines mysteriously thrust their curled moustaches from behind stone walls; something flitted past in the shadow near the ancient well on the triangular market-place; suddenly the somnolent whistle of the night watchman rang out, a good-natured dog growled in an undertone, the air fairly caressed one's face, and the lindens emitted so sweet a perfume that one's chest involuntarily inhaled deeper and deeper breaths, and the word: " Gretchen "—not quite an exclamation nor yet quite a query—fairly forced itself to one's lips.

The little town of Z. lies a couple of versts distant from the Rhine. I frequently walked to take a look at the majestic stream and, as I mused,— not without some effort,—on the sly widow, I would sit for long hours on a stone bench, beneath a huge, isolated ash-tree. A small statue of the Madonna, with almost childish face and a red heart on her breast, transfixed by swords, gazed sadly forth from among its branches. On the opposite shore was the small town of L., a little larger than the one in which I had settled down. One evening I was sitting on my favourite bench, gazing now at the river, now at the sky, and again at the vineyards. In front of me, tow-headed urchins were clambering over the sides of a boat, drawn up on the shore, and overturned with its tarred bottom upward. Small vessels were running under slightly inflated sails; the greenish waves were gliding past, faintly swelling and gurgling. Suddenly the sounds of music were wafted to my ear: I began to listen. A waltz was being played in the town of L.; a bass-viol was droning spasmodically; a violin was trilling indistinctly; a flute was piping valorously.

" What 's that? "—I enquired of an old man in a velveteen waistcoat, blue stockings and buckled shoes, who approached me.

" That,"—he replied, having preliminarily shifted the mouthpiece of his pipe from one corner of his mouth to the other,—" is students who have come from B., for a commers."

" I believe I 'll take a look at that commers," —I thought.—" By the way, I have n't been in L., as yet." I hunted up a wherryman and set off for the other shore.

II

IT is not every one, possibly, who knows what a commers is. It is a peculiar sort of triumphal banquet, at which the students of one land or fraternity (*Landsmannschaft*) assemble. Almost all the participants on a commers wear the costume,—established long ago,—of German students: a round jacket, large boots, and tiny caps with bands of familiar colours. The students generally assemble for a dinner, presided over by the Senior, that is to say, the Elder,—and feast until morning, drink, sing the songs, " Landesvater," " Gaudeamus," smoke and curse the Philistines; sometimes they hire an orchestra.

Just this sort of a commers was in progress

in L., in front of a small inn under the sign-
board of the " Sun," in a garden which abutted
on the street. Over the inn itself, and the garden,
flags were fluttering; the students were sitting at
tables under the clipped lindens; a huge bull-dog
was lying under one of the tables; on one side,
in an arbour of ivy, the musicians were installed
and were playing industriously, constantly rein-
forcing their strength with beer. On the street,
in front of the low fence of the garden, a considerable number of people were gathered: the good-
natured citizens of L. had not wished to let slip
the opportunity of staring at visitors from a distance. I also mingled in the crowd of spectators.
It cheered me to look at the faces of the students;
their embraces, exclamations, the innocent coquetry of youth, the ardent glances, the cause-
less laughter—the best laughter in the world,—
all this joyous ebullition of young, fresh life, this
impulse in advance—no matter where, so long as
it was forward,—this good-natured liberty
touched and kindled me. Why not join them?
I asked myself. . . .

"Ásya, art thou satisfied?"—suddenly said a
man's voice behind me, in Russian.

" Let us wait a little longer,"—replied another,
a feminine voice, in the same language.

I wheeled hastily round. . . My gaze fell upon
a handsome young man in a foraging-cap and a
roomy round-jacket. He was arm in arm with a

young girl of short stature, with a straw hat
which covered the whole upper part of her face.

" You are Russians? "—broke involuntarily
from my tongue.

The young man smiled and said:

" Yes; we are Russians."

" I did not in the least expect . . . . in such a
remote nook . . . ." I was beginning . . . .

" And we did not expect,"—he interrupted me;
—" what of that? so much the better. Allow me
to introduce myself. My name is Gágin, and this
is my " . . . . he hesitated for a moment,—" is
my sister. And may I ask your name? "

I mentioned my name, and we got into conversation. I learned that Gágin, while travelling for
pleasure, like myself, had arrived in the town of
L. a week previously, and had stuck fast there.
Truth to tell, I was not fond of making acquaintance with Russians abroad. I recognised them
from afar by their walk, the cut of their garments,
and, chiefly, by the expression of their faces. Conceited and scornful, often imperious, it was suddenly replaced by an expression of caution and
timidity. . . . The man would suddenly become
all alert, his eyes would roll about uneasily. . . .
" Good heavens! have n't I blundered? Are n't
people laughing at me? " that hurried glance
seemed to be saying. . . . A moment passed,—
and again the majesty of the physiognomy wa
restored, now and then giving way, in turn, to dull

perplexity. Yes, I avoided Russians, but I took an instantaneous liking to Gágin. There are in the world such happy faces, that every one likes to look at them, as though they warmed or caressed you. Gágin had precisely such a face, charming, caressing, with large, soft eyes, and soft, curly hair. He spoke in such a way that, without seeing his face, merely from the sound of his voice, you felt that he was smiling.

The young girl whom he had called his sister, seemed to me very pretty at the first glance. There was something individual, peculiar in the form of her dark-skinned, round face, with its small, slender nose, almost childish little cheeks, and bright, black eyes. She was gracefully built, and apparently not yet fully developed. She did not bear the slightest resemblance to her brother.

" Will you drop in and make us a call? "—said Gágin to me.—" I think we have gazed our fill at the Germans. Our fellows, it is true, would have smashed the glasses and broken the chairs, but these men are more discreet. Shall we go home—what thinkest thou, Ásya? "

The young girl nodded assent.

" We are living out of town,"—went on Gágin, " in a vineyard, in an isolated house, high up. We have a splendid site, as you will see. The landlady has promised to prepare some sour milk for us. But it will soon be dark now, and it will be better for you to cross the Rhine by moonlight."

ÁSYA

We set out. Through the small gates of the town (an ancient wall of cobble-stones surrounded it on all sides, and even the embrasures had not yet entirely gone to ruin) we emerged into the open country, and, proceeding for a hundred paces along the stone rampart, halted before a narrow wicket-gate. Gágin opened it and led us up the hill by a steep path. Grape-vines grew on both sides, on terraces; the sun had just set, and a thin scarlet light lay on the vines, on the tall stakes, on the dry earth thickly besprinkled with large and small flag-stones, and on the white walls of a small house, with black, sagging joists and four bright little windows, which stood on the very apex of the hill up which we were climbing.

"Here 's our dwelling!"—exclaimed Gágin, as soon as we began to approach the house;— " and yonder is the landlady bringing the milk. *Guten Abend, Madame!* . . . . We 'll set to eating immediately; but first,"—he added,—" look around you . . . . What do you think of the view? "

The view really was magnificent. The Rhine lay before us, between green banks; in one place it was flaming with the crimson hues of the sunset. The little town, nestling close against the shore, displayed all its houses and streets; hills and fields spread out widely in all directions. Down below it had been good, but up aloft it was still better: I was particularly struck by the purity and depth of the sky, the radiant transparency of the air. Cool and light, it softly undulated and surged in waves, as though it were more at its ease on the heights.

" You have chosen capital quarters,"—I said.

" It was Ásya who found them,"—replied Gágin.—" Come now, Ásya,"—he went on:—" See to things. Order everything to be served here. We will sup in the open air. The music can be heard better here. Have you noticed,"—he added, turning to me,—" that some waltzes are good for nothing when heard close to?—the sounds are insipid, harsh—while at a distance, they are splendid! they fairly set all the romantic chords in you to vibrating."

Ásya (her name was really Anna, but Gágin called her Ásya, and therefore you must permit me to do the same)—Ásya withdrew into the house, and speedily returned in company with the landlady. They carried between them a large tray with a pot of milk, spoons, sugar, berries, and bread. We sat down and began our supper. Ásya removed her hat; her black hair, cut short and brushed like that of a boy, fell in large rings on her neck and ears. At first she was shy of me; but Gágin said to her:

" Ásya, have done with thy shrinking! He does n't bite!"

She smiled and, a little while afterward, entered into conversation with me of her own accord. I have never seen a more restless being. She did not sit still for a single moment; she kept rising, running into the house, and running back to us again. She would begin to hum in a low voice, frequently broke out laughing, and that in a very strange manner:—it seemed as though she were laughing not at what she heard, but at various thoughts which came into her head. Her large eyes had a bright, direct, bold gaze, but sometimes her eyelids contracted slightly, and then her glance suddenly became deep and tender.

We chatted for a couple of hours. Day had long since vanished, and evening,—first all fiery, then clear and scarlet, then pale and confused,— had quietly melted and merged into night; and still our conversation continued, peaceful and gentle as the air which surrounded us. Gágin ordered a bottle of Rhine wine to be brought; we quaffed it, without haste. The music, as before, floated up to us; its sounds seemed sweeter and more tender; the lights had kindled in the town and on the river. Suddenly Ásya lowered her head, so that her curls fell into her eyes, became silent, heaved a sigh, and then said to us that she was sleepy, and went away to the house. But I saw that, without lighting a candle, she stood for a long time at the unopened window. At last the moon rose and played on the Rhine; everything grew bright, darkened, changed, even the wine in our facetted glasses began to glitter with a mysterious gleam. The wind subsided, as though it had folded its wings, and died out; perfumed, nocturnal warmth was exhaled from the earth.

" 'T is time for me to go!"—I exclaimed:— "otherwise I shall probably find no one to ferry me over."

"It is time,"—repeated Gágin.

We descended along the path. The stones behind us suddenly began to clatter; it was Ásya pursuing us.

"Art thou not asleep?"—her brother asked her; but she, without answering him a word, ran past us. The last dying fire-pots lighted by the students in the garden of the inn illuminated the under side of the foliage on the trees, which imparted to it a festive and fantastic aspect. We found Ásya on the shore; she was chatting with a wherryman. I sprang into the boat and took leave of my new friends. Gágin promised to make me a visit on the following day; I shook hands with him, and offered my hand to Ásya; but she merely gazed at me and shook her head. The boat floated off and glided over the swift river. The wherryman, a brisk old fellow, dipped his oars with tense effort into the dark water.

" You have entered the shaft of moonlight, you have broken it up,"—Ásya shouted to me.

ÁSYA

I lowered my eyes; around the boat the waves rocked darkly.

" Good-bye! "—rang out her voice once more.

" Until to-morrow,"—said Gágin, after her.

The boat made its landing. I got out and glanced around me. No one was any longer visible on the opposite shore. The shaft of moonlight stretched in a golden bridge across the entire width of the river. As though by way of farewell, the sounds of an old Lanner waltz hurtled over. Gágin was right: I felt that all my heart-strings were vibrating in response to those challenging strains. I wended my way home through the darkening fields, slowly inhaling the fragrant air, and reached my little chamber all softened by the sweet languor of random and limitless expectancy. I felt happy. . . . But why was I happy? I desired nothing, I was thinking of nothing. . . . I was happy.

Almost laughing aloud with the exuberance of pleasant and vivacious emotions, I dived headlong into bed, and was on the point of closing my eyes, when suddenly it occurred to me that not once during the whole course of the evening had I called to mind my cruel beauty. . . . " But what does it mean? "—I asked myself:—" Can it be that I am in love? " But without furnishing myself with an answer to this question, I apparently fell asleep on the instant, like a baby in its cradle.

III

ON the following morning (I was already awake, but had not yet risen), a knock resounded under my window, and a voice, which I immediately recognised as the voice of Gágin, struck up:

> "Sleepest thou? With my guitar
> I will awaken thee. . . ."

I made haste to open the door for him.

" Good morning,"—said Gágin, as he entered: —" I have disturbed you rather early, but just see what a morning it is. See the freshness, the dew; and the larks are singing. . . ."

With his gleaming, curly hair, his bared neck and rosy cheeks, he himself was as fresh as the morning.

I dressed myself; we went out into the little garden, ordered coffee to be brought out to us, and began to chat. Gágin communicated to me his plans for the future: being in possession of a comfortable property, and dependent upon no one, he was desirous of devoting himself to painting, and only regretted that he had become sensible rather late in the day, and had wasted a great deal of time in vain. I also mentioned my intentions;

yes, and by the way, I confided to him the secret of my unhappy love. He listened to me with condescension but, so far as I was able to perceive, I did not arouse in him any strong sympathy for my passion. After heaving a couple of sighs in imitation of me, out of politeness, Gágin proposed that we should go to his rooms and inspect his sketches. I immediately consented.

We did not find Ásya. According to the landlady's words, she had gone to " the ruin." A couple of versts from the town of L. there existed the remains of a feudal castle. Gágin opened all his portfolios for me. There was a great deal of life and truth in his studies, something free and broad; but not a single one of them was finished, and the drawing seemed to me to be slovenly and inaccurate. I frankly expressed my opinion to him.

" Yes, yes,"—he chimed in with a sigh,—" you are right; all this is very bad and immature, but what help is there for it? I have not studied as I should have done, and that cursed Slavonic laxity is asserting itself. When one dreams of work, he soars like an eagle; it seems as though he could move the earth from its place; but in the execution he immediately grows slack and weary."

I tried to encourage him, but he waved his hand in despair, and collecting all his portfolios in his arms, he flung them on the divan.

"If my patience holds out, I shall make something of myself,"—he muttered through his teeth:—"if it does n't hold out, I shall remain a hobbledehoy [1] of the gentry class. We had better go and look up Ásya."

We went.

IV

THE road to the ruin wound down a narrow declivity to a wooded valley; at the bottom of it ran a brook purling noisily among stones, as though in haste to merge itself with the great river which gleamed calmly beyond the dark border of sharply-serrated mountain crests. Gágin called my attention to several happily illuminated spots; in his words was audible, if not the painter, yet certainly the artist. The ruin soon came in sight. On the very apex of a bare cliff rose a four-cornered tower, all black, still strong, but cleft, as it were, with a long rent. Mossy walls joined the tower; here and there ivy was clinging; small, distorted trees hung from the grey battlements and crumbling arches. A stony path led to the gate, which was still intact. We were already approaching it, when suddenly a woman's figure flitted in front of us, ran swiftly over the heap of fragments, and placed itself on a projection of the wall directly over the chasm.

[1] An allusion to Von Vízin's famous comedy, "The Hobbledehoy."—TRANSLATOR.

"That certainly is Ásya!"—exclaimed Gágin:—"What a mad-woman!"

We entered the gate and found ourselves in a small courtyard, half overgrown with wild apple-trees and nettles. On the projection sat Ásya, in effect. She turned her face toward us and began to laugh, but did not stir from the spot. Gágin shook his finger at her, while I loudly reproached her for her imprudence.

"Stop,"—said Gágin to me:—"don't irritate her; you do not know her: she is quite capable of climbing the tower. But here, you had better wonder at the intelligence of the local inhabitants."

I looked about me. In one corner, sheltering herself in a tiny wooden shed, an old woman was engaged in knitting a stocking, and darting sidelong glances at us through her spectacles. She sold beer, gingerbread, and seltzer water to tourists. We placed ourselves on a bench, and began to drink tolerably cool beer out of heavy, pewter mugs. Ásya continued to sit motionless, with her feet tucked up under her, and her head enveloped in a muslin scarf; her graceful figure was distinctly and beautifully outlined against the clear sky; but I surveyed her with an unpleasant sensation. On the preceding evening I had noticed something constrained, not quite natural, about her. . . . "She wants to astonish us,"—I thought; "to what end? What childish prank is this?"

As though divining my thoughts, she suddenly flung a swift, piercing glance at me, broke out laughing again, and with two skips leaped from the wall, and running up to the old woman, asked her for a glass of water.

" Dost thou think that I want to drink? "—she said, addressing her brother.—" No; there are flowers on the wall yonder, which positively must be watered."

Gágin made her no reply; and she, glass in hand, went scrambling over the ruins, now and then halting, bending down and, with amusing importance, sprinkling a few drops of water, which glittered brightly in the sunlight. Her movements were extremely charming, but, as before, I felt vexed with her, although I involuntarily admired her lightness and agility. At one dangerous spot she intentionally shrieked aloud, and then screamed with laughter. . . . I was more vexed than ever.

"Why, she climbs like a goat,"—muttered the old woman, tearing herself for a moment from her stocking.

At last Ásya entirely emptied her glass, and, swaying in frolicsome wise, she returned to us. A strange smile slightly contracted her brows, nostrils, and lips; half-audaciously, half-merrily did the dark eyes narrow their lids.

"You consider my behaviour improper,"—her

face seemed to say:—" I don't care: I know that you are admiring me."

" Clever, Ásya, clever,"—saïd Gágin, in an undertone.

She seemed suddenly seized with shame, dropped her long eyelashes, and seated herself modestly beside us, like a culprit. Then, for the first time, did I get a thoroughly good look at her face, the most variable face which I had ever beheld. A few moments later it had turned pale, and assumed a concentrated, almost melancholy expression; her very features seemed to me larger, more severe, more simple. She had completely quieted down. We made the circuit of the ruin (Ásya followed behind us) and admired the views. In the meantime the hour for dinner was drawing near. On settling with the old woman, Gágin asked for another tankard of beer, and turning to me, exclaimed with a sly grimace:

" To the health of the lady of your heart! "

" And has he,—have you such a lady? "—Ásya suddenly inquired.

" Why, who has not? "—retorted Gágin.

Ásya became pensive for a moment; again her face underwent a change; again there made its appearance upon it a challenging, almost audacious smile.

On the way home she laughed and frolicked worse than ever. She broke off a long branch, laid it on her shoulders like a gun, and bound her scarf around her head. I remember that we met a numerous family of fair-haired and affected English people; all of them, as though at the word of command, stared after Ásya in frigid amazement with their glassy eyes, while she, as though to spite them, began to sing loudly. On reaching home, she immediately went off to her room, and only made her appearance at dinner, arrayed in her best gown, with her hair carefully arranged, her bodice tightly laced, and in gloves. At table she bore herself in very decorous manner, almost affectedly, barely tasted the viands, and drank water out of a wine-glass. She evidently wished to play a new part before me—the part of a decorous and well-bred young lady. Gágin did not interfere with her; it was obvious that he had got used to backing her up in everything. He merely cast a good-humoured glance at me from time to time, and shrugged his shoulders slightly, as much as to say:—" She is a child, be lenient." The moment dinner was over, Ásya rose, made a curtsey and, donning her hat, asked Gágin whether she might go to Frau Luise.

" Hast thou long been in the habit of asking permission? "—he replied with his invariable, on this occasion somewhat troubled, smile:—" Dost thou find it tiresome with us? "

" No; but I promised Frau Luise yesterday to go to her; and, besides, I thought you would be better off alone together; Mr. N." (she pointed at me) " will tell thee something more."

She departed.

" Frau Luise,"—began Gágin, endeavouring to avoid my eye,—" is the widow of a former burgomaster here, a kind-hearted but frivolous woman. She has taken a great fancy to Ásya. Ásya has a passion for getting acquainted with people from a lower class. I have observed that the cause of that is always vanity. I have spoiled her pretty thoroughly, as you see,"—he added, after a brief pause:—" and what would you have me do? I don't know how to be stern with any one, least of all with her. I am *bound* to be indulgent to her."

I held my peace. Gágin changed the subject. The better I knew him the more strongly was I drawn to him. I soon understood him. He was a regular Russian soul, upright, honourable, simple, but, unhappily, somewhat languid, without tenacity or inward ardour. Youth did not bubble up in him like a spring; it beamed with a tranquil light. He was very charming and clever, but I could not imagine to myself what would become of him as soon as he became a man. Be an artist? . . . . One cannot be an artist without bitter, incessant toil . . . . " and toil," I thought, as I looked at his soft features, and listened to his indolent speech,—" no! Thou wilt never toil, thou wilt not be capable of concentrating thyself." But not to love him was an impossibility; one's heart was fairly drawn to him. We spent four hours together, now seated on the divan, again pacing slowly to and fro in front of the house; and in the course of those four hours we definitively struck up a friendship.

The sun set, and it was time for me to go home. Ásya had not yet returned.

" What a wilful creature she is! "—said Gágin. —" I will accompany you, shall I? We 'll drop in at Frau Luise's on the way, and I will inquire if she is there. It is not much out of our road."

We descended to the town and, turning into a narrow, crooked alley, halted in front of a house two windows in breadth and four stories high. The second story projected over the street more than the first, the third and fourth projected more than the second; the whole house, with its ancient carving, its two thick pillars below, its pointed roof of tiles, and elongated spout, in the shape of a beak on the garret, seemed like a huge, crouching bird.

" Ásya! " — shouted Gágin: — " Art thou here? "

A tiny illuminated window in the third story opened, and we beheld Ásya's little, dark head. The toothless and purblind face of an old German woman peeped forth from behind her.

" I 'm here,"—said Ásya, coquettishly propping her elbows on the window-sill. " I 'm com-

fortable here. There, take that,"—she added,
tossing a spray of geranium to Gágin.—" Imagine that I am the lady of thy heart."

Frau Luise laughed.

" N. is going away,"—returned Gágin:—" he
wants to bid thee farewell."

" Really? "—said Ásya:—" In that case, give
him my spray, and I 'll return at once."

She clapped to the window and, apparently,
kissed Frau Luise. Gágin silently held out the
spray to me. I silently put it in my pocket,
walked to the ferry and crossed to the other side.

I remember that I was walking home thinking of nothing, but with a strange weight on my
heart, when suddenly a powerful, familiar scent,
but one which is rare in Germany, arrested my
attention. I came to a standstill, and beheld by
the side of the road a small bed of hemp. Its
fragrance of the steppes had instantaneously reminded me of my native land and aroused in my
soul a passionate longing for it. I wanted to
breathe the Russian air, to walk on Russian soil.
" What am I doing here, why am I dawdling in
foreign lands, among strangers? " I exclaimed;
the deadly burden, which I had felt at my heart,
was suddenly merged, in bitter, burning emotion.
I reached home in an entirely different mood
from that of the day before. I felt almost incensed, and for a long time could not recover
my composure. An irritation which I myself

found incomprehensible was rending me asunder.
At last I sat down, and calling to mind my crafty
widow (each one of my days wound up with
an official calling to mind of that lady), I got
out one of her notes. But I did not even open
it; my thoughts immediately took another direction. I began to think . . . . to think of Ásya.
It occurred to me that Gágin, in the course of our
conversation, had hinted to me at some difficulties,
some impediments to his return to Russia. . . .
" Is she really his sister? " I ejaculated aloud.

I undressed, got into bed, and tried to get to
sleep; but an hour later I was again sitting on my
bed, and again thinking about that " capricious
little girl with the strained laugh." . . . . " She
is formed like the little Galatea by Raphael, in
the Farnese gallery,"—I whispered:—" yes, and
she is not his sister. . . ."

And the widow's note lay quite quietly on the
floor, gleaming whitely in the rays of the moon.

V

On the following morning I again went to L.
I assured myself that I wanted to meet Gágin;
but I was secretly longing to see what Ásya would
do,—whether she would " play tricks," as on the
day before. I found them both in the parlour,
and, strange to say—perhaps because I had been

thinking a great deal about Russia during the
night and morning—Ásya seemed to me to be a
thorough Russian girl, and a low-class girl, almost a chambermaid, at that. She wore a poor
little old gown, had brushed her hair behind her
ears, and sat immovably at the window, embroidering at a frame, modestly, quietly, as
though she had never done anything else in all
her life. She said hardly anything, gazed calmly
at her work, and her features had assumed such
an insignificant, every-day expression, that I was
involuntarily reminded of our home-bred Kátyas
and Máshas. To complete the likeness, she began to sing in an undertone: " Mother dear, beloved one." I glanced at her sallow, extinguished
little face, recalled my musings of the night before, and felt sorry for something. The weather
was magnificent. Gágin announced to us that
he was going that day to make a sketch from
nature; I asked him if he would allow me to accompany him, whether I should be in his way.

" On the contrary,"—he replied:—" you may
be able to give me some good advice."

He donned a round hat, à la Van Dyck, and a
blouse, took a portfolio under his arm, and set
out; I ambled after him. Ásya remained at home.
Gágin, as he was departing, asked her to see that
the soup was not too thin: Ásya promised to
visit the kitchen. Gágin made his way to the
valley with which I was already acquainted,

seated himself on a stone, and began to sketch
an aged, hollow oak, with widely-spreading roots.
I threw myself down on the grass, and pulled
out a book; but I did not read two pages, and
he merely daubed his paper; we spent the time
chiefly in argument; and, so far as I can judge,
we argued with considerable cleverness and penetration, as to the precise way in which one should
work, what should be avoided, what rules should
be observed, and precisely what is the significance
of art in our age. Gágin decided at last that he
" was not in the mood to-day," lay down beside
me, and then our youthful speeches began to flow
freely,—now fervid, now thoughtful, now rapturous, but almost always the obscure speeches
wherein the Russian man is so fond of pouring
himself out. After having talked to satiety, and
filled with a sense of contentment, we returned
home. I found Ásya precisely the same as I had
left her; try as I would to watch her, not a shade
of coquetry, not a sign of a deliberately-assumed
rôle did I detect in her; on this occasion, it was
impossible to accuse her of lack of naturalness.

" A-ha! "—said Gágin:—" She has imposed
fasting and penance upon herself! "

Toward evening she yawned several times un-
affectedly, and went off early to her own room.
I soon took leave of Gágin, and on my way home,
I no longer meditated about anything: that day
had passed in sober sensations. I remember, how-

ever, that as I got into bed I involuntarily said
aloud:

"What a chameleon that young girl is!"—
And after reflecting a while I added:—"And
all the same, she is not his sister."

VI

Two whole weeks passed. I visited the Gágins
every day. Ásya seemed to shun me but no longer
indulged in a single one of the pranks which had
so astounded me during the first days of our
acquaintance. She appeared to be secretly em-
bittered or discomfited; she laughed less. I
watched her with curiosity.

She spoke French and German fairly well; but
in everything it was apparent that she had been
in feminine hands since her infancy, and had received a strange, an unusual bringing-up, which
had nothing in common with the breeding of Gágin. Despite his hat à la Van Dyck, and his
blouse, he exhaled the soft, half-enervated atmosphere of the Great Russian nobleman, but she did
not resemble a young lady of noble birth; in all
her movements there was something uneasy; she
was a wild tree which had only recently been
grafted; she was wine still in the process of fer-
mentation. By nature shy and timid, she was
vexed at her own bashfulness, and with irritation

she made desperate efforts to be bold and at her ease, in which she was not always successful. Several times I began to talk to her about her life in Russia, about her past; she answered my queries reluctantly. I learned, however, that for a long time before her departure abroad, she had lived in the country. I once caught her alone, over a book. With her head resting on both hands and her fingers deeply buried in her hair, she was devouring the lines with her eyes.

" Bravo! "—I said, stepping up to her: —" How diligent you are! "

She raised her head with dignity and gazed sternly at me.

" You think that I know how to do nothing but laugh,"—she said, and started to leave the room. . .

I glanced at the title of the book; it was some French romance or other.

" But I cannot commend your choice,"—I remarked.

" 'T is reading all the same! "—she exclaimed; and flinging the book on the table, she added:— " I had better go and play the fool,"—and ran off into the garden.

That same day, in the evening, I was reading to Gágin " Herman and Dorothea." At first Asya only darted past us, then suddenly she came to a halt, lent an ear, quietly sat down beside me, and listened to the reading to the end. On

the following day I again failed to recognise
her, until I guessed what had suddenly got into
her head: to be domestic and sedate, like Dorothea. In a word, she was to me a semi-enigmat-
ical being. Vain to the last degree, she attracted
me even when I was angry with her. Of one
thing only I became more and more convinced,
namely, that she was not Gágin's sister. He did
not treat her in brotherly fashion; he was too
affectionate, too lenient, and at the same time,
rather constrained.

A strange circumstance, apparently, confirmed
my suspicions.

One evening, as I was approaching the vineyard, where the Gágins lived, I found the gate
locked. Without thinking long about the matter, I made my way to a breach in the fence,
which I had previously noted, and leaped over it.
Not far from that spot, on one side of the path,
stood a small acacia arbour. I came on a level
with it, and was on the point of passing it . . . .
when suddenly Asya's voice struck my ear, uttering the following words with heat and through
tears:

" No; I won't love anybody except thee, no, no,
I will love only thee—and forever."

" Stop, Asya, calm thyself,"—said Gágin:—
" thou knowest that I believe thee."

Their voices resounded in the arbour. I caught
a sight of both of them through the interlacing

branches which were not thick. They did not notice me.

" Thee, thee alone,"—she repeated, throwing herself on his neck, and beginning to kiss him with convulsive sobs, and to press herself to his breast.

" Enough, enough,"—he repeated, passing his hand lightly over her hair.

For several moments I stood motionless. . . . Suddenly I started.—" Shall I go to them? . . . On no account! "—flashed through my mind. With swift strides I returned to the fence, sprang over it into the road, and set off homeward almost on a run. I smiled, rubbed my hands, marvelled at the accident which had suddenly confirmed my surmises (not for one moment did I doubt their correctness), and, yet I felt very bitter at heart. " How well they understand how to dissimulate! " I thought. " But with what object? What possesses them to mystify me? I had not expected that from him. . . . And what a sentimental explanation! "

VII

I slept badly, and rose early the next morning, strapped my travelling wallet to my back, and, having informed my landlady that she need not expect me back for the night, I set off on foot for the mountains, up the little river, on which Z.

lies. These mountains, a spur of the chain called
The Dog's Back (Hundsrück), are very curious
from a geological point of view; they are especially noteworthy for the regularity and purity
of the basaltic layers; but I was in no mood for
geological observations. I could not account to
myself for what was in progress within me; one
feeling was clear to me: a disinclination to meet
the Gágins. I assured myself that the sole cause
for my sudden dislike to them was anger at their
duplicity. Who had forced them to give themselves out for relatives? However, I tried not
to think of them; I wandered, without haste, over
the mountains and valleys, I tarried in village
eating-houses, peaceably chatting with landlords
and patrons, or lay on a flat, sun-heated stone,
and watched the clouds sail past; luckily the weather was wonderfully fine. In such occupations I
spent three days, and not without satisfaction,—
although my heart was heavy at times. The trend
of my thoughts was exactly in harmony with the
calm nature of that locality.

I surrendered myself to the quiet plan of accident, to chance impressions: succeeding one another without haste, they flowed through my soul,
leaving in it at last one general impression, in
which was merged everything I had seen, felt,
and heard during those three days—everything:
the delicate odour of resin in the forests, the cry
and pecking of the wood-peckers; the incessant

babbling of bright little brooks with spotted trout
on their sandy bottoms; the not too bold outlines
of the hills; the frowning cliffs; clean little ham-
lets with time-honoured, ancient churches and
trees; storks in the meadow; cosey mills with
briskly-revolving wheels; the cheerful faces of the
natives, their blue shirts and grey stockings;
creaking, sluggish wains drawn by fat horses,
and sometimes by cows; young, long-haired way-
farers on the clean roads, planted with apple and
pear-trees. . . .

Even now it is a pleasure to me to recall my
impressions of that time. A greeting to thee,
modest nook of the German land, with thy ingenuous satisfaction; with traces everywhere
about of industrious hands, of patient though
unhurried toil. . . . A greeting and peace to
thee!

I reached home at the very end of the third
day. I have forgotten to say that, out of vexation toward the Gágins, I had made an effort to
resurrect within me the image of the hard-hearted
widow;—but my efforts remained fruitless. I
remember that when I began to meditate about
her, I beheld before me a little peasant girl, five
years of age, with a round little face, and in-
nocently protruding eyes. She looked at me in
such a childishly-simple way. . . . I felt ashamed
of her pure gaze, I did not want to lie in her
presence, and instantly, finally, and forever I

made my farewell bow to the former object of my affections.

At home I found a note from Gágin. He was surprised at the suddenness of my decision, upbraided me for not having taken him with me, and begged me to come to them as soon as I returned. I read this note with displeasure, but on the following day I went to L.

VIII

GÁGIN welcomed me in friendly fashion, overwhelmed me with affectionate reproaches; but Ásya, as though of deliberate purpose, no sooner caught sight of me, than she burst out laughing loudly without any cause and, according to her wont, immediately ran away. Gágin was disconcerted, muttered after her that she was crazy, and entreated me to pardon her. I confess that I had become greatly incensed at Ásya; even without that I was not feeling like myself, and here again were that unnatural laughter, those strange grimaces. But I pretended that I had not noticed anything, and communicated to Gágin the details of my little trip. He narrated to me what he had been doing in my absence. But our speeches did not get on well; Ásya entered the room, and then ran out again; at last I announced that I had some work which must be done in haste, and that it was time for me to return home. At first Gágin tried to detain me; then, after looking intently at me, he offered to accompany me. In the anteroom Ásya suddenly came up to me and offered me her hand; I clasped her fingers lightly and barely bowed to her. Gágin and I got ourselves ferried across the Rhine and, as we passed my favourite ash-tree with the little statue of the Madonna, we sat down on the bench to admire the view. Thereupon, a remarkable conversation ensued between us.

At first we exchanged a few words, then fell silent, as we gazed at the gleaming river.

" Tell me,"—suddenly began Gágin, with his habitual smile:—" what is your opinion of Ásya? She must seem rather queer to you, does n't she? "

" Yes,"—I replied, not without some surprise. I had not expected that he would speak of her.

" One must know her well in order to judge her. She has a very kind heart, but a wretched head. It is difficult to get along with her. However, it would be impossible for you to blame her, if you knew her history. . . ."

" Her history,"—I interrupted. . . . " Is n't she your . . . ."

Gágin darted a glance at me.

" Can it be that you think she is not my sister? . . . . Yes,"—he continued, without paying any heed to my confusion:—" she really is my sister;

she is my father's daughter. Hearken to me. I feel confidence in you, and I will tell you all.

" My father was a very kind-hearted, clever, cultured—and unhappy man. Fate treated him no worse than she treats many others; but he was unable to withstand her first blow. He married early, for love; his wife, my mother, died very soon; she left me, a baby of six months. My father carried me off to the country, and for twelve whole years never went anywhere. He busied himself with my education, and would never have parted with me had not his brother, my blood-uncle, come to the country. This uncle resided permanently in Petersburg and occupied a pretty high post. He persuaded my father to surrender me into his hands, as my father would not consent to leave the country on any terms whatsoever. My uncle represented to him that it was injurious for a boy of my age to live in absolute isolation; that with such an eternally melancholy and taciturn preceptor as my father, I would infallibly fall behind the lads of my own age, and my very disposition might be ruined into the bargain. For a long time my father combated his brother's admonitions, but yielded at last. I wept at parting with my father; I loved him, although I had never seen a smile on his face . . . . but when I got to Petersburg I speedily forgot our gloomy and cheerless nest. I entered the yunkers' school, and from the school graduated into a regiment of the Guards. Every year I made a journey to the country for several weeks, and with every passing year I found my father more and more morose, engrossed in himself, and pensive to the point of timidity. He went to church every day, and had almost unlearned the art of speaking.

" During one of my visits (I was then over twenty years of age), I beheld for the first time in our house a thin, black-eyed little girl, ten years of age—Ásya. My father said that she was an orphan whom he had taken to rear—that was precisely the way he expressed himself. I paid no particular attention to her; she was shy, alert, and taciturn as a little wild beast, and as soon as I entered my father's favourite room, the huge, gloomy chamber where my mother had died, and where candles were lighted even in the daytime, she immediately hid herself behind his Voltaire chair, or behind a bookcase. It so happened, that during the three or four years which followed, the duties of my service prevented my going to the country. I received one brief letter from my father each month; he rarely alluded to Ásya, and then only in passing. He was already over fifty, but he still seemed a young man.

" Picture to yourself my consternation: suddenly, without a suspicion on my part, I received from the agent a letter in which he informed me of my father's mortal illness, and entreated me to come as speedily as possible if I wished to bid him farewell. I rushed off at headlong speed, and found my father alive, but already at his last gasp. He was extremely delighted to see me, embraced me with his emaciated arms, gazed long into my eyes with a look which was not precisely scrutinising nor yet precisely one of entreaty; and after having exacted from me a promise that I would fulfil his last request, he ordered his old valet to bring Ásya. The old man led her in; she could hardly stand on her feet, and was trembling all over.

" ' Here,'—said my father to me with an effort: —' I bequeath to thee my daughter—thy sister. Thou wilt learn all from Yákoff,'—he added, pointing at the valet.

" Ásya burst out sobbing and fell face downward on the bed. . . . Half an hour later, my father expired.

" This is what I learned: Ásya was the daughter of my father and of my mother's former maid, Tatyána. I vividly remember that Tatyána; I remember her tall, graceful figure, her comely, regular, intelligent face, with large, dark eyes. She bore the reputation of being a haughty and unapproachable girl. So far as I was able to make out from Yákoff's respectful reticences, my father had entered into relations with her several years after my mother's death. Tatyána was no longer living in the manor-house at that

277

time, but in the cottage of a married sister of hers, the herd-woman. My father became strongly attached to her, and after my departure from the country he had even wished to marry her, but she herself had not consented to become his wife, in spite of his entreaties.

"'The late Tatyána Vasílievna,'—concluded Yákoff, as he stood by the door with his hands behind him,—'was sagacious in everything, and did not wish to disgrace your papa.—"What sort of a wife am I for him?" says she. "What sort of a gentlewoman am I?"—That was the way she deigned to speak,—and she said it in my presence, sir.'—Tatyána was not even willing to remove to our house, and continued to live with her sister, along with Ásya. In my childhood I had seen Tatyána only on festival days, in church; with her head bound up in a dark kerchief, and a yellow shawl on her shoulders, she stood among the crowd near a window,—her severe profile was distinctly defined against the light glass,—and prayed with submission and dignity, making lowly reverences in old-fashioned style. When my uncle carried me off, Ásya was only two years old, and in her ninth year she lost her mother.

"As soon as Tatyána died, my father took Ásya to himself in the house. He had previously expressed a desire to have her with him, but Tatyána had refused this also. Imagine to yourself what

must have been Ásya's sensations when she was
taken to the master. To this day she is unable
to forget that moment, when they garbed her for
the first time in a silken frock and kissed her
hand. Her mother, as long as she lived, had
reared her very strictly; with her father she enjoyed complete freedom. He was her teacher;
she saw no one excepting him. He did not spoil
her—that is to say, he did not fondle her; but
he loved her passionately, and never denied her
anything; in his soul he regarded himself as culpable toward her. Ásya speedily grasped the
fact that she was the principal personage in the
house; she knew that the master was her father;
but she did not so speedily comprehend her false
position; vanity was strongly developed in her,
and distrust also; bad habits became rooted, sim-
plicity vanished. She wished (she herself once
confessed this to me) to make *the whole world*
forget her extraction; she was ashamed of her
mother and ashamed of her shame, and proud of
it. You see that she knew and does know a great
deal which one ought not to know at her age.
. . . . But is she to blame? Young forces had
begun to ferment in her, her blood was seething,
but there was not a single hand near by to guide
her. She was absolutely independent in everything! And is that easy to endure? She wanted
to be not inferior to other young ladies of noble
birth; she flung herself upon books. Could any-

thing judicious come of that? The life irregularly begun took an irregular turn, but her heart was not spoiled, her mind remained intact.

" And thus I, a young fellow of twenty, found myself with a girl of thirteen on my hands! During the first few days after my father's death, she was seized with a fever at the very sound of my voice, my caresses inspired her with aversion, and it was only gradually, little by little, that she grew accustomed to me. Truth to tell, later on, when she became convinced that I really did recognise her as my sister, and loved her as a sister, she became passionately attached to me; none of her emotions go by halves.

" I took her to Petersburg. Painful as it was for me to part from her, I could not possibly live with her; I placed her in one of the best boarding-schools. Ásya understood the necessity for our parting, but began by falling ill and nearly dying. Then she summoned her patience, and lived through four years in the boarding-school; but, contrary to my expectations, she remained almost exactly the same as she had been before. The principal of the boarding-school made frequent complaints to me about her: 'And it is impossible to punish her,'—she said to me:—'and she does not yield to kindness.'

"Ásya was extremely quick of understanding, and studied well, better than all the rest; but she absolutely refused to conform to the general

standard, became stubborn, and looked wild. . . .
I could not blame her over-much; in her position
she was bound either to cringe or stand aloof.
Out of all her companions she made friends with
one only—a homely, intimidated, poor girl. The
other young gentlewomen with whom she was
being reared, mostly from good families, did not
like her, and wounded and stung her to the best
of their ability. Ásya did not yield to them by
so much as a hair's breadth. One day, during a
lesson in religion,[1] the teacher began to speak of
vices. 'Flattery and cowardice are the worst
vices,' said Ásya aloud. In a word, she continued
to pursue her own road; only her manners im-
proved;—although, apparently, she is not a success in that respect either.

" At last she completed her seventeenth year;
it was impossible to leave her in the boarding-
school any longer. I found myself in a rather
difficult position. Suddenly a happy thought occurred to me: to resign from the service and travel
abroad for a year or two, taking Ásya with me.
No sooner thought than done; and here we are,
she and I, on the banks of the Rhine, where I am
trying to occupy myself with painting, while she
. . . . plays pranks and behaves queerly as of
old. But now, I hope, you will not judge her too
severely; and she—although she pretends that she

---

[1] "The law of God " is the Russian phrase. It occupies
a prominent place in all schools.—TRANSLATOR.

does not care a jot—values every one's opinion, yours in particular."

And again Gágin smiled with his tranquil smile. I clasped his hand warmly.

"All this is so,"—Gágin began again:—"but I shall get into difficulties with her. She is regular powder. So far, no one has struck her fancy; but woe is me if she should fall in love with any one! I never know how to treat her. The other day this is what she took into her head: she suddenly began to assert that I had grown colder toward her than of old, that she loved me alone. . . . . And thereupon, she fell to weeping so violently . . . ."

"So that is what . . . ." I began, and bit my tongue.

"But tell me, pray,"—I asked Gágin, "we are speaking frankly to each other,—is it possible that, up to this time, she has not taken a fancy to any one? She must have seen young men in Petersburg."

"She did not like them at all. No, Ásya must needs have a hero, a remarkable man—or a picturesque shepherd in a mountain gorge. But I have chattered too much with you, I have detained you,"—he added, rising.

"See here,"—I began:—"let 's go to your house; I don't want to go home."

"And how about your work?"

I made no reply; Gágin laughed good-hu-

mouredly, and we returned to L. At the sight
of the familiar vineyard and the little white house
on the top of the hill, I experienced a certain
sweetness,—precisely that, sweetness—in my
heart: it was as though honey were silently flowing through it. I felt at ease since Gágin's nar-
rative.

IX

ÁSYA met us on the very threshold of the house;
I expected another laugh; but she came out to us
all pale, silent, and with downcast eyes.

" Here he is again,"—said Gágin:—" and observe, he wanted to come back himself."

Ásya darted an inquiring glance at me. I,
in my turn, offered her my hand, and this time
warmly grasped her cold little fingers. I felt
very sorry for her; I now understood much in
her which had previously thrown me off the track;
—her inward uneasiness, her ignorance of how to
behave herself, her desire to show off,—all had
become clear to me. I had taken a look into that
soul; a secret burden oppressed her constantly,
her inexperienced vanity was tremulously perplexed and throbbing, but everything in her being
aspired toward truth. I understood why that
strange young girl attracted me; she attracted
me not alone by the half-savage charm diffused
over all her slender body: her soul pleased me.

ÁSYA

Gágin began to rummage among his drawings; I proposed to Ásya that she should take a stroll with me in the vineyard. She immediately assented, with blithe and almost submissive alacrity. We descended half-way down the hill, and seated ourselves on a broad slab of stone.

" And were n't you bored without us? "—began Ásya.

" And were you bored without me? "—I inquired.

Ásya darted a sidelong glance at me.

" Yes,"—she replied.—" Is it nice in the mountains? "—she immediately continued:—" are they high? Higher than the clouds? Tell me what you saw. You told my brother, but I did not hear anything."

" Why did you go away? "—I remarked.

" I went away . . . . because . . . . I won't go away now,"—she added with confiding affection in her voice:—" you were angry to-day."

" I? "

" Yes, you."

" Why, pray? . . . ."

" I don't know; but you were angry, and went away angry. I was greatly vexed that you went away in that manner, and I am so glad that you have come back."

" And I am glad that I have come back,"—said I.

ÁSYA

Ásya shrugged her shoulders, as children often do when they feel at ease.

" Oh, I know how to guess! "—she went on: —" I used to be able to know, from papa's cough alone in the next room, whether he was pleased with me or not."

Up to that day Ásya had never spoken to me of her father. I was struck by this. " Did you love your papa? "—I said, and suddenly, to my intense vexation, I felt that I was blushing.

She made no reply, and blushed also. Both of us remained silent for a while. Far away on the Rhine a steamer was sailing and emitting smoke. We began to gaze at it.

" But why don't you tell me about your journey? "—whispered Ásya.

" Why did you burst out laughing to-day, as soon as you caught sight of me? "—I asked.

" I don't know myself. Sometimes I feel like crying, yet I laugh. You must not condemn me . . . . for what I do. Akh, by the way, what is that legend about the Lorelei? That is her rock which we can see, is n't it? They say that she drowned every one at first, but when she fell in love she threw herself into the water. I like that legend. Frau Luise tells me all sorts of legends. Frau Luise has a black cat with yellow eyes. . . ."

Ásya raised her head and shook back her curls.

" Akh, I feel so comfortable,"—she said.

At that moment, abrupt, monotonous sounds

were wafted to our ears. Hundreds of voices were repeating a prayerful chant simultaneously, and with measured pauses; a throng of pilgrims was winding along the road below, with crosses and banners. . . .

" I 'd like to join them,"—said Ásya, as she listened to the bursts of voices which were grad· ually dying away.

" Are you so devout? "

" I 'd like to go somewhere far away, to pray, on a difficult exploit,"—she went on.—" Otherwise, the days go by, life will pass, and what have we done? "

" You are ambitious,"—I remarked:—"you do not wish to live in vain, you want to leave a trail of glory behind you. . . ."

" And is that impossible? "

" Impossible," I came near repeating. . . . But I glanced at her bright eyes and merely said: " Try."

" Tell me,"—began Ásya, after a brief silence, in the course of which certain shadows had flitted across her face, that had already paled again: —" were you very fond of that lady? . . . . You remember, my brother drank to her health on the ruin on the second day of our acquaintance."

I burst out laughing.

" Your brother was jesting. I have not been fond of any lady; at all events, I am not fond of any one now."

"And what pleases you in women?"—inquired Ásya, throwing back her head with innocent curiosity.

"What a strange question!"—I exclaimed.

Ásya was slightly disconcerted.

"I ought not to have put such a question to you, ought I? Pardon me; I have been accustomed to blurt out everything which comes into my head. That is why I am afraid to talk."

"Talk, for Heaven's sake; be not afraid!"—I interposed:—"I am so glad that you have, at last, ceased to be shy."

Ásya dropped her eyes and began to laugh softly and lightly; I did not know she could laugh in that way.

"Come, tell me,"—she went on, smoothing the folds of her gown, and laying them over her feet, as though she did not intend to move for a long time:—"tell me something, or recite something, as when you recited to us from ' Onyégin,' you remember. . . . ."

She suddenly became pensive. . . .

"Where is now the cross and the shadow of the bough
  Over my poor mother!"

she said in a low tone.

"That is not the way Púshkin has it,"—I remarked.

"I should like to be Tatyána,"[1] she went on,

---

[1] Tatyána is the famous heroine of Púshkin's poem,
"Evgény Onyégin."—Translator.

in the same thoughtful manner.—" Recite,"—she interjected with vivacity.

But I was in no mood for recitation. I gazed at her, all bathed in the sunlight, all composed and gentle. Everything was beaming joyously around us—the sky, the earth, and the waters; the very air seemed to be permeated with brilliancy.

" See, how beautiful it is,"—I said, involuntarily lowering my voice.

" Yes, it is beautiful,"—she replied with equal softness, and without looking at me.—" If you and I were only birds—how we would soar, would fly away. . . . We would fairly drown in that azure. . . . But we are not birds."

" Yet wings might sprout on us,"—I returned.

" How so? "

" If you live long enough, you will find out. There are feelings which raise us above the earth. Don't worry, you will have wings."

" And have you had any? "

" What shall I say to you? . . . I don't think I have flown up to the present moment."

Again Ásya became pensive. I bent slightly toward her.

" Do you know how to waltz? "—she suddenly inquired.

" I do,"—I replied, somewhat surprised.

" Then let us go, let us go. . . . I will ask my brother to play a waltz for us. . . . We will imagine that we are flying, that wings have sprouted on us."

She ran toward the house. I ran after her, and a few moments later we were circling round the little room to the sweet sounds of Lanner. Ásya waltzed beautifully, with enthusiasm. Something soft and feminine suddenly pierced through her virginally-severe face. For a long time afterward my arm felt the contact of her dainty waist; for a long time I seemed to hear her accelerated breathing near at hand; for a long time visions of dark eyes almost closed, in a pale but animated face, with curls sportively fluttering around it, flitted before me.

X

THAT whole day passed off in the best possible manner. We made merry, like children. Ásya was very charming and simple. Gágin rejoiced as he looked at her. It was late when I went away. On reaching the middle of the Rhine, I requested the boatman to let the skiff float down the current. The old man elevated his oars, and the royal river bore us onward. As I gazed about me, listening and recalling, I suddenly felt a secret restlessness at my heart . . . . and raised my eyes heavenward. But there was no rest in the sky either; besprinkled with stars, it was all

astir, moving, quivering: I bent over the river,
. . . . but there also, in those cold depths, the
stars were undulating and throbbing; it seemed
to me that there was tremulous animation everywhere, and the tremulousness within me increased. I leaned my elbows on the edge of the
boat. . . . The whisper of the wind in my ears,
the quiet purling of the water at the stern, and the
cool breath of the waves did not refresh me; a
nightingale began to warble on the shore and
infected me with the sweet poison of its notes.
Tears welled up in my eyes, but they were not the
tears of objectless rapture. What I felt was not
that troubled sensation which I had so recently
experienced of all-embracing desire, when the
soul widens out, reverberates; when it seems to it
that it understands everything and loves everything. No! the thirst for happiness had been
kindled in me. I did not, as yet, dare to call it
by name,—but happiness, happiness to satiety,—
that was what I wanted, that was what I was
pining for. . . . And still the boat was borne
onward, and the old boatman sat, and dozed, as
he bent over his oars.

XI

WHEN I set out for the Gágins' on the following
day, I did not ask myself whether I was in love
with Ásya, but I meditated a great deal about

her, her fate interested me, I rejoiced at our unexpected intimacy. I felt that only since the day
before had I known her; up to that time she had
turned away from me. And now, when she had
blossomed out at last before me, with what an en-
chanting light was her image illuminated, how
new it was to me, what secret witcheries bashfully
pierced through it! . . .

I walked briskly along the familiar path, incessantly glancing at the little house which gleamed
white in the distance; I not only did not think of
the future, I did not think even of the morrow;
I felt greatly at my ease.

Ásya blushed when I entered the room; I noticed that she had again arrayed herself gaily, but
the expression of her face did not consort with her
attire; it was sad. And I had arrived in such a
merry mood! It even seemed to me that, according to her wont, she was preparing to flee, but
exerted an effort over herself,—and remained.
Gágin was in that peculiar condition of artistic
ardour and fury which, in the shape of an attack,
suddenly takes possession of dilettantes when they
imagine that they have been successful, as they
express it, in " seizing nature by the tail." He
was standing, all dishevelled and besmeared with
paints, in front of a canvas stretched on a frame,
and, sweeping the brush across it with a flourish,
he nodded his head almost fiercely at me, retreated, screwed up his eyes, and again flung him-

self at his picture. I did not interfere with him, and sat down beside Ásya. Her dark eyes slowly turned to me.

" You are not the same to-day as you were yesterday,"—I remarked, after futile efforts to evoke a smile on her lips.

" No, I am not the same,"—she returned in a dull, deliberate voice:—" but that is nothing. I did not sleep well; I thought all night long."

" What about? "

" Akh, I thought of many things. It is a habit of mine since childhood; even at the time when I used to live with mamma. . . ."

She uttered that word with difficulty, and then repeated:

" When I lived with mamma. . . . I used to think, why it was that no one can find out what will become of us; and sometimes one has a presentiment of a catastrophe,—but it is impossible to be happy; and why it is that one must never tell the whole truth? . . . . Then I thought that I knew nothing, that I must study. I must be educated all over again. I am very badly brought up. I don't know how to play on the piano, I don't know how to draw, I even sew badly. I have no talents; people must find it very dull in my company."

" You are unjust to yourself,"—I replied:— " you have read a great deal, you are cultured, and with your intelligence . . . ."

ÁSYA

" Am I intelligent? "—she asked with such an ingenuous thirst for information, that I involuntarily burst out laughing; but she did not even smile.—" Brother, am I intelligent? "—she asked Gágin.

He made her no reply, and went on with his labours, incessantly changing his brushes, and elevating his arm very high.

" I sometimes don't know myself what there is in my head,"—pursued Ásya, with the same innocent mien.—" I am afraid of myself sometimes; God is my witness, I am.   Akh, I would like. . . . Is it true that women ought not to read much? "

" Not much reading is necessary, but . . . ."

" Tell me what I ought to read.   Tell me what I ought to do.   I will do everything you tell me,"—she added, turning to me with innocent trustfulness.

I did not at once hit upon anything to say to her.

" You won't find it boresome with me, will you? "

" Good gracious! "   . . . . I began. . . .

" Well, thanks! "—returned Ásya;—" but I was thinking that you would find it tiresome." And her hot little hand gripped mine forcibly.

" N.! "—exclaimed Gágin at that moment:— " is n't this background too dark? "

I went to him.   Ásya rose and withdrew.

XII

SHE returned an hour later, halted in the doorway, and beckoned to me with her hand.

" Listen,"—said she:—" if I were to die, would you feel sorry for me? "

" What ideas you have to-day! "—I exclaimed.

" I have an idea that I shall die soon; it sometimes seems to me that everything around me is bidding me farewell. It is better to die than to live thus. . . Akh! don't look at me like that; truly, I am not pretending. Otherwise I shall be afraid of you again."

" Were you afraid of me? "

" Really, I am not to blame, if I am such a strange creature,"—she replied.—" As you see, I cannot laugh any more. . . ."

She remained sad and preoccupied until the evening. Something was taking place within her which I did not understand. Her gaze frequently rested on me; my heart contracted quietly beneath that enigmatical gaze. She seemed calm, —but when I looked at her, I kept wanting to say to her, that she must not agitate herself. —I admired her, found a touching charm in her pallid features, in her undecided, deliberate movements—but for some reason or other, she took it into her head that I was out of sorts.

ÁSYA

" Listen,"—she said to me not long before I took leave:—" I am tortured by the thought that I am considered giddy. . . . Henceforth you must always believe what I shall say to you, only you must be frank with me; and I will always speak the truth to you, I give you my word of honour. . . ."

This " word of honour " made me burst out laughing again.

" Akh,—don't laugh,"—she said with vivacity: —" or I will say to you to-day what you said to me yesterday:—' Why do you laugh?' "—And after a brief pause, she added:—" Do you remember, you spoke of wings yesterday? . . . My wings have sprouted,—but there is nowhere to fly."

" Good gracious,"—said I:—" all roads are open to you. . . ."

Ásya looked me straight and intently in the eye.

" You have a bad opinion of me to-day,"—said she, contracting her brows in a frown.

" I? A bad opinion? Of you! . . . . "

" Why is it that you are just as though you had been dipped in the water? "—Gágin interrupted me:—" I 'll play a waltz for you, as I did yesterday;—shall I? "

" No, no,"—replied Ásya, clenching her fists: —" not on any account to-day! "

" I am not forcing you; calm yourself. . . ."

"Not on any account,"—she repeated, turning pale.

. . . .

"Can it be that she loves me?" I thought, as I approached the Rhine, which was flowing swiftly past in dark waves.

XIII

"Can it be that she loves me?" I asked myself the next day, as soon as I awoke.—I did not wish to look within myself. I felt that her image, the image "of the girl with the strained laugh," had imprinted itself on my soul, and that I should not soon rid myself of it.—I went to L. and remained there the entire day, but caught only a glimpse of Ásya. She was not well: she had a headache. She came down-stairs for a moment, with her brow bound up, pale, thin, with eyes almost closed; she smiled faintly, said:—"it will pass off, it is nothing, all will pass off, will it not?"—and went away. I found things tiresome, and, somehow, mournfully-empty; but I would not go away for a long time, and returned home late, without having seen her again.

The following morning passed by in a sort of semi-doze of consciousness. I tried to set to work, and could not; I tried to do things and not to think . . . . and did not make a success of that either. I wandered about the town; when I got home, I started out again.

" Are you Mr. N.? "—a childish voice suddenly rang out behind me. I glanced round; before me stood a small urchin.—" This is for you from Fräulein Annette,"—he added, handing me a note.

I unfolded it—and recognised Ásya's hasty, irregular chirography.—" It is imperatively necessary that I should see you,"—she wrote me.— " Come to-day, at four o'clock, to the stone chapel on the road near the ruin. I have committed a great indiscretion to-day. . . . Come, for God's sake, and you shall know all. . . . Say ' yes ' to the messenger."

" Will there be any answer? "—the boy asked me.

" Say that I answer ' yes,' " I replied. The boy ran off.

XIV

I came to my senses in my own room, sat down, and became immersed in thought. My heart was beating violently within me. I read over Ásya's note several times. I glanced at my watch: it was not yet twelve o'clock.

The door opened—Gágin entered.

His face was gloomy. He grasped my hand

and shook it vigorously. He seemed greatly perturbed.

" What is the matter with you? "—I asked.

Gágin took a chair, and sat down opposite me.

"Three days ago,"—he began with a constrained smile, and hesitating as he spoke,—" I astonished you by my tale; to-day I shall astonish you still more.—With any one else I should not, probably, have made up my mind . . . . to speak . . . . so plainly. . . . . But you are an honourable man, you are my friend, are you not?—Listen: my sister Ásya is in love with you."

I trembled all over and half rose from my seat. . . .

" Your sister, you say . . . . "

" Yes, yes,"—Gágin interrupted me.—" I tell you that she is crazy and will drive me out of my senses. But, fortunately, she does not know how to lie—and she trusts me.—Akh, what a soul that little girl has! . . . but she will certainly ruin herself."

" But you are mistaken,"—I began.

" No, I am not mistaken. Yesterday, you know, she was lying down almost all day; she ate nothing, but she did not complain of anything. . . . . She never complains.—I was not uneasy, although toward evening a slight fever made its appearance. At two o'clock this morning, our landlady woke me: ' Go to your sister,' she said: ' there 's something wrong with her.'—I ran to

ÁSYA

Ásya, and found her fully dressed, in a fever, in
tears; her head was burning, her teeth were chattering. 'What aileth thee?' I inquired:—'Art
thou ill?'—She threw herself on my neck and began to implore me to take her away as promptly
as possible, if I wanted her to remain alive. . . . I
understood nothing, I tried to soothe her. . . .
Her sobs redoubled . . . . and suddenly, through
those sobs I heard. . . . Well, in a word, I heard
that she loved you.—I assure you that you and
I, sensible people, cannot even imagine to ourselves how deeply she feels, and with what incredible violence feelings manifest themselves in
her: the attack comes over her as suddenly and
as irresistibly as a thunder-storm.—You are a
very charming man,"—pursued Gágin,—" but
why she should have fallen in love with you, I do
not understand, I must confess. She says that
she became attached to you at first sight. That
is why she wept the other day, when she assured
me that she did not wish to love any one except
me.—She imagines that you despise her, that you
probably know who she is; she asked me whether
I had not narrated her story to you,—and I, of
course, said that I had not; but her sensitiveness
is simply terrible. She wishes only one thing: to
go away, to go away instantly.—I sat with her until morning; she made me promise that we should
be gone from here to-morrow—and only then did
she fall asleep.—I reflected, and reflected, and

ÁSYA

made up my mind to have a talk with you. In my
opinion, Ásya is right: the very best thing is for
us both to go away from here. And I would have
taken her away to-day, had not an idea occurred
to me which stopped me. Perhaps . . . . who
knows?—my sister pleases you? If so, why
should I take her away?—And so I decided, casting aside all shame. . . . Moreover, I have noticed something. . . . I decided . . . . to learn
from you . . . ." Poor Gágin got entangled.—
" Pardon me, pray,"—he added:—" I am not
accustomed to such worries."

I grasped his hand.

" You wish to know,"—I enunciated in a firm
voice:—" whether I like your sister?—Yes, I do
like her. . . ."

Gágin looked at me.—" But,"—he said, falter-
ing,—" surely you will not marry her? "

" How do you wish me to answer such a question? Judge for yourself whether I can now. . . ."

" I know, I know,"—Gágin interrupted me.—
" I have no right to demand an answer from you,
and my question is the height of indecorum. . . .
But what would you have me do? One cannot
play with fire. You do not know Ásya; she is
capable of falling ill, of running away, of appointing a tryst with you. . . . Any other woman would know how to conceal everything and
wait—but not she. This is the first time it has
happened to her—and therein lies the mischief!

If you could have seen how she sobbed to-day at my feet, you would understand my apprehensions."

I reflected. Gágin's words: " of appointing a tryst with you," pricked me to the heart. It seemed to me shameful not to reply to his honourable frankness with frankness.

" Yes,"—I said at last:—" you are right. An hour ago, I received from your sister a note. Here it is."

Gágin took the note, ran his eyes hastily over it, and dropped his hands on his knees. The expression of amazement on his face was very amusing; but I was in no mood for laughter.

" You are an honourable man, I repeat it,"— said he:—" but what is to be done now? What? She herself wants to go away, and she writes to you and accuses herself of indiscretion . . . . and when did she get a chance to write this? What does she want of you? "

I reassured him, and we began to discuss coolly, so far as we were able, what we ought to do.

This is what we finally decided upon: with the object of preventing a catastrophe, I was to go to the tryst and have an honest explanation with Ásya; Gágin promised to sit quietly at home, and not to appear to know about her note; and we agreed to meet together again in the evening.

" I place firm reliance on you,"—said Gágin, gripping my hand:—" spare her, and me. And

ÁSYA

we will go away to-morrow, all the same,"—he
added, rising:—" for you will not marry Ásya,
assuredly."

" Give me until evening,"—I returned.

" Certainly; but you will not marry her."

He went away, and I flung myself on the divan
and closed my eyes. My head was reeling; too
many impressions had descended upon it at once.
I was vexed at Gágin's frankness, I was vexed
at Ásya; her love both delighted and upset
me. I could not comprehend what had made
her tell her brother all; the inevitableness of a
prompt, almost instantaneous decision worried
me. . . .

" Marry a little girl of seventeen, with her disposition,—how is that possible? "—I said, as I
rose.

XV

At the hour agreed upon I crossed the Rhine,
and the first person who met me on the opposite
shore was that same small urchin who had come
to me in the morning. Evidently he was waiting
for me.

" From Fräulein Annette,"—he said in a whisper, and handed me another note.

Ásya informed me that the place for our tryst
had been changed. At the end of an hour and a
half I was to go, not to the chapel, but to the

302

house of Frau Luise, knock at the lower door, and ascend to the third story.

" ' Yes ' again? "—the boy asked me.

" Yes,"—I repeated, and strolled along the bank of the Rhine. There was not time to return home, and I did not wish to prowl about the streets. Outside the town wall there was a tiny garden, with a sign announcing skittles and tables for lovers of beer. I went thither. Several Germans, already advanced in years, were playing skittles; the wooden balls rolled with a clatter; now and then exclamations of approbation resounded. A pretty serving-maid with tear-stained eyes brought me a tankard of beer; I glanced at her face. She swiftly turned aside and went away.

" Yes, yes,"—said a fat, red-cheeked burgher, who was sitting near by:—" our Hänchen is much afflicted to-day;—her betrothed has gone to be a soldier."—I looked at her; she had crouched down in a corner, and propped her cheek on her hand; the tears were dripping one by one through her fingers. Some one asked for beer; she brought him a tankard and returned again to her place. Her grief affected me; I began to think about my impending tryst, but my thoughts were anxious, cheerless thoughts. It was with no light heart that I was going to that meeting, there was no prospect of my surrendering myself to the joys of mutual love; what awaited me was the

303

keeping of my word which had been pledged, the
fulfilling of a difficult obligation.—" She is not
to be jested with,"—those words of Gágin pierced
my soul like arrows. And three days ago, in that
boat borne away by the waves, had I not languished with the thirst for happiness? It had
become possible—and I was wavering, I was re-
pulsing it, I was bound to put it from me. . . .
Its suddenness had disconcerted me. Ásya herself, with her fiery brain, with her past, her rearing,—that attractive, but peculiar being,—I must
confess that she frightened me. For a long time
did these feelings contend within me. The appointed hour was approaching. " I cannot marry
her,"—I decided at last:—" she shall not know
that I have fallen in love with her also."

I rose,—and laying a thaler in the hand of
poor Hänchen (she did not even thank me), I
wended my way to Frau Luise's house. The
evening shadows were already diffused through
the air, and the narrow strip of sky above the
dark street was crimson with the sunset glow. I
knocked feebly at the door; it immediately
opened. I stepped across the threshold and
found myself in total darkness.

" This way! "—an elderly voice made itself audible.—" You are expected."

I advanced a couple of paces gropingly, and
some one's bony hand grasped my hand.

" Are you Frau Luise? "—I asked.

"I am,"—the same voice answered me:—"I am, my very fine young man."—The old woman led me up-stairs, by a winding staircase, and halted on the landing of the third story. By the faint light which fell through a tiny window I descried the wrinkled face of the burgomaster's widow. A mawkishly-crafty smile distended her sunken lips, and puckered up her dim little eyes. She pointed out to me a tiny door. With a convulsive movement of the arm I opened it, and slammed it behind me.

XVI

In the small room which I entered it was decidedly dark, and I did not at once perceive Ásya. Enveloped in a long shawl, she was sitting on a chair near the window, with her head turned away and almost concealed, like a frightened bird. I felt unspeakably sorry for her. She turned her head still further away. . . .

"Anna Nikoláevna,"—I said.

She suddenly straightened herself up fully, and tried to look at me—and could not. I seized her hand; it was cold, and lay like dead in my palm.

"I wanted," . . . . began Ásya, making an effort to smile; but her pale lips did not obey her: —"I wanted. . . . No, I cannot,"—she said, and fell silent. In fact, her voice broke at every word.

I sat down by her side.

"Anna Nikoláevna," I repeated, and I also was unable to add anything further.

A silence ensued. I continued to hold her hand and gaze at her. She, as before, shrank all together, breathed with difficulty, and quietly bit her under lip, to keep from weeping, to restrain the welling tears. . . . I gazed at her: there was something touchingly-helpless in her timid impassivity; it seemed as though she had barely made her way to the chair with fatigue, and had fairly collapsed upon it. My heart melted within me. . . .

"Ásya,"—I said, in a barely audible voice.

She slowly raised her eyes to mine. . . . Oh, glance of the woman who is in love, who shall describe thee? They implored, those eyes, they trusted, they interrogated, they surrendered themselves. . . . I could not resist their witchery. A thin fire ran through me, like red-hot needles; I bent down and pressed my lips to her hand. . . .

A tremulous sound, resembling a broken sob, resounded, and I felt on my hair the touch of a weak hand, which was quivering like a leaf. I raised my head and saw her face. How suddenly it had become transfigured! The expression of terror had vanished from it, her gaze had retreated somewhere far away, and drew me

ÁSYA

after it; her lips were slightly parted, her brow
had become as pallid as marble, and her curls were
floating backward, as though the wind had blown
them. I forgot everything, I drew her to me—
her hand obeyed submissively, her whole body
was drawn after the hand; her shawl slipped
from her shoulders, and her head sank softly on
my breast and lay there beneath my ardent
lips. . . .

"Yours,"—she whispered, in a barely audible
voice.

My arms were already stealing round her
waist. . . . But suddenly, the memory of Gágin illuminated me like a flash of lightning.—
"What are we doing?"—I cried, and drew back
with agitation. . . . "Your brother . . . . he
knows all. He knows that I am with you."

Ásya dropped into a chair.

"Yes,"—I went on, rising and walking away
to the other end of the room.—"Your brother
knows everything. . . . I must tell him everything. . . ."

"You must?"—she said indistinctly. She
evidently could not yet recover herself, and understood me imperfectly.

"Yes, yes,"—I repeated, with a certain ob-
duracy:—"and for that you alone are to blame.
—Why did you betray your secret? Who forced
you to tell your brother all? He came to me to-
day himself and repeated to me your conversation

307

with him."—I tried not to look at Ásya, and paced the room in long strides.—"Now all is lost, all, all."

Ásya endeavoured to rise from her chair.

"Stay,"—I exclaimed:—"stay, I beg of you. You have to deal with an honest man,—yes, with an honest man.—But, for God's sake, what agitated you? Had you observed any change in me? But I could not dissimulate before your brother when he came to me to-day."

"I did not summon my brother,"—Ásya's frightened whisper made itself heard:—"he came of his own accord."

"Just see what you have done,"—I went on.—"Now you want to go away. . . ."

"Yes; I must go away,"—said she, as softly as before:—"and I asked you to come hither merely for the purpose of bidding you farewell."

"And do you think,"—I retorted,—"that it will be easy for me to part from you?"

"But why did you tell my brother?"—repeated Ásya, in perplexity.

"I tell you that I could not do otherwise. If you had not betrayed yourself . . . ."

"I locked myself in my chamber,"—she returned ingenuously:—"I did not know that my landlady had another key. . . ."

This innocent excuse, on her lips, at such a moment, almost drove me frantic then . . . . and even now I cannot recall it without emotion. Poor, honest, sincere child!

" And now, all is at an end! "—I began again. —" All. Now we must part."—I cast a stealthy glance at Ásya . . . . her face flushed swiftly. She was both ashamed and alarmed, I felt it. I myself was walking and talking as though in a fever.—" You did not allow the feeling to develop which was beginning to ripen; you yourself have ruptured our bond, you did not trust me, you doubted me. . . ."

While I was speaking, Ásya bent forward lower and lower,—and suddenly fell on her knees, bowed her head on her hands, and burst out sobbing. I ran to her, I tried to raise her, but she would not let me. I cannot endure woman's tears; I immediately lose my self-control at the sight of them.

" Anna Nikoláevna, Ásya,"—I kept repeating:—" pray, I implore you, for God's sake, stop. . . ." Again I took her hand.

But, to my great surprise, she suddenly sprang to her feet,—with the swiftness of lightning flew to the door, and vanished. . . .

When, a few moments later, Frau Luise entered the room, I was still standing in the middle of it as though I had been struck by a thunderbolt. I did not understand how that meeting could have ended so speedily, so stupidly—and when I had not said the hundredth part of what

I had meant to say, of what I ought to have said,
—when I myself had not yet known how it
would turn out. . . . .

" Has the Fräulein gone?"—Frau Luise asked
me, elevating her yellow eyebrows to her very
wig.

I stared at her like a fool—and left the room.

XVII

I MADE my way out of the town and set off
straight across the open country. Vexation,
fierce vexation gnawed me. I overwhelmed myself with reproaches. How could I have failed
to understand the cause which had made Ásya
change the place of our tryst, how could I have
failed to appreciate what it had cost her to go to
that old woman, why had I not held her back?
Alone with her, in that dim, barely-lighted room,
I had found the strength, I had had the heart—
to repulse her, even to upbraid her. . . . And now
her image haunted me, I entreated its forgive-
ness; the memory of that pale face, of those moist
and timid eyes, of the uncurled hair on the bowed
neck, the light touch of her head on my breast
burned me. " Yours " . . . . I heard her whisper. " I have acted according to my conscience,"
I assured myself. . . . Untrue! Had I really
desired such a solution? Was I in a condition

to part from her? Could I do without her? "Madman! madman!" I repeated viciously. . . .

In the meantime night had descended. With huge strides I wended my way to the house where Ásya lived.

XVIII

GÁGIN came out to meet me.

"Have you seen my sister?"—he shouted to me from afar.

"Is n't she at home?"—I asked.

"No."

"She has not returned?"

"No. . . . I am to blame,"—went on Gágin: —"I could not hold out: contrary to our compact I went to the chapel; she was not there: so she did not come?"

"She was not at the chapel."

"And you have not seen her?"

I was obliged to admit that I had seen her.

"Where?"

"At Frau Luise's.—I parted from her an hour ago,"—I added.—"I was convinced that she had returned home."

"Let us wait."—said Gágin.

We entered the house and sat down side by side. We maintained silence. We both felt extremely embarrassed. We kept incessantly ex-

changing glances, gazing at the door, listening.
At last Gágin rose.

" This is outrageous! "—he exclaimed:—" My
heart will not keep still. She is torturing me, by
Heaven. . . . Let us go and seek her."

We went out. It was completely dark already
out of doors.

" What did you and she talk about? "—Gágin
asked me, pulling his hat down over his eyes.

" I only saw her for five minutes altogether,"
—I replied:—" I talked to her in the way we had
agreed upon."

" Do you know what? "—he returned:—" We
had better separate; we may hit upon her the
more promptly in that way.—In any case, come
hither an hour hence."

XIX

I DESCENDED briskly from the vineyard, and
rushed to the town. Swiftly did I make the
round of the streets, looking everywhere, even
into Frau Luise's windows; returned to the Rhine
and ran alone the shore. . . . From time to time
I met feminine forms, but Ásya was nowhere to
be seen. Irritation was already beginning to tor-
ment me. A secret alarm tortured me, and it was
not alarm only that I felt. . . . No, I felt re-
pentance, the most burning compassion, love—

yes! the tenderest love. I wrung my hands, I
called on Ásya athwart the gathering mists of
night, at first in a low tone, then ever more and
more loudly; I repeated a hundred times that
I loved her, that I swore never to part from her;
I would have given everything in the world to
hold her cold hand once more, to hear once
more her gentle voice, to behold her once more before me. . . . She had been so near, she had come to
me with entire resolution, in full innocence of
heart and feelings, she had brought to me her
unsullied youth . . . . and I had not pressed
her to my breast, I had deprived myself of the
bliss of seeing how her lovely face would have
blossomed forth with the joy and tranquillity of
rapture. . . . That thought nearly drove me
mad.

" Where can she have gone, what has she done
with herself? "—I exclaimed in the grief of impotent despair. . . . Something white suddenly
gleamed on the very brink of the river.—I knew
that spot; there, over the grave of a man who
had been drowned seventy years before, stood a
stone cross, with an ancient inscription, half
buried in the ground.—My heart died within me.
. . . . I ran to the cross: the white figure disappeared. I shouted: "Ásya! " My wild voice
frightened me—but no one answered. . . .

I decided to go and inquire whether Gágin had
found her.

ÁSYA

XX

CLAMBERING alertly up the path of the vineyard, I descried a light in Ásya's room. . . . This reassured me somewhat.

I approached the house; the lower door was locked. I knocked. An unlighted window in the lower story was cautiously opened, and Gágin's head made its appearance.

" Have you found her? "—I asked him.

" She has returned,"—he replied to me in a whisper:—" she is in her room, and is undressing. All is as it should be."

" God be thanked! "—I exclaimed with an inexpressible outburst of joy:—" God be thanked! everything is splendid now. But you know we must confer together further."

" Some other time,"—he replied, softly drawing the casement toward him:—" some other time, but now good-bye."

" Until to-morrow," I said:—" to-morrow everything will be settled."

" Good-bye,"—repeated Gágin. The window closed.

I was on the point of knocking at the window. I wanted to tell Gágin then and there that I asked for his sister's hand. But such a wooing at such a time. . . . " Yes, to-morrow,"—I said to myself:—" to-morrow I shall be happy. . . ."

To-morrow I shall be happy! There is no to-morrow for happiness; neither has it any yesterday, and it recks not of the future; it has the present, and not even a day at that—but a moment.

I do not remember how I got to Z. My feet did not bear me thither, neither did a boat convey me; I was lifted aloft on some sort of broad, mighty pinions. I passed the bush where a nightingale was singing, I halted and listened for a long time; it seemed to me that it was chanting my love and my bliss.

XXI

WHEN, on the following morning, I began to draw near to the familiar little house, I was struck by one circumstance: all its windows stood wide open, and the door also was open; some papers or other were trailing about in front of the threshold; the servant-maid with a broom made her appearance beyond the door.

I went up to her. . . .

"They have gone away!"—she blurted out, before I could manage to ask her whether the Gágins were at home.

"Gone away?" . . . I repeated. . . . "What do you mean by 'gone away?' Whither?"

"They went away this morning, at six o'clock,

ÁSYA

and did not say where. Wait, you are Mr. N., I
think?"

"I am Mr. N."

"The landlady has a letter for you."—The
maid went up-stairs and returned with the letter.
—"Here it is, if you please."

"But it cannot be. . . . What does it mean?"
—I was beginning. The maid stared dully at me
and began to sweep.

I unfolded the letter. It was from Gágin;
there was not a line from Ásya. He began by beg-
ging me not to be angry with him for his sudden departure; he was convinced that, on mature
consideration, I would approve of his decision.
He could discern no other issue from the situa-
tion, which might become difficult and dangerous.
—"Last night,"—he wrote,—"while we were
both waiting in silence for Ásya, I became definitively convinced of the necessity of a separation.
There are prejudices which I respect; I understand that you cannot marry Ásya. She has told
me all; for the sake of her peace of mind, I must
yield to her repeated, urgent entreaties."—At the
end of the letter he expressed his regret that our
acquaintance had come to so speedy an end,
wished me happiness, pressed my hand in friendly
wise, and implored me not to try to hunt them
up.

"What prejudices?"—I cried, as though he
could hear me:—"What nonsense! Who gave

316

him a right to steal her from me?" . . . . I clutched my head.

The maid-servant began to call loudly for the landlady; her fright made me recover my senses. One thought kindled in me:—to find them, to find them, at any cost. To accept this blow, to reconcile myself to this conclusion of the matter was impossible. I learned from the landlady that they had gone aboard a steamer at six o'clock, and sailed down the Rhine. I betook myself to the office; there I was informed that they had bought tickets for Cologne. I went home with the intention of immediately packing up and following them. I was obliged to pass Frau Luise's house. . . . . Suddenly I heard some one calling me. I raised my head, and beheld in the window of the room where I had met Ásya on the day before, the burgomaster's widow. She was smiling with her repulsive smile, and calling to me. I turned away, and was about to pass on; but she screamed after me that she had something for me. These words brought me to a standstill, and I entered her house. How shall I express my feelings, when I beheld that little room once more. . . .

" As a matter of fact,"—began the old woman, pointing out to me a tiny note:—" I ought to have given you this only in case you came to me of your own accord; but you are such a very fine young man. Take it."

I took the note.

ÁSYA

On the tiny scrap of paper stood the following words, hastily scrawled in pencil:

"Farewell, we shall see each other no more. 'Tis not out of pride that I am going away,—no; I cannot do otherwise. Yesterday, when I wept before you, if you had said to me but one word, only one word—I would have remained. You did not say it. Evidently, it is better so. . . . Farewell forever!"

One word. . . . Oh, madman that I am! That word. . . . I had repeated it with tears in my eyes the night before, I had scattered it on the wind, I had reiterated it amid the empty fields . . . . but I had not said it to her, I had not told her that I loved her. . . . But I had not been able to utter that word then. When I met her in that fateful chamber there was within me, as yet, no clear consciousness of my love; it had not even awakened while I was sitting with her brother in irrational and painful silence. . . . It had flamed up with irresistible force only some moments later when, affrighted by the possibility of unhappiness, I had begun to seek her and and call to her . . . . but then it was too late. "But this is impossible!" I shall be told. I know not whether it be possible,—I do know that it is true. Ásya would not have gone away had there been even a shade of coquetry in her, and if her position had not been a false one. She was

not able to endure what any other woman would
have borne; I had not understood that. My evil
genius had stopped the avowal on my lips during my last meeting with Gágin in front of the
darkened window, and the last thread at which I
could still clutch had slipped out of my hands.

That same day I returned, with my trunk
packed, to L., and embarked for Cologne. I remember that the steamer had not yet left the
wharf, and I was mentally bidding farewell to
those streets, to all those places which I was destined to behold no more,—when I caught sight
of Hänchen. She was sitting by the shore, but
not sad; a young and handsome man was standing by her side, laughing and narrating something to her; while, on the other side of the Rhine,
my little Madonna was still gazing out as sadly
as ever from the dark greenery of the ash-tree.

XXII

IN Cologne I came upon traces of the Gágins:
I learned that they had gone to London, and I set
out in pursuit of them; but in London all my re-
searches proved vain. For a long time I would
not submit, for a long time I persisted; but I was
finally compelled to renounce all hopes of over-
taking them.

And I never beheld them—I never beheld
Ásya again. Obscure rumours reached me con-

cerning him, but she had vanished from me forever. I do not even know whether she is alive. One day, several years afterward, I caught a glimpse, abroad, in a railway carriage, of a woman whose face vividly reminded me of the never-to-be-forgotten features . . . . but I was, in all probability, deceived by an accidental resemblance. Ásya has remained in my memory the same little girl as I knew her at the best period of my life, as I saw her for the last time, bowed over the back of a low, wooden chair.

I am bound to confess, however, that I did not grieve too long over her: I even thought that Fate had ordained matters rightly in not uniting me to Ásya; I comforted myself with the thought that I probably should not have been happy with such a woman. I was young then and the future, —that brief, swift future,—seemed to be limitless. May not that which has been repeat itself, I thought, and in still better, still more beautiful form? . . . I have known other women,—but the feeling awakened in me by Ásya, that glowing, tender, profound emotion, has not been repeated. No! No eyes have taken the place with me of those eyes which once were fixed upon me with love, and to no heart which has reclined on my breast has my own heart responded with such sweet and joyous swooning! Condemned to the solitude of an old bachelor without family, I am living out the wearisome years; but I preserve like sacred treasures her tiny notes and the withered spray of geranium, that same spray which she once tossed to me from the window. It still emits a faint fragrance, but the hand which gave it to me, that hand which I was fated to press but once to my lips, may have long been mouldering in the grave. . . . And I myself . . . . what has become of me? What is left in me of those blissful and troubled days, of those winged hopes and aspirations? Such a faint exhalation of an insignificant plant outlives all the joys and woes of a man—outlives even the man himself.